While hiking in Montana, the author came across a decaying mound of cast-off artifacts at the base of the Rocky Mountains. He surmised that the discarded items were part of the hopes and dreams that early settlers had for their new life in the Oregon Territory. He wondered what must have gone through their minds when they were forced to relinquish these precious treasures, and how much that loss altered their future.

The author's experience in Montana and the memory of his Grandfather's dog, Bones, ultimately led to the story of Billy Bones.

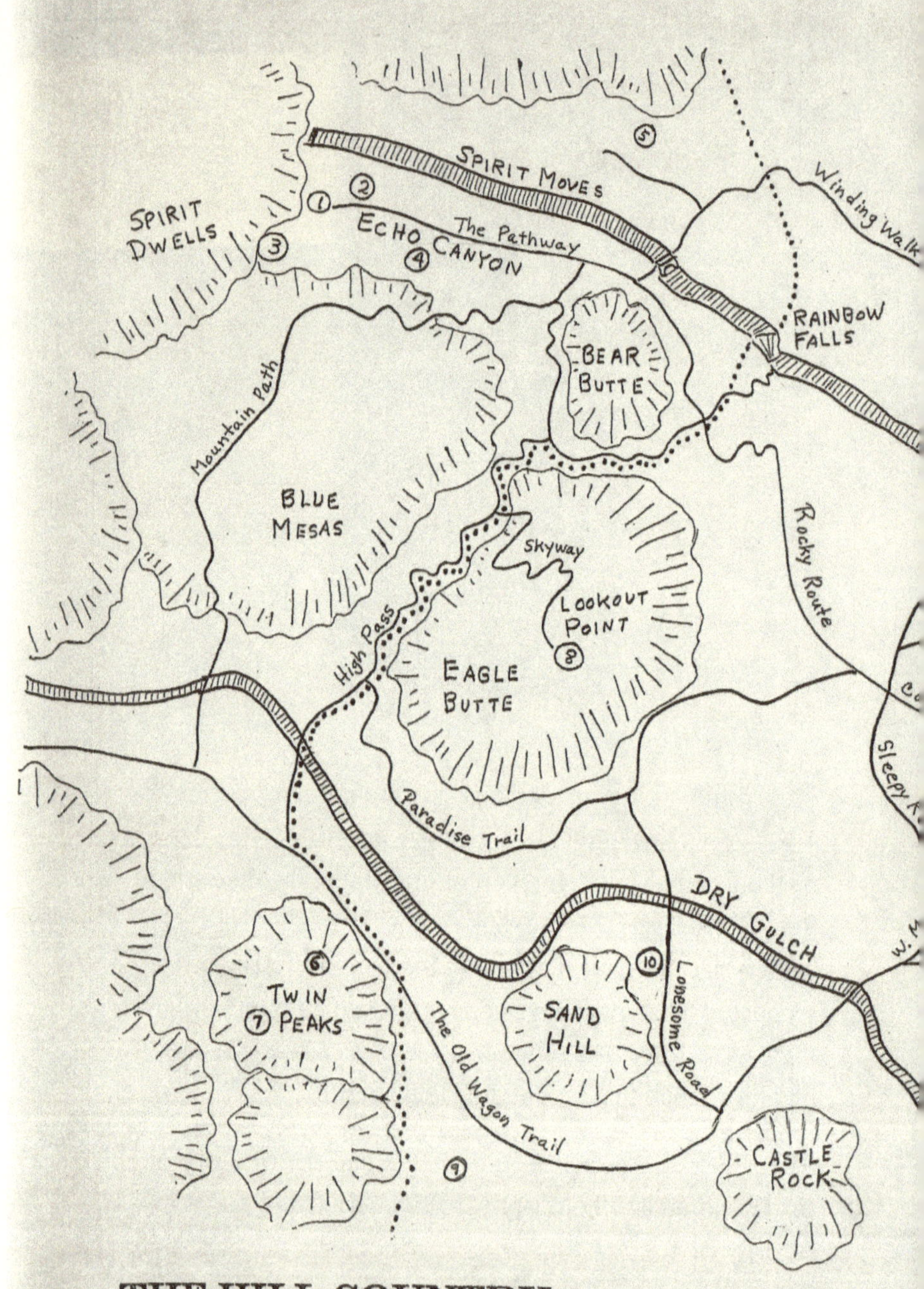

THE HILL COUNTRY

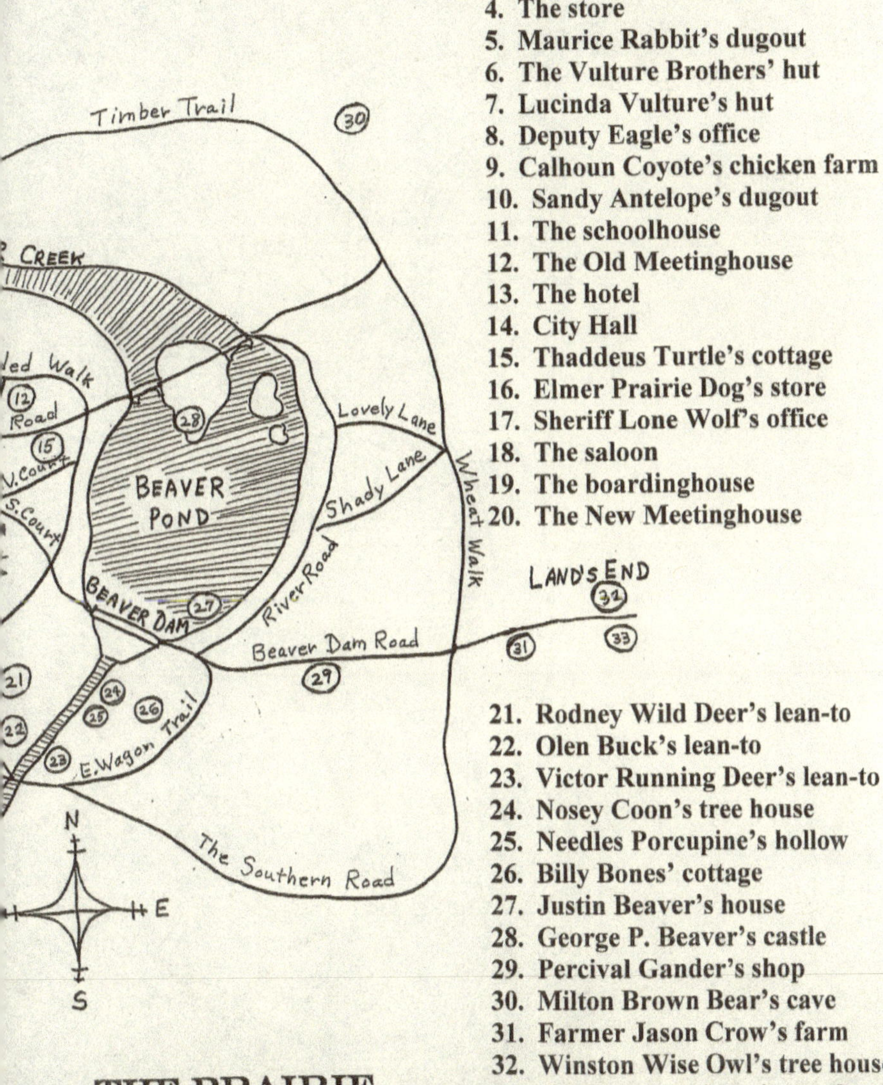

1. The lodge
2. Arthur Elk's hut
3. Omar Mountain Goat's cave
4. The store
5. Maurice Rabbit's dugout
6. The Vulture Brothers' hut
7. Lucinda Vulture's hut
8. Deputy Eagle's office
9. Calhoun Coyote's chicken farm
10. Sandy Antelope's dugout
11. The schoolhouse
12. The Old Meetinghouse
13. The hotel
14. City Hall
15. Thaddeus Turtle's cottage
16. Elmer Prairie Dog's store
17. Sheriff Lone Wolf's office
18. The saloon
19. The boardinghouse
20. The New Meetinghouse

21. Rodney Wild Deer's lean-to
22. Olen Buck's lean-to
23. Victor Running Deer's lean-to
24. Nosey Coon's tree house
25. Needles Porcupine's hollow
26. Billy Bones' cottage
27. Justin Beaver's house
28. George P. Beaver's castle
29. Percival Gander's shop
30. Milton Brown Bear's cave
31. Farmer Jason Crow's farm
32. Winston Wise Owl's tree house
33. Hester Ground hog's tree house

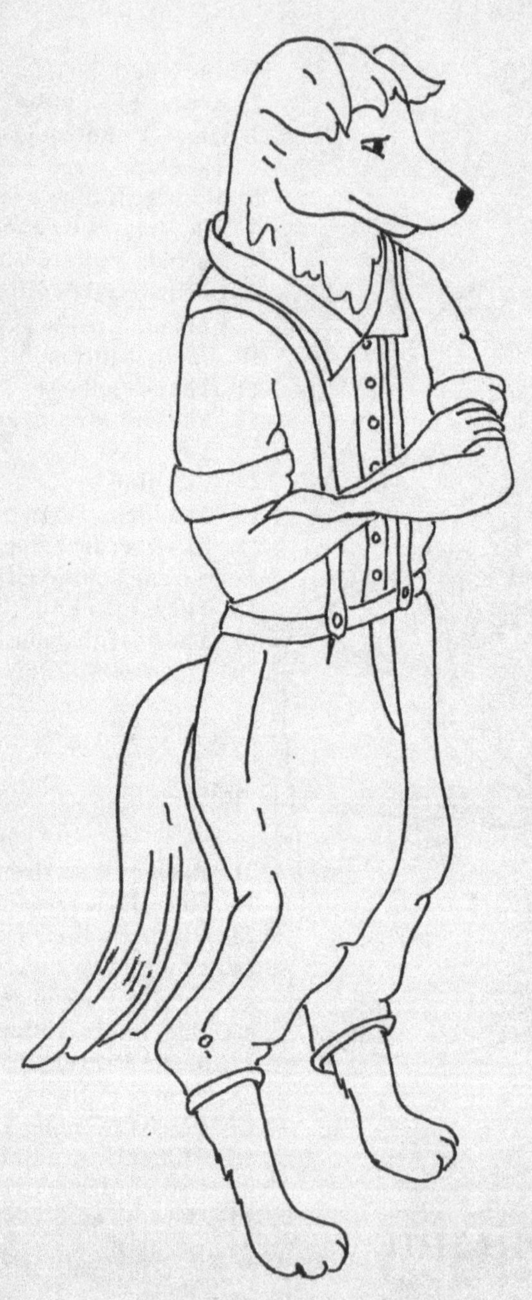

BILLY BONES

Book One

BEYOND THE TALL GRASS

RON OAKS

ACON RING PUBLISHING

http://www.aconring.com/

ISBN 978-1-7323499-0-2   Hardcover
ISBN 978-1-7323499-1-9   Paperback
ISBN 978-1-7323499-2-6   eBook

FIRST EDITION

Credits
Cover Painting by Howard Garrett
Illustrations by Ron Oaks

Edited by Anne Ostroff, Louise Carlson, and Laura Oaks
Cover and Interior Design by Delaney-Designs.com
Photography by Sandy Rothberg

To Jan and Laura

Table of Contents

BOOK ONE: BEYOND THE TALL GRASS

PART ONE: INTO THE GOLDEN MIST

❦

PART TWO: ON TO THE GRAND FAIR

Table of Contents

BOOK ONE: BEYOND THE TALL GRASS

PART ONE: INTO THE GOLDEN MIST

PART TWO: ON TO THE GRAND FAIR

Illustrations

PAGE 166: "Billy, I'd like you to meet Sandy Antelope
and Arnold Big Horn. They're my new runnin'
partners since you abandoned me to work on
that precious house of yours."

PAGE 203: "Tell him yourself, buddy!" said Billy, suddenly
stepping to one side and giving the coyote a
quick shove.

PAGE 239: As Victor headed back to his space in line,
Rodney suddenly jumped out in front of him.
His eyes were filled with hate, but his voice
was even.

PAGE 254: "After my father is mayor, you won't be so
high and mighty any more, Mr. Smarty-pants!"
screamed Patsy.

PAGE 280: The breeze billowed around her long blue skirt
and scarf, accenting the exquisiteness of her
face and body.

PAGE 289: "You don't want the sheriff comin' after you,
do you, Nosey?" "Would he do that?" inquired
Nosey, suddenly changing his attitude.

Cast of Characters

BOOK ONE: BEYOND THE TALL GRASS

HUMANS IN THE NINTEENTH CENTURY
Warren Nathaniel Stone – schoolmaster taking books to Oregon Territory
Jimmy Stone – W. N. Stone's grandson
Ben Johnson and his wife – young couple going to Oregon Territory

HUMANS IN THE PRESENT
William Stuart Sr. (Will) – purchased land along the old wagon trail
William Stuart Jr. (Bill) – son of William Stuart Sr.
William Stuart III (Billy) – grandson of William Stuart Sr.

ANIMALS IN THE ENCHANTMENT'S PRAIRIE
Billy Bones (Bones) – shepherd dog who enters The Enchantment
Victor Running Deer – young buck who enters with Billy Bones
Winston Wise Owl – the wise gatekeeper, mentor to Billy Bones
Hester Groundhog – Winston's neighbor and confidant
Mayor George P. Beaver – mayor of the Prairie
Constance Beaver – Mayor George P. Beaver's wife
George (Georgie) Beaver– the mayor's nephew, guide for Billy and
       Victor
Justin and Gladys Beaver – parents of Georgie Beaver
Cornelius Van Mink – moderate councilor on the City Council
Thaddeus P. Turtle – spiritual leader of the Old Meetinghouse
Percival (Percy) Gander – tailor and collector of used furniture
Brother Fabian Lynx – spiritual leader of the New Meetinghouse
Sister Sarah Mourning Dove – former spiritual leader of New
       Meetinghouse
Rodney Wild Deer (the Rogue Deer) – Victor's rival for Melinda Doe
Melinda Doe – Victor Running Deer's love interest
Olen and Myrtle Buck – parents of Melinda Doe
Lester, Leon, and Leroy Coyote – friends of Rodney Wild Deer
Calhoun Coyote – father to Lester, Leon, Leroy and Lenny
Leonard (Lenny) Coyote – Calhoun's youngest son

Sandy Antelope and Arnold Big Horn – running friends of Billy and
Victor
Alvin Muskrat – friend of Billy and Victor
Nolen (Nosey) Coon and Needles Porcupine – rascally friends of Billy
Johnny Otter – swimming rival of Georgie Beaver
Conrad Van Mink – swimmer in the Open Race
Phineas T. Fox – on board of councilors for New Meetinghouse, City
Hall
Philip P. Fox – brother of Phineas
Farmer Jason Crow – on board of councilors for the New Meetinghouse
Gwendolyn and Gerard Crow – wife and son of Farmer Jason Crow
Elmer Prairie Dog – proprietor of General Store, becomes mayor of
Prairie
Edwina and Patsy Prairie Dog – wife and daughter of Elmer
Irma Prairie Dog – sister-in-law of Edwina
Whiskers – old cat who lived on farm with Billy Bones in the outside
world
Chester and Fanny Hawk – owners of chicken pie booth in the Grand
Fair
Wendell Red Breast – moderate councilor, baritone at Summer Concert
Melba Thrush – soprano at Summer Concert
Hosea Brown Thrasher – tenor at Summer Concert
Gloria Meadowlark – mezzo-soprano at Summer Concert
Walter Lone Wolf – sheriff of the Prairie
Harold Eagle – deputy of the Prairie and the Hill Country
Milton Brown Bear and Bison Bob – deputies to Sheriff Lone Wolf
Wiley Weasel and Rattlesnake Pete – two characters often in trouble
Charlie Pheasant – councilor on the City Council

ANIMALS IN THE ENCHANTMENT'S HILL COUNTRY
Lucinda Vulture – spiritual head of the Hill Country
Felix, Festus, and Floyd Vulture – sons of Lucinda
Arthur Elk – guard of the Tribal Council
Maurice Rabbit – painter on the Tribal Council, befriends Billy Bones
Omar Mountain Goat – chief of the Tribal Council
Gaylord Cougar, Lucretia Lizard, and Orville Bat – on Tribal Council

BILLY BONES

❦

Book One

❦

BEYOND THE TALL GRASS

PROLOGUE

If you happen to be fortunate enough to find a particular spot just east of the great mountains where the prairie meets the foothills, you might see it. Of course you would have to arrive on the morning of the summer solstice when the mist is still rising off the pond created by the dam that the beavers built. You would have to approach the spot very carefully, lie close to the ground, and peek beyond the tall grass. The passageway with its strange golden hue opens for only a few moments between the two ancient trees. If you are a human, you can only wonder at what lies just beyond, for you would not be invited to enter.

PART ONE

INTO THE GOLDEN MIST

CHAPTER ONE

THE MIRACULOUS TRANSFORMATION

On the morning of June 21, as Billy Stuart III was finishing his morning chores on his grandfather's farm, he glanced over to watch the mist rise slowly off the pond. His shepherd dog, Bones, was right on his heels. Suddenly the dog began sniffing the air and whining softly. At the same moment a young buck sprang from the corn patch and bounded toward the wildlife preserve. Instinctively Bones lunged after it and disappeared around the corner of the patch. The young boy laughed and called after him, "Here Bones! Come back, boy! You'll never catch that crazy deer!" Bones, already caught up in the thrill of the chase, continued to pursue the buck.

The frightened deer finally paused to rest in front of two ancient trees that stood on either side of an old wagon trail that ran through the farm. The young shepherd dog also halted behind a small hillock and peered between the long blades of grass at the frightened deer.

As he watched, Bones felt the earth seem to shift, and a fresh breeze hit his face. Simultaneously his attention was diverted as the space between the two trees began to glow and then miraculously tear open behind the deer, revealing an altered version of the same land. Although the dog could not comprehend what was happening, he knew something was drastically different, and it made him uneasy and a bit confused.

However, with the clear focus of a shepherd dog, Bones' attention quickly shifted back to his prey. He sensed his chance to catch the distraught creature and sprang even after it. When the young buck saw the dog bounding toward him, its head and pert ears bobbing just above the level of the grass, he panicked again. He turned sharply, surged forward, and plunged through the strange opening. Bones, fearful of losing his prey, leaped in after him. The portal lingered for a few moments in radiant splendor, moved out of sync with the surrounding world, and closed. By the time Billy Stuart reached the clearing, everything around the old trees had returned to normal, and both animals, along with the mysterious window, had vanished without a trace.

If Billy Stuart had arrived just a moment sooner, he would have noticed that colors inside the opening were vivid and alive and that the sun shone with a more golden light. He would have seen that the wild flowers grew in greater profusion, and the trees surrounding the pond were more magnificent in size and hue. All and all, he would have surmised that the vision beyond the shimmering arch resembled a page from one of his children's books, unexpectedly and gloriously thrust open. But he missed the moment.

Once past the golden rift, the startled shepherd dog felt himself somehow tripping over his own feet. Finally losing his balance completely, he fell hard on his head and began tumbling over and over until he lay in a clump on the cool green grass of his new surroundings. Following his old instinct, he tried to get up on all fours and corner his prey, also lying in a heap on the ground. For some reason he felt sluggish and awkward and was unable to reach the fallen deer.

At that moment Bones became aware of what sounded like human voices crying in desperation for hopes and dreams forever lost. Overriding this was a kind of distant music like the sounds of rushing water, mixed with bird-songs and the fluttering of many wings. The singing came closer and closer until it hovered over him, holding him captive in its ever-increasing intensity. Ultimately it surrounded him, penetrating his very being, and filling his breast with an exhilaration he had never before experienced.

In the midst of the shepherd dog's euphoria, a young man's face appeared above him. The dog could tell it was not his human's face but that of an older boy with hair and eyes darker than Billy Stuart's. The young man gazed at him for a moment, smiled, and then faded away. After much time passed, the singing slowed, whirled softly above the dog, and disappeared as mysteriously as it had arrived. Afterward he fell into a deep slumber.

Bones woke with a start. His first awareness was of a new clarity and understanding. Thoughts in the form of human language flooded his conscious mind. "Where…

where am I?" he managed to ask himself, as unfamiliar colors of blue, green, and brown swarmed in front of him.

Gradually the shepherd dog sensed that he was somehow a new creature and that everything within him had profoundly changed. Again he asked, "What is happening to me, and who am I?" A feeling of wonderment mixed with great alarm cascaded over him. He vaguely remembered chasing a deer into a radiant opening between two trees, but somehow the memory seemed distant, as if it belonged to another creature in another time.

"But who am I? Where is my human?" the dog wondered again, confused as he sat upright. To his surprise he found that he had positioned himself like a human animal. He looked around and saw the deer, not six feet away, also sitting upright and glaring at him with large intelligent eyes. The young buck was also strangely transformed. Although his back legs still ended in hooves, his upper body had arms and hands that resembled the human animal, and his head was upright on his broad shoulders.

The canine slowly looked down and saw his own arms and hands and was astonished at his own miraculous change. Instinctively he looked around for any sign of the boy as feelings of joy, amazement and confusion continued to flood through him. "I think I still belong with the humans, but something has happened to me, something remarkable," he determined.

At that instant, without warning, the deer sprang up and jumped onto the startled dog, pinning him to the ground and pointing a newly-discovered finger dangerously close to his eye. "Why…why did you….did you want to hurt me?" the deer blurted.

The dog was shocked and perplexed by the voice of the youthful buck and at his own understanding of the words he was hearing. Now he knew for certain that he was the same animal called Bones who had chased the deer sitting on top of him.

"I…I…" the young dog was baffled by the sound of his own voice. He tried again with some effort. "I didn't…I didn't mean to hurt you!"

"Then…then why…why were you chasing me?" bellowed the deer again, forcing the words out and struggling to keep the dog's newly-formed arms pinned on the ground.

"Because…" the young dog sputtered, trying to sort through events in the other world, somehow still clouded, "because I like to chase things. I…I think it is f…fun."

"Fun!" yelled the distraught deer, as he swung a strong right arm that grazed the chin of the startled dog. With great effort the canine managed to twist free and crawl away from the sudden onslaught. A new feeling of panic gripped him as he realized he was in imminent danger of being seriously hurt. The deer immediately leaped after him, catching him around the legs.

Soon the two creatures were rolling over and over, pummeling one another with wild blows about the head and body. Finally after they were completely exhausted, they turned over on their backs and stared up at the sky. For Bones it was the first time he had ever experienced color, and he instinctively knew that it was blue.

Eventually the shepherd dog's attention returned to the young deer. "I swear…I swear," repeated the panting dog, "I would not have hurt you."

"Ha!" gasped the tired buck. "A likely story!"

"But…but how do you…do you manage to talk?" inquired the dog, glancing back over at the buck.

"Same as you I imagine. Maybe it has somethin' to do with that noise…that music," answered the deer.

"But how are we able to talk…like the humans?" queried the shepherd dog again, beginning to gain control of his breathing.

"Well, there are no humans here!" interrupted a new commanding voice.

CHAPTER TWO

THE GATEKEEPER

The shepherd dog and the deer sat up instantly and saw a large-headed bird wearing a black tie, striped trousers, and a swallow-tailed coat with no sleeves standing directly in front of them. He had a hand-like appendage stretched out at the end of his wings, like the dog.

"I see the two of you are giving thanks for the wonderful gifts you've been given by brawling and yelling like young ruffians." The old bird's chastisement caused the dog to look away, ashamed. Out of the corner of his eye he noticed the deer had done the same.

"Well, we'll blame your youth and the fact that you're new to the charms of this place," said the owl with more compassion. "I can only pray that underneath that display of tomfoolery you have good hearts."

"Who…who are you?" questioned the young dog, regaining his courage. "Your face looks like one of the owls that sit on the rafters of the old man's barn, only you're quite a bit larger than they are."

"They call me Winston Wise Owl," said the large bird, trying to sound humble. "As for my size, well, I'm a Great

Horned Owl, you see. The owls in that old man's barn were probably common barn owls and are a bit smaller." After a moment of silence the owl smiled and continued, "As for me, I came here the same as you, only I flew through that golden portal many years ago. In fact, I hardly recall the old life. Most of our citizens have forgotten, you know. I still remember because I live so close to the entrance. I'm like the gatekeeper. I feel it's my duty to remember so I can help the new ones who enter."

"Those who enter, but…but aren't we the only ones who entered?" asked the deer.

"Slow down, my young friend. Let me explain," began the old owl. "You see, the wondrous rift opens only for a few moments once a year. I'm afraid we'll have to wait until next year before anyone else comes through."

"What do you mean – we'll have to wait until next year? And what's this opening you're talking about?" asked Bones.

"What we call our 'Enchantment' and the outer world come together for just a few moments every year on the day of the summer solstice. That's when animals are allowed to enter. For some reason humans cannot," explained Winston. "There are many things that are beyond our understanding here, but I suppose that's how it's meant to be. Not everything can be understood," he continued pensively. Winston looked back at the two new beings. "On all other days The Enchantment is closed to the outside world. That's the way it's been since the Great Rift occurred over eighty years ago." The owl smiled knowingly at the confused arrivals. "But now I think it's time for the two of you to make amends."

"With him? After what he did?" complained the deer.

"Yes, with him," commanded the owl. "He's a dog, you see, and they were born to chase things. Be still now and give him your hand. I think, by the look in his eye, he's got a good heart."

Bones was anxious to make friends with the deer and immediately held out his newly- transformed appendage. He could see, however, that the deer was reluctant to do the same. Finally with some trepidation, the deer shook his hand. As the hands clasped, the dog could feel the bony structure of the deer's transformed hoof. When he pulled his hand back, he looked down at his own fingers.

As he stretched them out to their full length, he marveled to himself, "So like the humans…it's hard to believe!"

After some exploration of his own hands, the deer finally turned back to the owl. "You keep referrin' to a good heart. Is that one of the gifts we received after that strange music we heard?"

"No, my anxious friend," explained the owl. "The gifts are those of the mind and the voice and the body. Those gifts, along with old memories from the human's world are the only things you're given when you enter. You can't be given a good heart. That's part of your own nature. Ah, but enough of that; on to more pressing issues. Do either of you have a name?"

"Back on the farm, the boy and the old man called me Bones," replied the dog, full clarity of his former life suddenly returning to him. The boy. He'd almost forgotten about the boy. An ache filled his chest. He was silent.

"You may choose another if you like," said the owl sympathetically.

"No, no, I think I'd like to keep that name." A vision of the little towheaded boy calling him and kneeling with his arms around him flashed through his mind again. "But I'd also like another name." He thought then of the old man and what he had called the boy. "Billy! I'd also like to be called Billy…Billy Bones."

"Then Billy Bones it is!" Winston Wise Owl turned to the buck. "And you my long-legged friend, what about a name for you?"

The deer turned away. "I…I've lived alone most of my life. I…I can't ever remember havin' a name."

"Then we must choose one for you," said the owl kindly.

"How about Running Deer?" suggested Bones. "He was runnin' away from the old man's cornfield when I was first chasin' him, and I never did catch up to him until we got to this magical place where <u>he</u> kind a' caught me, so to speak." The dog tried to smile as he showed his bruised chin.

"Then Running Deer it must be." The owl looked over at the young deer, who did not seem convinced. "Well, at least for the time being. Now let's go to my house and prepare you for your new adventures. I live in one of those two lone trees close to where you entered."

Winston turned to leave, while the two unlikely companions struggled to stand upright, Billy on his remaining back paws and Running Deer on his back hooves. Although Billy felt this was the natural thing to do with his newly transformed body, it took some time to adjust to his new height. He noticed that the deer was having just as much difficulty. After several awkward attempts at gaining control of their balance, the two animals finally succeeded and followed the old owl up the path.

Suddenly the dog stopped. A great yearning pervaded his being. "Wait," he said hesitantly. "I don't think I can go with you. I…I think maybe I should go back."

The owl turned to the young dog and frowned. "But Mr. Bones, I'm afraid you don't understand. As I explained to you, the rift's already closed."

"But Billy…Billy will miss me. He…he still needs me!" insisted the dog.

"Ah yes, the boy," the owl said gently, "I thought as much. But as I explained earlier, you can't go back for at least another year. Even then I'm afraid it won't be the same." He hesitated a moment and then continued. "This is your adventure, Billy Bones. You've been given a rare gift, and you must make the most of it. Come now, follow me to my tree house, and I'll tell you more over a cup of tea and a bit of sustenance. Then we must be off to see the tailor. You two need something to wear!"

"Something to wear?" questioned the dog. "I don't understand."

"Ah now, that's a good question. I know that in the outside world, only human animals wear clothes. I guess with us, it's one of the ways we express ourselves," confessed the owl. "It has something to do with the old memories."

For some strange reason a vision of Billy Stuart getting out of bed that very morning flashed through the shepherd dog's mind. He recalled that the first thing the young boy did was pull on a pair of pants and a loose-fitting shirt that buttoned up the front.

"I guess it never occurred to me that that's what he did every morning. I guess I just took it for granted," thought the dog. "I wonder what color his shirt was anyway? And I wonder what happened to Billy's parents? 'Cause I'm sure now that the boy called the old man 'Grandpa.'"

CHAPTER THREE

BILLY STUART AND BONES

Billy Stuart had come to live with his "Grandpa," Will Stuart, after his mother's fatal car accident. His father, Bill Stuart Jr., had tried to raise the young towheaded boy by himself, but his high-powered job kept him constantly on the move.

"Geneva does her best to take care of Billy while I'm gone," Bill Jr. confided to his father over the phone, "but she's my housekeeper. I can't expect her to take his mother's place, and he misses her so much. What he really needs is family!" After many disturbing phone calls, it was finally decided that the grandfather's farm was the best place for young Billy.

Will Stuart was a retired math professor and a widower. He had purchased his property from the son of the original homesteader. He had always planned to find a small farm where he could have a garden, raise a few chickens and geese and sheep, and go fishing whenever he pleased.

The old homestead that backed up to a wildlife preserve was the perfect spot for Will. He kept the pasture and a small acreage of sweet corn for himself and rented the rest of the land out to a local wheat farmer, except for an old road that led down to a beaver pond at the edge of the reserve. Apparently this road had been part of a wagon trail used by pioneers traveling westward toward the Oregon Territory. Preservation of the old trail and the two aging trees that stood on either side of it had been written into the deed when he bought the place.

The sad young boy stayed mostly in his room when he first arrived at the farm. After a couple days he ventured out onto the porch and sat on a bench facing the highway. His grandfather's dog, Bones, was resting on a step nearby. Billy suddenly realized that Bones had crawled over to him and started nudging his hand. After a time, Billy reached out and absentmindedly stroked the dog's head and back. In a few minutes Bones jumped up on him and began licking his hands and face. Soon Billy was giggling and scuffling with the dog, and by late afternoon the boy and the dog were exploring every corner of the grandfather's farm. By the time the week was out, a strong unbreakable bond of love and friendship had developed between them.

Bones had some truly remarkable qualities. Generally referred to as a shepherd dog, he was actually a mixture of collie, German shepherd, and various kinds of sheepdog. His coat was tan, with a smudge of white on his face and an even larger splash across the front of his throat.

It was not just Bones' intelligence or happy disposition however, that separated him from other dogs. He had an uncanny ability to sense when something extraordinary was about to happen. Such a bizarre incident occurred in early spring. Billy and Bones were playing among the hardwood trees on the far side of the beaver pond that lay west of his grandfather's farm. Without warning, a strong wind ahead of an approaching storm caused the branches to sway erratically. As Billy and Bones started for home, the dog suddenly darted in front of the boy and knocked him over backwards. Just then a huge overhanging limb broke and crashed to the ground, landing in the path just ahead of them where the boy would have been running. Billy looked at Bones in amazement, but the dog just wagged his tail and headed for home.

When school started in the fall, Billy found it especially hard to leave Bones and the farm. Fortunately Bones made it easier for him. Every morning the dog would walk with him to the bus stop, and every afternoon the dog would wait for him at the end of the lane. For some inexplicable reason the dog seemed to know exactly when Bus Number Twelve was going to arrive. It was a relief to the boy and the dog when June came around, and they could spend every waking hour together.

On the morning of June 21, however, Billy Stuart's happiness took a tragic turn when Bones chased a young deer out of Will Stuart's cornfield and then strangely disappeared. The heartbroken boy and his grandfather searched everywhere, but the shepherd dog was nowhere to be found.

CHAPTER FOUR

THE WONDROUS TREE HOUSE

Strewn along the path to the two lone trees that stood near the edge of the tiny world called The Enchantment was a host of brilliantly colored wild flowers. The shepherd dog Billy Bones stopped from time to time to marvel at clusters and knelt to smell their fragrance, as he and Running Deer followed Winston Wise Owl back to the owl's tree house. In the dog's prior state he had never been aware of such beauty. He noticed the deer seemed to also be subject to bouts of wonderment. Every so often the young buck would turn around and around, as if he were trying to take in the sights and smells of his new environment.

"Ah, Mr. Bones, Mr. Running Deer, taking time to smell the flowers, I see!" said Winston Wise Owl patiently. The old bird seemed pleased.

Before long the three companions reached the lone trees at what appeared to be the boundary of The Enchantment. The two leafy giants, magnificent against the mist and gold of the land's edge, stood like two natural cathedrals, their emerald branches twisting skyward.

"I never noticed the size of these trees," marveled the young dog. "From beyond the tall grass where I was waitin' before we entered, they seemed most ordinary."

"Where you were stalkin' me, you mean!" cried the deer.

"Enough of that now my friends; in time you'll understand," soothed the owl. "As for the size and splendor of these trees, ah well, that's part of The Enchantment! You see, the old memories apparently left us with what they perceived to be ideal. Like the hopes and dreams the settlers must have had for their new life out west."

"Or beautiful?" added Billy Bones.

"Yes, or beautiful," agreed Winston, as he walked toward the tree on the north side of the path. A circular staircase led to a paneled door part-way up the tree.

Billy stopped and stared at the old door. A vision of a hole in the old tree flashed in front of him.

"What is it?" asked the owl.

"That's strange. I remember the hollow in that tree. It was right there where the door is now," insisted the dog.

"Of course, my friend, that's the way it would've appeared to you on your family's farm."

"Oh," said the dog in a soft voice. Somewhere in the back of his mind there was something else he wanted to tell the owl—something about the hollow hole and the strange young man he had seen during his transition, but for some reason he could not recall what it was.

"Follow me," said the old bird, as he started up the wooden steps. "My home is in the hollow of this tree."

The main floor of Winston's home contained his library and a place for dining. Comfortable old armchairs sat around the room, and the bookcases held a large collection of leather-bound books.

The owl allowed the two animals time to browse through his library and pick up some of the books. Billy found to his amazement that he could read their titles. A great longing filled his breast, as if an ancient memory was awaking within him.

"The old man, my first human, had a lot a' books in his main room," the dog began hesitantly. "He used to let me lie down by his chair while he read and smoked his pipe, but his library was nothin' like this! Where did so many wonderful books come from?"

The owl looked thoughtful. "Before The Enchantment some human animals hid these books in the cavity of my tree. I think one of them must have died here, 'cause there's an old grave just north of us. I was named after him, you know. On the cross above his grave it said "W. N. Stone," only it was blurry, and the animals who lived in The Enchantment at the time I entered thought it said Winston. And since it was my tree where the books were found, they decided to call me Winston, Winston Wise Owl. I found out his real name later when I looked inside the book covers." He glanced over at the dog. "Like you, I was astounded that I could read the words."

Billy lowered his head. Even though Winston inspired trust, the dog was somewhat embarrassed that the owl could so easily discern his elation.

"Let me show you the upstairs," hooted the owl, interrupting the dog's thoughts.

Partway up the stairs the old owl stopped. He had been explaining the different features of his home and his cherished possessions, but now he had a look of special pride. A grandfather clock stood at the rear wall of the first landing. "And this is my greatest treasure. They say it's at least 150 years old!" He went on to explain, "You see, most of the furniture we have was built by our own animals, but this long case clock was found in the foothills out west of town. Like my books it was apparently left by the human animals who traveled through here before The Enchantment."

The old bird paused for a moment. A sad wistful look crept into his eyes. "Ah, to think of all those dear possessions which were too heavy to carry over the mountains. And all that energy and those wonderful memories locked up inside of them. I truly believe…." He paused again. "I truly believe that energy had something to do with the formation of our wonderful Enchantment. I really do!"

Suddenly there was a great pounding at the front door, and the tour came to an abrupt halt as the old owl rushed down the stairway, followed by his anxious guests.

"Winston, are you there?" cried a frantic voice. "Winston, I need to talk to you!"

Standing outside Winston's open door was a formally-dressed, very agitated beaver. Because he had been in a rush to get up the stairs, his top hat had slid to a rakish angle.

"Ah, good morning, Mayor, and what brings you all the way out here?" inquired the surprised owl. "And what on earth's the matter? You seem completely out of sorts!"

"Sorry to bother you, Winston," puffed the smartly attired rodent, "but I think we have a serious situation on our hands!"

"Well, come on in. But before we discuss your emergency, let me introduce you to these two young animals who just arrived through the rift this morning," said Winston, ushering the beaver into his library.

"Oh, I'm sorry! Do forgive my interruption. I forgot all about the summer solstice today. I should've known you'd have guests," exclaimed the beaver, removing his hat.

"No, no, it's only proper that they should meet our most upstanding citizens first," smiled Winston. "Billy Bones and Running Deer, this is our good mayor, George P. Beaver."

The beaver smiled politely, nodded, and shook hands with the newcomers. "I'm pleased to make your acquaintance, and may I be the first to welcome you to our little community."

Remembering his earlier errand, the mayor excused himself and pulled his old companion to the side of the room. As Billy's hearing was still exceptional, he could not help but catch the entire conversation.

"I realize, Winston, that you're presently occupied, but our community is about to undergo a great upheaval, and I must talk to you," began the beaver. "It seems that Fabian Lynx is causing more trouble at the New Meetinghouse. Rumor has it that he wants to be their new spiritual leader. He seems to have the prairie dogs on his side. It could turn out to be a real disaster!"

"But what about Sister Sarah Mourning Dove?" questioned the concerned owl.

"Fabian has focused on some obscure passage that the Ancient Ones wrote in one of the appendixes to *The Great Book of Rules*. It implies that a bird cannot be the chosen leader of a gathering. He's been trying to use it to depose the poor dove," explained the beaver.

"I knew there was something sinister about that cat when he came through the rift last year," recalled Winston, "but I had no idea he'd move so fast. He's got a hatred for all things human, you know. Apparently they kept him caged up in one of their zoos. He was escaping the keepers when he accidentally came across the opening in the rift."

"No wonder he's always speaking out against the human artifacts!" exclaimed the mayor.

"I'll talk to Thaddeus Turtle and get some advice while you visit the moderate members of the City Council," suggested Winston. "Thaddeus is probably working in his study at the Old Meetinghouse right now."

With a nod to the two young animals, George P. Beaver descended the staircase and hurried off in the direction of the little village nestled in the heart of The Enchantment.

As Billy watched the elegantly-dressed beaver depart, he wondered who this Fabian Lynx was and why he hated humans so much. All of his dealings with the old man and the boy had been positive, and he had nothing but love and respect for them.

CHAPTER FIVE

THE GOOD NEIGHBOR

Winston guided Billy Bones and Running Deer back down to the yard and turned their attention to the magnificent tree on the right.

"Now my good friends, there's someone else I'd like you to meet. I'm confident she can handle your immediate needs. I think I'd better attend to the mayor's concerns," stated Winston Wise Owl, as he led them across the yard.

Snugly constructed in a hollow at the bottom of the equally enormous tree to the south was a lovely little dwelling. English ivy had grown up on either side of quaint Dutch doors and surrounded two small connected windows with whitewashed shutters on the right. Under the windows was a large flower box overflowing with purple and white petunias.

Before Winston Wise Owl could knock, the top door swung open, and a good-natured face popped into view. "Ah Hester, I thought I saw you peeking through the window," chided the owl.

"Well I certainly wouldn't want to miss anything that brought the mayor way out here on such a beautiful morning," retorted the jolly creature.

"It seems they're experiencing some trouble at the New Meetinghouse," confided the owl. "But come outside. I'd like you to meet our latest arrivals from the other world."

The owl helped Hester Groundhog open the bottom door, and she moved sprightly out onto the steppingstone. She was dressed in a long patterned dress of the old-fashioned style with a clean white dust cap on her head and an equally clean white apron around her waist.

"Hester, I'd like you to meet Billy Bones and Running Deer. Billy Bones and Running Deer, this is Hester Groundhog. She's one of our finest gardeners and certainly one of our best cooks, and goodness knows, she's managed to put up with me all these years."

"Well, we certainly have been good neighbors," laughed the groundhog, "even though Winston tries my patience at times when he doesn't let me in on everything."

"Hester, I was wondering if you'd look after these two until I can send the mayor's nephew back to show them around," continued the owl. "I promised them some refreshments, and I'm sure they'd like to see your garden. Oh and if you don't mind, tell them about the Grand Fair. From the looks of Mr. Running Deer here, I'd say he's a prime candidate for the Big Race. I'd wager he could give that Rogue Deer a run for his money!"

"Now Winston, don't go putting ideas into their heads. Just leave them to me." Hester paused and looked meaningfully at Winston. "Now what's all the fuss about?"

Winston looked uncomfortable for a few moments while Hester waited. "Oh what's the use; you're going to hear about it soon enough anyway. Fabian Lynx and some of the members of the New Meetinghouse are trying to remove Sister Sarah Mourning Dove and put Fabian in her place. I'm going to talk to Thaddeus right now and see if we can put a stop to this nonsense!"

Hester nodded. "I'll be glad to entertain these two newcomers until Georgie arrives. Now off with you! I know you're anxious to please the good mayor!" As the groundhog stepped saucily into her tiny abode, Billy mused that perhaps Hester could say things to Winston that others could not.

Leaving the two amused creatures in Hester's capable hands, the owl flew off toward the center of town and the Old Meetinghouse.

Before long the groundhog returned with freshly baked buns, blueberry jam, and hot tea. While the new arrivals ate on a table outside her cottage, she explained to them about the Grand Fair. "This is an especially important celebration because we're having an election, and all the candidates for mayor and City Council will be out and about, giving speeches and the like. And the rest of the week, there'll be judging competitions and games and such. I myself will be entering the baking division. The Big Race is on the third day. It's a foot race around town."

"And that's the race Mr. Wise Owl had in mind for Running Deer?" Billy interrupted.

"Yes, I believe so," said Hester, as a disturbing noise caused her to turn and look down the path that led westward toward the beaver pond.

Two black birds were approaching on foot. Billy Bones instantly recognized them as crows. He had often seen them cawing and squabbling about the old man's farmyard. The larger of the two crows seemed to be sobbing uncontrollably. She wore a white apron and a pink bonnet and appeared to be the mother of the smaller male she was dragging behind her.

"But there are also a number of other races. Georgie can tell you more about them if you're really interested," Hester suggested, as she wiped her hands on her apron and headed toward the distraught bird.

As the crows reached the shaded area between the two great trees, the mother crow wailed even louder. "Oh Hester, is Winston around? I must see him at once! I simply must!"

"I'm sorry, Gwendolyn, but he's flown off to consult Counselor Turtle. But what on earth's the matter? Has someone been hurt?"

"No, no, it's my husband and that bunch of fools down at the New Meetinghouse. They're going to ruin everything. I just know it!"

"Now calm down and explain to me what's happened," soothed the groundhog.

"They're trying to remove Sister Sarah as spiritual counselor and put Fabian Lynx in her place. Oh Hester, she's been so good to us! How can they be so cruel?"

"I think that's why Winston went to see Counselor Turtle, Gwendolyn. I think maybe he's looking into that very thing right now. But what about your husband? Can't you talk to him?"

"Oh, you know how Jason is, Hester. He tells me to be quiet and let him make the decisions. He says I don't understand such matters," the crow sobbed.

It was at this juncture that Gwendolyn Crow felt her son tugging on her apron. "What is it, Gerard? Can't you see that I'm upset here?" she cried, as she slapped the feathered hand that extended out from the young crow's wing.

Gerard did not answer but only pointed at Billy Bones and Running Deer, who were by this time standing uncomfortably behind Hester's table.

"Hester, there are two animals standing behind your table, and they have no clothes on," stated Gwendolyn flatly.

"Yes, I know. They just came through the magic portal this morning."

"Oh my goodness, the opening was this morning? I should've known. Oh my, they must think I'm a total basket case, carrying on like this," Gwendolyn muttered; as she let Hester lead her and Gerard over to the table.

"Mr. Bones and Mr. Running Deer, this is Mrs. Gwendolyn Crow and her son Gerard. They live along the fence line just a short way down the path," said Hester, as she shifted her attention back to the crow. "Gwendolyn, let me give you a loaf of walnut bread that I baked this morning. I'll tell Winston of your concern as soon as he returns."

As Hester hurried off to her kitchen, Gwendolyn continued her apologies. "You must think I'm terrible, carrying on like that. It's just that I get so flustrated… is that the word? Yes, well anyway, Jason says I just get so discombobulated. You see, Sister Sarah is such a dear friend. I can't bear to see her mistreated like this."

Gerard started pulling on his mother's apron again. Finally she leaned over and allowed him to whisper something in her ear.

"Gerard still wonders why you aren't wearin' clothes." The crow smiled and looked back down at her son. "It's because they haven't seen Percival Gander yet, dear. Don't you remember when Mr. Lynx came through the portal last year? We saw him and Mr. Wise Owl pass by our kitchen window on their way to Percy's Shop. Mr. Lynx wasn't wearing any clothes either. Remember?"

When Hester returned from her kitchen, she quickly handed a loaf of bread to Gwendolyn and began escorting her back down the path. Gerard followed obediently but turned around one last time and waved shyly to the two animals still standing awkwardly behind the table.

After the two crows were safely on their way, Hester padded back to the table and motioned for Billy and Running Deer to sit down and resume their meal. "I'm sorry about that, but as you can see, Gwendolyn's terribly concerned about Sister Sarah Mourning Dove. The crows go to the New Meetinghouse, and Gwendolyn and Sarah are close friends," the groundhog explained. "But I'm afraid her husband Jason has decided against Sarah."

"Wasn't that what Mr. Wise Owl was concerned about, Miss Groundhog?" asked Billy.

"Yes, I'm afraid it was," agreed Hester.

As soon as the meal was over, Hester Groundhog showed the two visitors her garden. Near her home the plantings consisted of carefully designed bushes and many varieties of flowers. Farther to the south were cultivated rows of fresh garden products, also artistically edged with bushes and flowers.

"How long have you worked on your garden?" asked Billy. "It must've taken you years to create such beauty."

"At first, I just planted my vegetables," Hester smiled. "The ideas for the landscaping came gradually. You see, time treats us differently here. One of the real miracles of The Enchantment is that we're allowed to live a long life so that we can work to accomplish our dreams. My dreams are simple. They revolve around my house and my garden and what I can share with others."

As Billy listened to Hester's answer, he realized how much he liked the diligent groundhog and the wise owl and how he already felt some connection to the lonely deer. These good creatures and the magnificence of The Enchantment had aroused a new sense of excitement within him, but he was also intrigued by the concerns of the anxious mayor and the overwrought crow. "What's this Fabian Lynx trying to do anyway?" he wondered. "And why is it upsetting them?"

CHAPTER SIX

THE ROGUE DEER

After a short nap on the soft grass near Hester Groundhog's garden, Billy Bones and Running Deer were awakened by a good-natured voice: "Hi there!" The two animals jumped up, startled and rubbed their eyes. Before them stood a strapping young beaver with a broad toothy grin, dressed in a red vest, bow tie, and short pants. "I'm Georgie! They call me that so I'm not confused with my uncle, George P. Beaver. I'm here to show ya' around."

Billy reached out a hand. "I'm Billy Bones, and my lanky companion here is Running Deer. At least that's what we've been calling him until he comes up with a better name."

The beaver shook their hands with great gusto, and just as energetically turned to depart along the only path that led westward. "Come on, the tailor's waitin'!"

Billy had an immediate liking for the eager Georgie, but he had to run to catch up with him. More reserved, Running Deer followed behind. In the distance Billy could see the richly-colored trees that circled the beavers' pond and lined the stream that meandered south. Even farther west, golden foothills led up into the mountains and gleamed with a radiance that Billy had never before seen. Surrounding all of this, of course, was the ever-present mist with its golden hue, whose mysterious beauty filled the shepherd dog with a sense of awe and wonder.

"Do you ever get used to the magnificent colors here?" asked the dog.

Georgie laughed. "Most everyone who enters here asks me the same thing. But I've always lived here. So of course I don't know what it was like before The Enchantment started."

"And when did it start?" asked the deer.

The beaver stopped at a crossroads that suddenly appeared between two fields of ripe grain. "I've heard that it was more than eighty years ago." He gave the deer a sidewise glance. "But then, what do I know?"

Georgie smiled again and quickly changed the subject. "Do you see that sign over there?" He gestured to a newly painted sign that pointed in four directions. "If you follow the path south, you'll eventually cross the ford in the river and then head west up into the foothills." He playfully turned in the opposite direction and pointed. "This path is called Wheat Walk. Many of the crop farmers live along the fence line." He finally pointed westward. "But if we go straight, we'll go toward our dam, where you can cross into town. Percy Gander lives along that road, and that's where we're headed. He's our tailor. He also collects all kinds a' useful stuff that comes in handy when animals are just startin' out. You'll like him, though he is a bit odd, especially when you first meet him."

Suddenly and seemingly out of nowhere, a large buck came sprinting around the curve and ran headlong into Running Deer. Both deer went sprawling into the wheat field that bordered the intersection.

As the strange deer jumped to his feet, Billy could see that he was about the same size as Running Deer. Unlike the other animals, he wore only a pair of trousers and a red bandana tied loosely around his neck. On his left cheek he had an old scar that caused him to sneer slightly as he spoke. "What's the matter with you? Why don't you watch where you're standin'?" he yelled at Running Deer. "Who are you anyway? I never seen you around! And why ain't you wearin' no clothes?"

Georgie rushed over to Running Deer who was still sitting on the ground catching his breath. "This is Running Deer, Rodney. He just came through the opening this morning. And this is Billy Bones. They haven't had a chance to see Percy yet!"

"Who's talkin' to you, Chubby? Stay out of this, if you know what's good for you!" snapped the agitated deer, pushing the young beaver aside.

Running Deer by this time had managed to rise but still found it difficult to speak. Unexpectedly and without warning, the deer called Rodney started to lunge at him. Using the utmost speed, Billy moved between them and caught Rodney by his forearms.

"This was an accident, my friend. There's no need for fighting here," pleaded the shepherd dog.

Rodney gave Billy a disdainful glance, yanked his arms

away, and started limping northward. Billy could see that he was in quite a bit of pain. "Just stay out of my way… all of you, especially your ugly friend over there!" Rodney snarled, as he pointed toward Running Deer.

The small group watched in silence as Rodney moved up the Wheat Walk path. When Billy felt Rodney was out of earshot, he let out a sigh, "Whew, what was that all about?" Outside of his initial misunderstanding with Running Deer, this was the first animal he had encountered who was not amiable at all.

"That was Rodney Wild Deer, but most people call him the Rogue Deer. He pretty much stays to himself, 'cept for Lester, Leon, and Leroy. They're the three coyote brothers he sometimes runs with. He was by himself today, so he's probably practicin' for the Big Race. He usually wins, you know. My dad says it's best to stay out of his way!" warned Georgie.

Running Deer turned away unexpectedly and started walking in the direction of the enraged buck. Billy could see that his new companion was upset, so he and Georgie waited quietly until the young buck gathered his composure.

"Why do you suppose he got so angry with Running Deer?" whispered Billy to Georgie.

"Cause he's bad news, and I imagine he's jealous of havin' another buck in town."

"Why's that?" wondered Billy.

"Well, there's this doe he likes called Melinda. Maybe he thinks Running Deer will be some competition for him.

I know Melinda's dad doesn't like him comin' near his daughter."

After the deer composed himself and walked back to the beaver and the dog, the trio continued their journey west on Beaver Dam Road.

CHAPTER SEVEN

PERCIVAL'S SHOP

Percival's shop was on the left side of the road. The main story of the shop was built high above the ground, and a long ramp led up to the main door. Billy recognized that the building resembled the chicken coops in the old man's barnyard. A memory of the boy going up the long ramp after hen's eggs flashed through his conscious mind, and he felt a strange lump in his throat that hurt when he swallowed.

When the animals reached the front of the shop, Georgie strode up the ramp and knocked on the door. Almost immediately a long-necked gander stuck his head out of a window.

"Well my goodness, my goodness me, what do we have here? What do we have here?" the goose repeated, pulling his head back inside and then suddenly out again.

Georgie motioned toward his companions. "Percy, these two animals just arrived from the other world. Mr. Wise Owl said they're in need of your services. May we come in?"

"Well, my goodness, my goodness, yes! Bring them in! Bring them in!"

In a few moments, the gander pushed the door open and stood in the doorway motioning for them to enter. He had on a mustard-yellow vest, neatly buttoned from top to bottom and a long measuring tape that dangled around his neck.

Billy and Running Deer glanced skeptically at one another as they climbed hesitantly up the ramp. Once inside the visitors noticed rows of clothing on both sides of the shop.

"Introduce your friends, Georgie. Yes, please, oh my, yes!" said the excited gander.

Georgie introduced Billy first. "This shepherd dog goes by the name of Billy Bones."

Billy held out his hand, but was surprised when the high-energy gander took a measuring tape and held it along Billy's outstretched arm, sizing him up for a possible shirt. "Ah yes, Billy, and what kind of garment are we looking for? Yes, what are we looking for?" He said this more to himself than to Billy. He then took his measuring tape and held it in front of the dog's chest, eyeing it carefully.

"I'm not sure… I haven't thought…" Billy muttered rather helplessly, but Percival had already approached Running Deer.

"And what are we looking for here?" He repeated the motion of sizing up the deer's chest measurements with his tape. "Oh my, yes, oh my, you may be a problem, may be a problem!"

The deer backed away slightly and looked at the beaver for help.

"And this is Running Deer," Georgie interjected, hoping to relieve the tension on the young buck's face. The beaver then turned to the deer. "Percy needs to know your size so he can find an outfit for you. Everyone in our little community wears something. My Dad says it's got something to do with the human animals who came before us. But then, what do I know?"

By the time Georgie finished his explanation, Percival had already waddled down the aisle in the direction of the large sizes. He brought several articles to the center of the room and continued questioning the animals about what they would prefer. Billy, of course, had memories of what the young boy wore so knew something of what he might desire. Running Deer, on the other hand, seemed to have no preference for any type of clothing.

After trying a number of garments on the uncomfortable deer, the concerned gander finally stepped back and announced, "It's the name! You need another name, ah yes, a first name, oh my, yes, a first name! Let see now, Rodger, Rodger Running Deer. No, no, too much like Rodney.

"Mr. Wise Owl wants Running Deer to enter the Big Race," volunteered Billy. "Perhaps a name for a good runner…?"

"Ah yes, something a winner might have. Ah yes, a winner. Let's see now, there's Wynn, Wynn Running Deer. No, no, not quite right, not quite right. Let's see, Speedy, Victorious, Vic… Wait. That's it: Victor…Victor Running Deer! What a delightful name! What a delightful name! Very nice, yes, very nice…."

Having settled the question of a name for the deer in his own mind, Percival succeeded in finding for him a long pair of trousers and a striking dark brown vest that could be worn open. Victor said nothing about the clothes and seemed to be content with his new name. For Billy Bones, Percival settled on a royal blue shirt and a pair of pants with two waist straps holding them up. He stood back and examined both carefully.

"Yes, oh my, yes, that will do, that will do nicely, oh my, yes!" Percival exclaimed with a satisfied nod. He turned the animals around for one last look. This time, however, both Billy and Victor obeyed without question. Georgie sat nearby on a counter. He had an amused look on his face. "Oh my, yes, that will do. That will do nicely," repeated Percival, as he turned and waggled away.

The two newcomers looked quizzically at Georgie. "What do we do now?" asked the dog. "Do we just keep the clothes? I don't quite understand."

"If you ever find somethin' you don't want, just bring it over to Percy. He'll store it and give it to whoever's in need. He's got a big storage room downstairs," Georgie explained.

As the satisfied costumers turned to leave, the gander returned to the center of his shop. He was carrying a long white robe of exceptional quality. He glanced up at the three. "I see you like my work. It's for Fabian Lynx. He's being chosen to take over the New Meetinghouse. Yes, quite a story that. Yes, quite a story. Don't know what to think… what to think! Must talk to Winston… Yes, must talk to Winston about that!"

As Georgie, Billy, and Victor were leaving the shop, they met an entourage of conservatively dressed citizens. Billy noticed that a number were prairie dogs. He vaguely remembered barking at them and chasing them down into their holes in the other world.

The handsome animal leading the group, however, was something quite different. He looked like a large cat with ears that strangely seemed to have been torn or clipped. Like the others, he too was conservatively dressed in a white shirt and ribbon tie under his green vest and dark coat. Unlike the others, he had an air of great importance and charm. He folded his hands and nodded as he whisked by the beaver and the deer. When he came to the dog, however, he stopped, eyed him carefully, and then marched up the ramp into Percival's shop. His respectful followers waited obediently on the path outside.

"Who was that?" whispered Billy. "I'd hate to be his enemy!"

"That was Fabian Lynx. And if what Percy said is true, I'm afraid it's now Brother Fabian Lynx!"

CHAPTER EIGHT

THE OLD MEETINGHOUSE

After a quick stop at the beaver pond to inform the mayor's nephew that he was needed at Land's End, Winston Wise Owl continued his flight to the Old Meetinghouse. He felt again the stiff breeze ruffle the feathers of his powerful wings. He loved to fly.

From a distance the Old Meetinghouse spire, the New Meetinghouse spire, and the City Hall Clock Tower provided a storybook charm to the little village. The three belfries made Winston recall the pictures in the book of fairy tales that he kept in a trunk at the foot of his bed, the one that said, "To my beloved grandson, Jimmy."

On this particular occasion, however, Winston was not concerned with architecture. He was reflecting on the dog and the deer. He hated to leave them so soon after their headlong entry into The Enchantment. He was especially concerned about the dog. He still had such a steadfast relationship with his human family. "And yet, there's something different about this Billy Bones," he mused, "something almost spiritual. I…I can't quite put my finger on it."

As Winston landed on the east lawn of the Old Meetinghouse, he forced his attention back to the matter at hand. The disturbing news he heard from the mayor earlier in the day could have far-reaching consequences if something was not done quickly. Since the information concerned matters of moral leadership, Winston needed the advice of his old friend, Counselor Thaddeus B. Turtle. He and Thaddeus had entered the golden portal during the same summer solstice many years ago, and he felt they were kindred spirits.

As he had expected, Winston found Thaddeus in his study in back of the assembly hall. The dignified turtle was sitting at his desk working on his weekly meditation for the Sunday meeting at the Old Meetinghouse. As usual, his glasses were balanced partway down his beak-like nose, and the clean white stole around his neck was slightly askew.

Thaddeus looked up over his glasses as Winston approached him. "Well, I see that you still don't believe in knocking!"

"Please don't get up on my account," the owl retorted. He enjoyed the friendly banter between them. "I'll just sit right here and make myself at home." The owl proceeded to sit in a comfortable old armchair in front of the turtle's desk and waited for the terrapin to look up again from his work.

"You've come about the business at the New Meetinghouse, I take it, unless you've another one of your outlandish ideas on moral welfare to debate," grunted the turtle.

Winston was aware that Thaddeus liked the heated discussions as well as he did. In fact, the turtle had borrowed some books on ancient philosophers that never found their way back into his library. The owl sat straighter in his chair and inquired, "Then you've heard what they're planning to do to Sister Sarah? The mayor hiked all the way out to my tree house this morning just to tell me."

"Our *Great Book of Rules* can be used to support many points of view," stated the terrapin flatly. "This time it seems Fabian Lynx is using it against Sarah. He contends that a bird cannot be the leader of a gathering, and he's been quoting paragraphs from *The Great Book of Rules*, something about 'no winged animal should be first among them.' I think it goes back to one of the memories before The Enchantment."

"But that's out-and-out prejudice!" interrupted Winston. "Besides, she's been their adviser and counselor for years. True, I don't always agree with her strict adherence to certain rules, but she's done a lot for the citizens of this community. The only conclusion I can come to is that he covets the job himself!"

"And to think that Fabian has been in The Enchantment for only one year!" commented Thaddeus. "Surely the members of the New Meetinghouse can't be swayed so easily."

At that precise moment, a soft tap on the south door interrupted their conversation.

"Who do you suppose…?" The old turtle got up from his desk, slowly plodded over to the door, hesitantly opened it, and peered out. There stood the object of their concern, Sister Sarah Mourning Dove.

Winston could see that Thaddeus did not recognize the dove at first. She had removed her short white robe and her white bonnet and had donned a light blue shawl and a straw bonnet. She had been crying.

"Why Sister Sarah, what on earth's the matter?" asked Thaddeus B. Turtle.

The dove entered the room without answering. When she saw Winston, now standing by his chair, she stopped. "Oh I'm sorry, is this a bad time? It's just that I…I…." She turned away and wiped her eyes with a small handkerchief clutched in her hand.

"It's all right, Sarah," soothed the turtle. "Winston and I were just speaking of the difficulty you're having at your meetinghouse. I'm sure he's just as concerned about your situation as I am."

Winston surmised that Sarah Mourning Dove was just as happy to be able to cry on two old shoulders as on one. She continued bravely, "I know we haven't always been in complete agreement, but I felt that we had an understanding, a mutual respect, so to speak. So I thought I'd come to you. I'm at a loss…I'm simply at a loss!"

"Now now," said Winston who had always been fond of the little bird, "why don't you just sit on this chair and tell us everything."

The little bird boosted herself up on the old chair, her small legs dangling in the air. She looked altogether lost and forlorn. Both old companions waited patiently for her to gain her composure and speak.

"They literally threw me out this morning," Sarah finally sighed. "The gathering said that I wasn't really qualified to be their leader anymore since I was a bird. One of the guides at the New Meetinghouse even read a paragraph from *The Great Book of Rules* to support their position!"

"Well, what did you tell them? Did you explain to them that you can support almost any point of view with the *Book of Rules* if that is your intent?" asked Winston, his cheeks fairly puffing with indignation.

Sarah looked over at Winston with some surprise. "I don't know if I agree with that statement, Mr. Wise Owl, but I do know that sometimes things can be interpreted incorrectly. But of course, the truth is always there."

"Well then, perhaps the guides have misinterpreted the passage," said Thaddeus, trying to avoid a philosophical debate. "In any case, what was your reply?"

"I just didn't say anything. I mean, I was flabbergasted. I should've seen it coming. Certainly the signs were all there, and I should have realized."

"And just who did they get to replace you?" Winston was becoming angry.

"They elected Fabian Lynx right there on the spot. Now he's Brother Fabian Lynx!"

"Why that…that….!" Winston was almost shouting.

"Careful, my friend," warned Thaddeus, putting a comforting hand on the owl's shoulder. He then turned his attention back to Sarah. "Is there anything we can do to stop this?"

"I'm afraid not, counselor. Fabian and a number of the guides are already on their way to Percival's shop for a white robe. That will make it official you know."

The owl crossed to the door. He was seething. "I think maybe I need to fly over there and see if I can stop Percy from making that robe!"

"I'm afraid you're too late. It seems that Fabian ordered the robe weeks ago. Apparently it's waiting for him at the shop," lamented Sarah.

"Why that devious…he's planned this whole thing all along!"

Winston stepped out of the building and stretched his wings.

"Exactly what are you planning to do?" inquired the worried turtle.

"First, I'm going to try to reason with the guides at the New Meetinghouse. If that doesn't work, at least I can give them a piece of my mind!"

Sister Sarah, who was now just plain Sarah, slipped by the turtle and moved outside. She seemed somewhat calmer and more in control now that she had the good turtle and the wise old owl on her side. "Do be careful, Winston. I think Fabian's not a good enemy to have. He also made some derogatory remarks about you…and especially about your books!"

Winston Wise Owl looked quizzically at Sarah Mourning Dove for a moment and then spread his huge wings and flew off toward Percival's shop.

CHAPTER NINE

THE CONFRONTATION

Billy Bones was interested in staying at Percival's shop and hearing more about Fabian Lynx, but Georgie Beaver was already heading up the path toward the beaver dam. When Billy reached the pond, he instinctively rushed to the water's edge, knelt down on his knees, and started lapping up the cool water with his tongue. By the time he raised his head, he could see that Georgie was amused. He realized that perhaps this was not the way creatures inside The Enchantment drank. The only consolation was that Victor had done the same thing.

"I guess that's not the way you get a drink around here, huh?" remarked the dog.

"Well, we usually dip it out with our hands or use a cup," chuckled the beaver. "I'm only smilin' because most newcomers do the same thing."

As soon as Georgie finished talking, Billy turned his attention back to the beaver dam. It was thick and sturdy and appeared to be an engineering masterpiece. "I don't remember the dam lookin' like this. As I remember it was rough and jagged with lots of branches and mud showin' around the edges."

"Well, that's how the original one looked. It was built by my great-grandad and his family before The Enchantment," the proud beaver began. "The large earthworks that we're standin' on and the spillway were put in afterwards. And look at this great roadway! Now everybody can use it to get across the water. I live over there." Georgie pointed to a house with whitewashed walls and great beams that rose out of the water close to the shoreline. "We'll go over there tonight for supper, if you want to. Mom's invited us." He hesitated for a moment and then pointed to a castle-like structure rising out of the water close to an island in the center of the pond. "And look over there! That's where my uncle, old George P., lives. Pretty fancy, huh?"

The pond seemed to fill what looked like a larger, more ancient riverbed. Billy gazed in wonder at its beauty and the little homes snuggled around it. His greatest admiration, however, was for the magnificent trees with their thick gnarled branches that seemed to reach unbelievable heights.

"I still can't believe these trees!" exclaimed Billy, breaking the silence. "I used to play with the boy by this pond. I know what these trees looked like!"

At that moment, a shadow passed over the three young animals, and they could hear the "whump, whump" of the wings of a large bird. They looked up and saw a great horned owl moving along the path that led back to Percival's shop.

"It's Mr. Wise Owl!" cried Georgie. "He doesn't usually fly that low unless somethin' is wrong, or he's good and mad!" The beaver suddenly started to run in the direction of the great bird. "Come on! Let's see what he's fired up about! We don't want to miss this!"

By the time the three companions got back to Percival's shop, Winston had already grazed the heads of the surprised guides of the New Meetinghouse and was circling to make a landing. His descent from the sky was equally theatrical. He made it appear that he would land directly on top of the smug prairie dogs, who had placed themselves in front of the group. Instinctively the little rodents panicked and backed into the startled guides behind them. At the last moment Winston slowed his approach and landed safely on the path some ten feet in front of them.

Georgie, who had placed himself and his two new companions off to one side of the path, whispered to Billy and Victor proudly, "Isn't he terrific? I wish I could do that!"

As Billy listened to Georgie and observed Winston's defiant stand against the guides, he knew intuitively that something of great significance was about to happen.

"And who's in charge of this fiasco?" Winston demanded.

A fox and a crow, who Billy guessed must be Gwendolyn Crow's husband, took a rather concerned prairie dog by either arm and led him forward.

"Elmer Prairie Dog runs the General Store on Main Street," whispered Georgie Beaver to Billy and Victor.

"Elmer here is chairman of our council. I reckon he's

in charge," declared the crow, chomping on a wheat stalk he held in his beak.

"Yes, Elmer's the one to talk to," agreed the fox. "But speakin' for myself, I can say I wasn't exactly thrilled by your entrance. Somebody could've gotten hurt, you know!"

"You seemed to have survived all right, Phineas," remarked the owl sarcastically. He then turned his attention back to the crow. "As for you, Farmer Crow, I always credited you with more sense than to go along with a scheme like this!"

"I'd say that ain't none o' your concern, Winston," said the crow.

"When a good bird like Sister Sarah is unjustly treated, I would say that it becomes pretty much everybody's concern! I'm sure Gwendolyn is having no part of this nonsense."

"My wife goes along with whatever I say! Besides, if that's what the *Great Book o' Rules* says, then that's what we do."

"Now Mr. Wise Owl, we had a fair election," muttered Elmer Prairie Dog, trying to compose himself. "This was no rash decision. Once it was pointed out to us that a winged creature could not be head of the gathering, we knew we had to act."

"And just who pointed that out to you?" inquired the owl.

"Well, I…" the prairie dog hesitated. "As I remember, it was our dear Brother Fabian."

"Is he in Percival's shop, this very minute, donning the white robe of office that he miraculously ordered weeks ago?" questioned the owl.

"Yes, Brother Fabian is there, as you probably know," admitted Elmer.

"Doesn't it seem odd to you that the animal replacing Sarah Mourning Dove is the same one who pointed out to you that a bird should not be the head of your gathering?"

"But it says in *The Great Book of Rules…*" protested the rodent.

"The words in *The Great Book of Rules* can be manipulated to support whatever meaning you want, you old fool!"

The guides suddenly bristled and began whispering to one another.

"Oh, oh!" warned Georgie softly to Billy and Victor, "they're not going to like that."

"And who is calling whom an old fool?" said a loud voice, coming from inside the doorway to Percival's shop.

Because of the brightness of the noonday sun, Billy could not see the figure in the doorway clearly. As he strode down the ramp however, the dog was stunned by the appearance of the large handsome lynx. He was absolutely radiant in his long white robe, which seemed to sparkle in the sunlight.

It seemed to Billy that Brother Fabian Lynx could not have chosen a better moment to appear on the scene. The owl's entrance was powerful, but the lynx's arrival was equally as dramatic. Winston appeared to have been caught off guard. "Why Mr. Fabian Lynx, it seems like only yesterday when I helped you through the magic portal. It appears you've come a long way since then!"

"Don't play games with me, Winston Wise Owl. It won't work, and by the way it's Brother Fabian to you now," stated the cat, as he momentarily made eye contact with Billy.

"Oh, I'm sorry, Brother Fabian, I didn't realize you were so sensitive," parried the owl.

"Sarcasm won't work on me either, Winston," responded the cat, "but yes, thanks to The Great Spirit, I've come a long way. He's guided my decisions over the past year."

"Oh, The Great Spirit's led you, has he?" The owl shook his head. "Fabian, Fabian, don't blame your little deceptions on The Great Spirit. You orchestrated this take-over yourself, and you know it!"

The atmosphere surrounding the two combatants had become increasingly tense. No one made any movement except Percival, who kept sticking his long neck in and out of the window. No one spoke, and there was an uncomfort-able long silence while the two glared at one another.

Finally Brother Fabian smiled, glanced down at them and spoke. His voice was calm and serene. "I say to you again, Winston Wise Owl, that The Great Spirit has led me in this decision with the help of *The Great Book of Rules,* study, and meditation. I'm sorry for Sarah Mourning Dove. I know she did her best, and I've therefore offered to let her be my assistant."

"Your assistant! And how long do you think that would last?" yelled the owl angrily. "You're nothing but a hypo-crite, Fabian Lynx, but these good guides aren't ignorant! They'll eventually see you for what you really are!"

The big cat lifted his head slightly, and the sunlight made his eyes sparkle. "You can call me names all you wish, Winston Wise Owl, and I hope The Great Spirit forgives you." He then pointed a finger directly at the owl. "And now I say this to you, Mr. Winston Wise Owl, look to yourself! You and your wicked books! There's but one truth, and that's found in *The Great Book of Rules* written by the Ancient Ones. I'm fully aware of some of the evil teaching located in the pages of many of your books, and I won't rest until they're all confiscated and burned!"

Without waiting for a reply, the crafty lynx turned on his heels and strode down the path leading back to the little town. Shocked, his obedient guides trotted after him.

Percival waited until the entourage was out of sight and then waddled nervously down the ramp and over to where Winston was standing. "Oh my, oh my, what have I done? What have I done?" moaned the gander. "I was only thinking of my work! I should have refused to make the robe! Yes, I should have refused!"

"The fault's not yours, Percival," answered Winston affectionately. "You were only doing your job. If anything, the fault's mine. I underestimated our charming Brother Fabian. I'm afraid we lost this battle, but time is on our side. I won't underestimate him again."

Billy Bones was the next to approach the owl. He had watched the confrontation with great interest and had already chosen sides. "Is there anything we can do, Mr. Wise Owl?"

"Ah, thank you, Mr. Billy Bones," sighed the owl appreciatively, "but this is my fight. Now go finish your tour with Georgie. You have much to see before nightfall."

Winston nodded gently to each of the young animals and to the gander and then turned and slowly trudged up toward his tree house at Land's End, where the golden mist marked the edge of The Enchantment.

CHAPTER TEN

MAIN STREET

The majority of the Prairie's charmed village was in a secluded pocket of land bordered on the east by the beaver pond and on the west by the golden hills. As Georgie Beaver guided Billy Bones and Victor Running Deer back across the dam and on to Court Street, he pointed out a number of little homes nestled in the trees and on the slopes leading down to the pond. Many inhabitants of these delightful houses leaned out of their windows for a cheery hello or popped out of their doors for a quick introduction and a sincere welcome to their little community.

After the trio passed City Hall, Georgie showed Billy and Victor the brightly-painted buildings on Main Street. Although they varied in color and style, they all had a late Victorian period look about them. Further south, more stores and quaint little shops lined both sides of the street, ending with the old saloon on the west and the town boardinghouse on the east.

Georgie then crossed over to the General Store belonging to Elmer Prairie Dog at the corner of Court and Main. "My Grandfather and Elmer's dad built this old store together. Dad said they were really good friends. He said that when the conservative prairie dogs broke away from the Old Meetinghouse and formed the New Meetinghouse, things were never the same again. Too bad, that's what I say!"

Knowing that his companions would need the services of the General Store, Georgie decided to take them inside for a quick tour. Edwina Prairie Dog was minding the store for her husband. She looked up suspiciously when Georgie and the town's newest members entered. She was dressed rather conservatively with a neat little apron at her waist. Her irritable wide-eyed daughter, Patsy, wearing a big ribbon on her head and a lacy petticoat beneath the hem of her skirt, was busy rearranging goods on a shelf.

As soon as Georgie introduced Billy and Victor, Edwina began plying them with questions about their arrival and their experiences so far in the little community. Because of the memory of their first encounter with Fabian Lynx and Elmer Prairie Dog, Billy was hesitant to respond. Out of the corner of his eye, he noticed that Victor was having similar difficulty. Eventually Georgie came to their rescue and related part of the day's adventures.

"We were in front of Percival's shop when Fabian Lynx appeared in his white robe. He looks very nice in it," Georgie concluded, trying to stay clear of the actual confrontation.

"Ah, Brother Fabian," Edwina interrupted, "what a blessing he's been to us! To think we allowed a bird to lead us all these years, and we didn't even know better!"

"Mr. Wise Owl says that Sister Sarah's been deeply wronged!" interjected Georgie, expressing his loyalty.

"Ha! You mustn't listen to that old fool. He's just upset 'cause he's a bird himself," said Edwina, as she turned and walked briskly behind the counter.

Taking a cue from her mother, Patsy marched over to Georgie and chided, "Brother Fabian says that my father should run for mayor during the Grand Fair. He says that he has just as much right to be mayor as your uncle, and even more so 'cause there are more prairie dogs than beavers and there always have been. So there!" She stuck out her tongue at the shocked beaver and moved quickly back to her shelf.

As Patsy was venting her feelings, two woodland birds, a prairie dog named Irma—who turned out to be Edwina's sister-in-law—and an old cat who had been sitting on a bench out front entered the store. The cat seemed to be especially curious about Billy Bones.

Suddenly a commotion in the street broke the tension between Georgie and the prairie dogs. Irma rushed to the door and called back to her sister-in-law, "It's Brother Fabian, Edwina! He's with your husband and a number of the guides from the New Meetinghouse. They're coming this way. Oh, and Brother Fabian has on his beautiful new white robe. He looks magnificent! There's a whole crowd gathering!" With those words she turned and rushed out into the street followed by Edwina, Patsy, the two birds, Georgie, Billy, Victor, and finally the old cat.

When Brother Fabian Lynx arrived at the crossroad of Court and Main, he climbed up on the corner steps leading into the store and held up his arms. He stood well above the rest of the large crowd, and the sun caught the back of his head, causing his golden fur to shine like a halo. His robe was splendid. The crowd became silent, anticipating his remarks.

"I feel The Great Spirit has moved among us today and that wonderful things are about to happen that will make this charmed community a better place to live." The lynx paused and motioned for Elmer to come up and stand by him. He towered over the little rodent. "To help us in this endeavor, the guides at the New Meetinghouse are planning to back Elmer Prairie Dog for mayor during the election at the end of the Grand Fair!"

As Fabian raised Elmer's arm, the rest of the members of the New Meetinghouse cheered and applauded loudly. Many others in the crowd, including Georgie and the two woodland birds, seemed stunned. The two birds twittered softly to each other and then hurried off to spread the news to their neighbors.

Georgie quickly pulled his two companions aside. "A beaver's been mayor for as long as I can remember. I gotta tell my uncle what's happened!" he said. "A prairie dog will be real competition for him. Just walk one block west of here, and you'll see why. We call it Prairie Dog Town 'cause it's got all these underground houses. I shouldn't be gone long. Wait for me in front of City Hall."

As Billy and Victor watched Georgie dash off toward the beaver pond, a smooth resonant voice caused both animals to turn back toward Preston's store. "Victor

Running Deer and Billy Bones, if I understand correctly, I was hoping to get a chance to meet you when circumstances weren't so chaotic. I'm afraid the little confrontation at Percival's shop has put everybody in a bad light." Brother Fabian shook hands with Victor and then turned to Billy. As he shook Billy's right hand, he clasped the dog's right arm with his left hand. Billy was amazed at the strength and warmth of the lynx's touch, felt all the way to his backbone. Unexpectedly however, a picture of two humans coming at him with a large stick and a whip simultaneously flickered across his conscious mind. The image caused Billy to withdraw his hand.

"What's the matter, Mr. Bones?" asked Brother Fabian, looking at the dog quizzically.

"I'm sorry. I thought I saw something. I must have been mistaken," lied Billy.

The lynx smiled out of the corner of his mouth and then stood aside so he could introduce the new candidate for mayor. "And I'm sure you know Elmer Prairie Dog from the announcement made only a few minutes ago."

The proprietor of the General Store, who had been standing in the shadow of the handsome cat, bowed slightly and shook hands with both animals. "Welcome to our little town. If I can be of service to you at any time, please don't hesitate to call on me."

"And we'd like to invite you both to visit the New Meetinghouse on Sunday morning," continued Brother Fabian. "I think you'll find our gathering very friendly."

As Fabian and Elmer continued their welcome,

Billy's concentration was being broken by a very unusual phenomenon. It looked like the head of an old stag with huge antlers still in the velvet was floating toward them over the heads of the crowd, now dispersing in the other direction down Main Street.

When the mysterious vision got closer, Billy Bones could see that it was a real deer dressed in a collarless gray shirt rolled up at the sleeves and dark trousers held up by suspenders. He seemed to be walking directly toward them. When the old buck got within six feet of them, he stopped and waited for Elmer Prairie Dog and Brother Fabian Lynx to finish their conversation. Elmer was pointing out the boardinghouse at the end of the street as a possible place to stay, when he became aware of the stag directly behind him.

"Oh, Olen, I'm sorry. I didn't see you standing there," said the prairie dog apologetically. "Mr. Olen Buck, this is Victor Running Deer and Billy Bones, the newest arrivals in our community. Mr. Buck here is one of the finest members of our deer population. He and his wife live in the thicket south of the dam." Seeming to sense that the deer was on a mission, Elmer and Brother Fabian excused themselves and crossed the street to Elmer's store.

"Mr. Running Deer," said the old stag, turning his attention immediately to Victor. "I came as soon as I heard there was another deer in our community. We're small in number, but we take care of our own. I'm very happy to meet you!"

The dog could see that the younger deer was visibly moved by the amicability of the older deer. "I bet Victor's lived alone most of his life," Billy mused to himself. "No wonder that encounter with Rodney Deer upset him so much."

"And I'm very happy to meet you, sir. It's very kind of you to come and greet us," responded Victor appreciatively, as the two deer shook hands.

"My wife said that I was to invite you for supper and offer you a place to spend the night." The old stag turned politely to Billy. "And of course your friend's welcome also."

Victor lowered his head and responded for the two of them. "That's very kind of you, sir, but I'm afraid we've already been invited to supper by Georgie Beaver's mother."

"Oh I don't think she'll mind if I take you off her hands. Besides, Victor, I don't think you'll fit inside her house!" laughed the older deer. "And there's another reason you might be interested in coming to us tonight. There's an old lean-to in the thicket just across the stream you might want to claim. I'll show it to you later this evening or in the morning if you like. There's a nice patch of sweet corn that goes along with it. Unfortunately the previous occupant is no longer with us."

"I think you should go with him," Billy urged. "I'll wait for Georgie and explain where you are. I'm sure he won't mind."

"Well, in that case, I think I'll take you up on that offer, sir," smiled the young deer.

"Good, then it's settled!" said Olen, putting a hand on Victor's shoulder. He then turned back to Billy. "Tell

Georgie we'll catch up with you in the morning at Terry Deer's old place."

As the two happy deer headed south toward the thicket, Billy realized that he was alone for the first time since his arrival inside The Enchantment. He also realized that he had not had a chance to really cement a lasting relationship with Victor, and he wondered if the buck still held a grudge against him. His thoughts went back to Brother Fabian. A shiver of anxiety ran through him. He was confused by the vision of the mean-spirited humans that had flashed through his mind when he shook the lynx's hand. His uneasy solitude did not last long, however.

CHAPTER ELEVEN

WHISKERS

"Bones, is that really you?" asked the old cat, who had eyed Billy Bones earlier in the General Store. He had been waiting patiently on the bench in front of the store and hobbled over to where the dog was standing. He had on overalls and an ancient felt hat.

"I'm sorry, but do I know you?" asked the shepherd dog.

"It's Whiskers, you young whippersnapper! Don't you remember me? Ah, but you were just a pup when I left!"

"Whiskers!" Billy's anxiety suddenly turned to joy, as he threw his arms around the old cat and lifted him off the ground. "Whiskers, I thought you went away and died! But here you are, you old codger!"

"Hey, careful now, I'm still an old, old cat, and I'm alive only 'cause I wandered into this place. Thank goodness we get to live a long time here!" Billy put Whiskers gently down. The cat continued, "I remember how you used to pester me all the time. Ah, but you were a good-natured pup."

Billy Bones smiled at his old friend and then quietly turned away. "I'm confused, Whiskers. They say I can't go back. You didn't know the boy. He came to live with the old man after you disappeared. He needs me, Whiskers, I know he does!"

"Have they told you it won't be the same if you go back? You won't be able to talk or think with the same kind of clarity. You would be givin' up a lot," explained the cat.

"No, I haven't thought that far. Everything's still so new to me," admitted the shepherd.

"Ah well, you got plenty a' time to decide. You can't go back for a year anyhow."

"I guess you're right. Anyway, Georgie said I should look at the prairie dog homes just west of here," said Bones, nodding in that direction.

"If you don't mind walkin' slowly, I'll tag along with you," said Whiskers.

On the way the cat explained about the old prairie dog town that had existed before The Enchantment. "Many of the original home sites are still bein' used, but they've been made a lot bigger underground. See, only the door-ways and one or two windows on each house are visible." As the shepherd dog scanned the many entrances, he was especially impressed with the brightly colored doors and the pots around them overflowing with flowers.

Before leaving the Prairie Dog Town, Billy gazed west-ward again toward the foothills. A fresh breeze caressed his cheek as he shielded his eyes from the glare of the afternoon sun. "And how about over there, Whiskers? Is that part of The Enchantment?"

"Yep, they call it the Hill Country. But you can't just mosey over there. You gotta get special permission from their Tribal Council. They call us the Prairie. They broke away from this here part of The Enchantment long time ago. Guess they didn't like our *Great Book o' Rules.* They got what they call a code."

Billy looked again at the Hill Country that faded mysteriously into the mist surrounding The Enchantment. "I know I'd like to go there someday, Whiskers. I bet it's beautiful!"

When the two old friends got back to City Hall, Georgie was waiting for them. "Where's Victor?" the beaver asked.

"Mr. Olen Buck and his wife offered to feed him and keep him overnight. Mr. Buck said he thought you wouldn't mind. He said they would see us in the morning at Terry Deer's old place."

"Well, he's in good hands," agreed Georgie. "Are you ready? Mom's waitin' for us."

Billy looked back at Whiskers, who smiled and nodded at the two young animals. "You run along, Bones. If you ever get lonesome, I'll be sittin' on one of them benches along Main Street or down at the boardin' house. Right now, I need my rest. My bones are gettin' weary!"

"Come on then!" Georgie hollered, as he headed for the beaver dam. Billy Bones was glad to be with the young beaver again. He liked his company.

CHAPTER TWELVE

THE HOUSE ON THE POND

From a distance the white-washed walls of Georgie Beaver's home out on the pond sparkled in the late afternoon sun.

"Not only do we have an entrance 'cross the land bridge," bragged Georgie, "but we got an underwater passage that comes up into the house."

When the two companions reached the open space east of the land bridge, Georgie's mother Gladys was waiting for them. After Georgie explained to her that Victor Running Deer would be staying with Olen Buck, she seemed somewhat relieved. "At least I won't have to tell him that he can't stand up in my house because my ceilings are too low," she laughed. "But just in case, I planned a picnic out here in the clearing. I hope that's all right."

After a good meal of fish and vegetables and a delicious apple pie for dessert, Georgie's father Justin offered to help Billy fix up a place to live. Justin was energetic and good-natured and liked to work with his hands. He dressed much the same as Olen Buck except that he wore a brown carpenter's apron that he seldom removed. "There are several sites south of here along the East Wagon Trail before you come to the ford in the stream. Georgie, why don't you show 'em to Billy in the morning on your way down to Terry Deer's old place?" suggested the older beaver.

While Justin was giving his advice, Gladys cleared away the dishes and puttered back and forth between the little house and the picnic area. Like Hester Groundhog, she preferred the older style of dress and constantly wore an apron and a dust cap around home.

After the beavers and Billy conversed for the better part of an hour, Georgie suddenly jumped up and announced, "It's time for my swim. Billy, do you wanna join me?" And without waiting for an answer, he crossed the land bridge and entered the house.

The little home inside was snug and tight. An all-purpose room with a huge fireplace took up most of the space. Georgie's little room was on the west end. A bunk built into the wall and a small dresser took up one side, and an opening that led down into the water filled the other. The young beaver removed his clothes and climbed down the ladder. "Hurry up, before it gets dark!" he yelled, as he hit the water with a splash.

Billy quickly removed his new shirt and trousers and climbed down after him. When he reached the inside pool, Georgie turned to him and grinned, "I hope you can swim underwater. It's only a short ways outside. Just follow me." Before the dog could respond, the beaver made a nose-dive and was gone. After several efforts Billy managed to stay underwater long enough to get into the underwater passage. He finally ended up swimming with his head against the ceiling of the tunnel. By the time he reached the pond on the other side, he was fairly winded.

"I see you have a hard time stayin' underwater. Looks like you would be a great floater," observed the beaver. "Well come on, I'll race you 'cross the pond." As it happened, Georgie had to double back to make sure Billy was all right.

"I'm OK, Georgie; I guess I'm just not a very fast swimmer!" laughed the dog.

Without warning a head popped up between them. "Hey Georgie, who's your friend? I see he's even more of a slowpoke than you are. I hope you're not plannin' to enter him in the race too!" The playful animal did a quick dive and instantly emerged on the shepherd dog's other side. "Hi! I'm Johnny Otter. You must be new. I ain't never seen you before!"

"Hi! I'm Billy Bones. This is my first day here."

"Well, maybe you can give Georgie some pointers. He tries every year to beat me in the swimmin' race at the Grand Fair, but it ain't never gonna happen!" Johnny splashed some water at Georgie and laughed, "Maybe if he slimmed down some, he might have a chance. Well… see ya' around!" And with those challenging remarks, the mischievous otter twisted around in the water and swam toward the large island in the middle of the pond.

"That braggart! I'd like to show him some day," Georgie snorted.

"Can he really beat you? You seem pretty fast to me."

"I work on it every day, but I can't seem to get up enough speed. Maybe if the race was longer, I think I could take him. I got better endurance," confided the beaver.

"Maybe you should ask for a longer race this year," suggested Billy.

"Come to think of it, they do have one, but it's part of a team medley." Georgie stopped talking and rolled over on his back. "Maybe if you and Victor helped me… Nah, you probably wouldn't want to do that, and I can't say I blame you."

"Help you do what?" asked the dog. "Come on, you've got to tell me now!"

"Well, OK…." The hopeful beaver turned back over on his stomach. "You see, on the fifth day of the Grand Fair, they got this race called the Great Medley. It's a team effort, and it takes three animals. It involves a long-distance run, a long-distance swim around the big island out there, and a shorter distance run," explained Georgie.

"I've got to tell you. I'm probably not very good at short races, but I might be able to tackle the longer one. I bet Victor could handle the short one though. Let's talk to him tomorrow, that is if he still wants to associate with me." Billy Bones paused for a moment. He was tired of treading water, but he thought he better explain himself. "You see, I was chasin' him when we entered the opening this morning. I have a feeling he might be glad to get rid of me, but hey, it can't hurt to ask."

As Billy continued to tread water, his mind wandered

back to Victor's departure. The animal he had entered The Enchantment with and said his first words to had walked away with the old stag without looking back. Or had he? Billy vaguely remembered the deer turning his head slightly, as if he meant to say something.

Billy felt strangely lonely for Victor. Even though their first encounter had been a turbulent one, he believed they were somehow connected, as if their separate fates were in some way dependent on a deep and abiding friendship with one another.

After Georgie swam several more laps across the width of the pond, the two animals headed back to the beaver's house. "Would you like some company tonight? I could sleep on the hammock that my dad hung up for Victor," Georgie offered.

"Thanks, I would like that, Georgie," said the grateful dog. After the two animals dried off, they said goodnight to Justin and Gladys and headed out to the picnic area.

The hammocks had been strung up nice and tight, and Gladys provided each of them with a pillow and a blanket. It was almost dark by the time the two young animals settled in for the night.

"This must seem really strange to you," said Georgie. "Nobody here talks much about the outer world."

"I'd be curlin' up on the foot of the boy's bed about now. At least I'm used to a bed, unlike Victor who was born in the wild," admitted the dog. "I keep thinkin' I'll wake up in the morning and all this will be gone, and I'll have forgotten how to talk and walk upright. Everything's happening so fast!"

"Mr. Wise Owl says that's because of the old memories. They work right away, but then what do I know?" said the beaver humbly.

"You think a lot of Mr. Wise Owl, don't you, Georgie?" said Billy unexpectedly.

"Yeah, I do," answered the beaver.

"And what about Brother Fabian…?"

"My Dad says he's not to be trusted. What do you think?"

"I think deep down he's very troubled," said Billy slowly.

"Well anyway, goodnight," yawned Georgie.

"Goodnight," answered Billy.

The shepherd dog had many more questions for his new friend, especially about what they had eaten that evening. Finally it weighed so heavily on his mind that he just had to ask.   "Ah, Georgie…there is one more thing. I was wondering…?"

"Yeah?"

"It's about the fish we ate for supper tonight. I was just wonderin' why we were allowed to eat them?"

The beaver turned toward the shepherd dog, whose face he could barely see in the darkness. "All I can tell ya' is for some reason the fish in the water along with domestic chickens weren't affected when The Enchantment first came into existence."

"But why domestic chickens?" interrupted Billy, voicing some concern. "I mean, isn't Percival a domestic bird? And he went through the change."

"Well…my dad says that according to the Ancient Ones, a couple a' chickens wandered into The Enchantment during the last few seconds when the first rift was closin'. And then apparently they strayed back into the mist that separated the two worlds and didn't come out again 'til after the change was over, so they weren't affected by it. Dad says it was probably a good thing though, 'cause it gave the meat-eating creatures somethin' to eat besides fish."

"I see…I think…. Oh, and Georgie?

"Yeah?"

"Thanks! Thanks for everything today."

"Hey, I didn't do anything. Now get some sleep," said the good-natured beaver, who was himself soon fast asleep.

Even though Billy was fairly exhausted, he could not sleep right away, as events of the day kept racing through his mind. When the shepherd dog finally dozed off, he dreamed he was walking through a golden mist. He could occasionally see a towheaded boy just ahead of him, but he could never quite catch up to him.

CHAPTER THIRTEEN

THE GOLDEN MIST

Billy Bones suddenly woke in his hammock early in the morning of June 22 and fell roughly on the ground. A familiar sound had wakened him. A dense fog had settled over the pond, and he was not quite sure where he was. Then he heard it again. "Bones! Here boy! Come here, boy!" It was the boy's voice, and it was close to him.

"Hey Bones, where are you, boy? Come here, pal!" This time it was the old man calling. He sounded farther away. "Let's search up the trail. If he was anywhere near the pond, he would have come by now. Maybe he's near the clearing where you saw him last!"

"But he must be around here somewhere, Grandpa. He wouldn't just run off. I know it!" The boy's voice echoed eerily in the mist. The shepherd dog could tell that he had been crying. "Here, Bones! Here, boy!"

A stab of pain and loneliness struck the dog's heart. He tried desperately to bark, but his effort was weak and useless. He got down on all four legs in order to follow the cries but felt something was terribly wrong. As he looked toward the dam, he thought he saw two figures walking up the path toward the edge of the trees. He began to follow but was hampered by the strange garments over his chest and legs. By the time he reached the trees, he could barely discern the smaller figure disappearing between two fields of wheat. He pulled at the upper garment and heard a ripping noise as it tore off his chest. It fell by the wayside, a shredded piece of blue cloth.

When Billy reached Percival's shop, he tried to remember where he was. Then he heard the boy's cry again, much farther away. "Here, Bones! Here, boy!"

Panic suddenly gripped the dog. He found himself tearing at the strap on his shoulder and pulling and kicking at the legs of his trousers until he was free of the remaining clothing. He tried to continue on all fours but finally remembered to stand on two feet. He began running up the path again in the direction of the boy's shout at a much faster pace.

By the time Billy Bones reached the crossroads, he thought he saw the outline of the boy and the old man nearing the ancient trees at Land's End. A terrible longing filled him as he ran faster and faster until the two giant trees loomed directly in front of him.

Billy halted momentarily under the trees to catch his breath. When he glanced around and saw the owl's tree house and the groundhog's snug little cottage, the memories of his first day inside The Enchantment finally came flooding back to him. Suddenly without warning, the shepherd dog heard a final call, "Bones!" Without hesitation, he plunged into the golden mist just beyond the two guardians of The Enchantment.

Once inside the mist at Land's End, the atmosphere thickened to a dark gold, and Billy Bones was lost. He dashed aimlessly back and forth for a short time before finally realizing that he was getting nowhere. All he could hear or feel was the loud thumping of his heart and the sound of his lungs trying to take in the dense air.

After Billy forced himself to calm down, he became aware of the mystical sounds he heard after he jumped into the rift the day before. When he tried to move toward them however, a much heavier sound like wind rushing through a tunnel increased in volume until it turned him in another direction, causing the sound to fade again. He tried several times to move toward the louder sounds, but each time the outcome was the same.

After some time when Billy had adjusted to the strange darkness, he thought he could see a person on his knees in the distance. He rushed toward the spot only to discover that it was an older boy kneeling at a gravesite. He was startled to discover that he recognized the boy's face. It was the same one that had looked down at him during his transformation soon after he entered The Enchantment. Not far away from the young man were two more people, a man and a woman, beckoning to the boy to join them. They seemed to be totally unaware of Billy's presence. The dog tried to touch the teenager's shoulder, but his hand passed through the boy's homespun shirt. The lad stood up slowly, looked back down at the grave, and then joined his ghostly companions. By the time Billy trotted over to where they were standing, they had totally vanished.

At that moment the shepherd dog once again glimpsed the shadows of his humans walking away from him. He tried to catch them but found himself in a wooded area outside the dense mist. Then he heard the sound of someone chopping wood close by. When he investigated, he saw the back of a figure wearing a plaid shirt and overalls. He had an ax in his hand and appeared to be resting momentarily. Thinking it could be the old man, the dog moved closer, but when the figure turned around, Billy saw that it was a large brown bear. With great disappointment the dog dashed back into the dense mist. He could just hear the bear call after him, "Hey you, don't go in there! I won't hurt you!"

Once inside the heavy curtain, Billy Bones started running instinctively. Several times he thought he saw the fleeting backs of the two humans he so dearly loved. "Wait, Billy, wait," he finally called but realized almost immediately that they would not recognize the sound of his speaking voice.

After what seemed like hours, the young dog stepped out into a cornfield. In the distance he could see the spires of the two meetinghouses and City Hall, and he knew that he was still inside The Enchantment. With great determination he stepped back into the heavy mist until he stumbled onto a small stream. He tried to follow the stream toward the sounds of the rushing winds but found himself turned around again, wading upstream toward the beaver dam.

With a mighty effort he again moved back into the mist, urged on by the unwavering love of his young human.

Eventually he found himself climbing, and he knew he must be in the foothills. He forced himself to move along the land's edge for hours until he reached what seemed to be a rather steep valley between two good-sized hills. As he started to cross it, he could just make out a team of horses that was losing control of a wagon carrying heavy trunks and furniture. Suddenly the horses screamed and lost their balance, causing the wagon to break away and roll back down the hill directly at him. Billy ducked, but the wagon rushed right through him and crashed onto the rocks below. When Billy turned to look down into the valley, part of the mist had magically lifted, allowing him to see a long line of wagons heading up the trail to where he stood. From his vantage point he could see miles of discarded belongings, broken wagon parts, and human animals milling about trying to get rid of whatever they could before making the sharp ascent up into the hills.

Deeply moved by what he was witnessing, Billy started to walk slowly down the slope until he found himself again in the clear air of The Enchantment. The wagons, discarded items, and desperate people were all gone. He made his way over to a large flat rock and sat down. In the Prairie below him he could make out Prairie Dog Town, Main Street, and the populated section around the pond. Way in the distance he could see the two lone trees at Land's End. Somehow he had managed to move halfway around the charmed little world.

Billy Bones did not know how long he had traveled in and out of the mist, and he did not care. His heart was broken, and he knew now that what Winston Wise Owl, Georgie Beaver, and Whiskers had been trying to tell him was true. If he could not escape when the two worlds were close enough for him to hear his human's call, he could not escape at all. He would just have to wait until the next summer solstice and make the most of his time inside The Enchantment. He rolled over on his back, looked at a sky still bluer than any he had ever seen and fell asleep.

CHAPTER FOURTEEN

THE SEARCH

Winston Wise Owl liked to do his serious thinking and reading in the early hours of the morning. He had been asleep for only a couple of hours when he was awakened by Georgie Beaver's knocking on the front door. When the owl opened the door, he was still in his red and white striped cap and nightgown.

"Sorry to bother you so early, Mr. Wise Owl, but we think something serious has happened to Billy Bones. We thought we'd better tell you right away!" declared the anxious beaver.

The old owl looked at the worried faces of Justin Beaver and Percival Gander at the foot of the stairs. Out of the corner of his eye he could see Hester Groundhog scurrying across the pathway. "Give me a second to get dressed, and I'll be right down," said Winston gravely.

The owl quickly changed and climbed down the outside staircase. Justin nodded to him as he reached the bottom step. "Good morning, Winston. I'm afraid Georgie and Percival have come to me with some rather grim news. Since you asked my son to be Billy's guide, I thought it was only proper that you should be the first one informed."

"Thank you, I appreciate that," said Winston. "I should have gotten back to Georgie last evening, but so much happened yesterday, I'm afraid I got sidetracked."

"Perhaps Georgie and Percy should tell you, since they made the discovery. Georgie, tell Mr. Wise Owl about yesterday and this morning," said Justin.

Georgie bowed his head. Winston could tell that the beaver was devastated. "I showed Billy around, sir, just as you asked. Yesterday afternoon on Main Street, Victor Running Deer decided to go home with Mr. Buck for the evening, and Billy went home with me. Billy had supper with us, and then we went swimmin'. After that we both slept out in front of our place in hammocks. And when I woke up this morning, Billy was gone!"

"Maybe he just went for a walk and got lost," suggested the owl, finding it difficult to remain calm.

"I thought of that right away, sir, because of the thick fog," observed Georgie. "But when I started up the path to look for him, I found this." He pulled out the torn pieces of blue cloth from his pocket. "This is all that's left of the shirt that Percival gave him to wear!"

"And this is the rest of his clothes!" said the gander, showing the owl Billy's trousers. "Something woke me up, so I ran outside. It looks to me like foul play, yes, foul play!"

"When I reached Percy's shop, he was standin' in the middle of the path holding Billy's pants. I showed him what I found, and then we went to get my dad!" added Georgie.

"Percival, do you remember what woke you up and caused you to look outside?" inquired the old owl, trying to make some sense of the story.

The gander thought for a moment. He hadn't considered that. "Oh my, oh my, there was something…yes, something!"

"Did you hear Billy cry out, or perhaps you heard someone fighting?" asked Hester.

"No, no, it wasn't Billy that I heard, not Billy. It was someone else." Percival tried to remember. "I think it was a younger voice calling for somebody!"

"Georgie, did anyone talk to Billy yesterday, anyone who might have influenced him in any way? And were you with him the whole day?" asked Winston.

"We were greeted by so many people. It's hard to recall," answered the young beaver solemnly, "but I did leave Billy and Victor for about an hour in the afternoon to tell my uncle that Elmer Prairie Dog was runnin' for mayor."

"Did you find out later if he had talked to anyone else during that time?" asked Justin.

"Well, he did talk to Fabian Lynx and Elmer Prairie Dog, but I don't think anything came of it, from what he told me later. Oh, I remember now who else he talked to. He met Whiskers, the old cat who sits around Main Street. Apparently they lived on the same farm and knew each other. Whiskers told him to visit whenever he got lonely."

"At least that's someone we can ask," said Winston, hopefully.

"Bones!" interrupted Percival Gander suddenly. "The voice was calling for Bones. Yes, Bones, I remember now! It was kind of distant, but I heard it just the same!"

"So whoever called knew him by the name Bones," said Justin.

"And that could be Whiskers," said Georgie. "He called him Bones."

"Or somebody before that," said Winston.

"Like Victor Running Deer?" asked the young beaver.

"Even before that!" said the wise owl pensively. "We are still close to the solstice, and it was a really dense fog this morning. It's been known to happen, especially with domestic animals."

"What's that?" inquired the young beaver curiously.

"Perhaps it was his human from the other world. Percival's very sensitive to matters of the heart. Maybe that's why he heard it too," speculated the owl.

"So it could be that Billy tried to enter into the mist at Land's End," stated Hester, immediately aware of the dangers. "Did you tell him what would happen?"

"I must confess that I never got the chance," said Winston. "This messy business with Sarah Mourning Dove...I'm afraid you might be right, Hester. Our young friend might've been drawn into the mist."

"Well, let's hope not! At least we can start with Whiskers. I'll go to the boardinghouse and find out what he knows," volunteered Justin.

"And I'll try to find Victor. Maybe he knows somethin'," added Georgie hopefully.

"And I'll notify the sheriff in case there was foul play involved," said the owl, trying to organize things. "Then I'll get Deputy Harold Eagle to help me search the Hill Country in case Billy entered the mist and got lost!"

"And what can I do?" asked Hester, eager to be a part of the search.

"You wait here in case he returns on his own. In fact, we'll all meet here in a couple hours. If you find anyone who knows anything, bring 'em back with you! I'll take this torn shirt to Sheriff Walter." And without waiting for a reply, the owl spread his great wings and flew off toward the sheriff's office on South Main Street next to the saloon.

The open space directly in back of the sheriff's office was a discreet place for Winston Wise Owl to land. He slipped quietly between the office and the saloon and knocked on the front door. Winston knew that the good sheriff kept his silver badge of office polished and his black felt hat on the top of his desk, brushed and available for action. Almost immediately Sheriff Walter Lone Wolf opened the door. He was a tall dignified animal wearing a black vest and trousers.

"Why, Mr. Wise Owl, what can I do for you?" asked Walter respectfully.

"May I come in? A situation has arisen that I'd like to talk to you about," stated the owl.

"By all means, Mr. Wise Owl," said the sheriff, placing an old chair in front of his desk. "Here, have a seat."

"Two new animals came in yesterday morning during

the summer solstice," began Winston. "One was a shepherd dog, and he's got strong ties to his human family in the other world. He is missing. No one's seen him this morning. It seems he either met with foul play or maybe was drawn back into the mist at Land's End."

"Well, if he entered the mist and hasn't come out yet, I'm sorry for him," said Walter. "As we both know, he could be hurt or permanently lost."

"I realize that," agreed the owl, "but from what I could tell he's got a pretty strong constitution, and he seemed to be smart too. I think he may make it back out safely."

"I'll defer to your judgment on that," said the sheriff. "But as you know, I prefer to deal with facts."

"Oh, right" said Winston remembering his evidence. He pulled the torn shirt out and handed it to Walter Lone Wolf. "Georgie Beaver found this on the path to Percival Gander's shop" he said as he handed it over to the Sheriff.

The Sheriff looked at the garment, running his finger carefully along the tears and carefully regarding them. "Hmmm. This could definitely help" stated Walter, getting right to business.

After discussing the details of Billy's disappearance, the decision was reached to deputize several local citizens whom Sheriff Lone Wolf trusted and to make some inquiries before meeting at the owl's tree house at noon.

Lookout Point on Eagle Butte was the next stop on Winston's schedule. Deputy Harold Eagle had his little office in the front of a small cabin just off the point. From this spot Harold could look over the whole community and also the Hill Country, where the Tribal Council had given him authority to settle small disputes and disturbances.

The colorful eagle liked to wear a plaid swag across his chest and speak with a Scottish brogue. "Ah, the poor shepherd dog! 'Tis a real shame he's run into such a mess on only his second day with us. Tell me, what can I do to help?"

"I was hoping you would assist me in searching all the borders from the air. It's not likely that Billy reached the Hill Country, but if you could even search there. I'm sure you'd be more welcome than I am," suggested the owl.

Around the middle of the day Winston Wise Owl returned to the meeting point between the two lone trees. He discovered that Hester had prepared a lunch for the participants and spread it out on the wooden table north of her tree. Justin had talked to Whiskers, but the cat had not seen Billy since the previous day. Georgie arrived without Victor Running Deer. It seems the deer chose not to come. Winston also learned that Victor and the old stag were rebuilding the lean-to in the thicket where Terry Deer had once lived. Apparently Victor met Olen's daughter and could think of little else.

Sheriff Lone Wolf had better news. He brought Milton Brown Bear down from the north woods. The bear was still carrying his ax. The massive bruin explained how he had encountered Billy. "When I turned around, the poor dog had a wild look about him. I'm not sure he was in his right mind. He stared at me for a moment, and then he turned and ran straight into the mist. I tell you, I never saw anything like it!"

"Well, at least we know what happened to him. Now if we can just locate him," sighed the old owl. All morning he had tried to remain composed and unruffled, but his stomach was churning with worry and concern.

When Deputy Eagle arrived, the lunch Hester provided had been almost fully devoured by the hungry participants.

Fortunately Gladys Beaver came to the rescue by bringing some freshly baked fish. The eagle ate eagerly and seemed most satisfied. "I flew up and down all the borders. I even flew several times across the Hill Country but saw nothin'. I'm sure if the poor creature entered the mist near here, he couldn't have gotten very far."

"He did get as far as the woods though? That's no easy task," stated Milton Brown Bear, "but I could swear he headed south again. At least it appeared that way."

"We've got to think positively and assume he got out!" said Hester with determination. "That means he's probably somewhere close by."

"She's right!" agreed Sheriff Lone Wolf. "We need to keep searchin'. My deputies have gone south below the dam. Milton and I will continue searching the woods to the north. Justin, you and your son and Percival keep lookin' for him east of the pond."

"Winston and I'll keep searchin' from the sky," said Harold. "We've got at least six more hours of daylight."

As the afternoon waned, the number of concerned souls joining the hunt doubled, and by evening it had tripled. No sighting of Billy had been made, however, except for the brief encounter in the woods with Milton Brown Bear.

Winston noted that Georgie seemed especially concerned that Victor had not joined the search. "Olen Buck and the other deer have always tended to mind their own business," explained the owl, trying to calm the young beaver's apprehension.

The next day many of the faithful continued to look for the dog, but by the end of the third day, most had given up. With a heavy heart the sheriff thanked everyone and called off the search. "We've done all we can. We can only hope that if Billy's still alive, he'll find us."

As the crowd headed home, Georgie turned to Winston and his father. He felt desperate. "We can't give up now! I know he's still alive! He must be!"

Justin put his arm around his son's shoulder and said softly, "Let's go home now. Winston and the sheriff have done all they can. Perhaps something'll turn up in the morning."

"I'll help you." Victor Running Deer was approaching them in the growing darkness. Winston was pleased that Victor had finally found his voice. The owl was afraid that the deer still harbored a grudge against the dog who had chased him through the golden opening. When Winston turned back to Georgie, he could see that the beaver had turned his face away. When the beaver finally looked back, he had tears in his eyes and so did the deer.

CHAPTER FIFTEEN

THE THREE VULTURES

It was late afternoon when Billy Bones was rudely awakened by three curious vultures who were prodding him with sharp sticks and a long pole. The dog found it difficult to focus on what was happening and tried desperately to gather his wits about him.

"Ow! Stop that!" Billy tried to protect himself but discovered that his wrists and ankles had been tied with dirty pieces of rope. "What are you doin'? Get these off me!"

Billy would soon learn that the vultures had the unlikely names of Felix, Festus, and Floyd. They had found him sleeping on a flat rock in the Hill Country near the mist. Because he was a stranger and unclothed, they immediately assumed the worst.

"Are you a spy or are you a sorcerer?" inquired Felix, sticking his homely beak close to the struggling dog. At the same time Festus jabbed the dog's legs and shoulders from behind.

"I don't know what you're talkin' about, and would you please stop poking me with that stick!" cried Billy. Suddenly he turned and grabbed one of Festus' skinny legs with his two hands still tied at the wrists.

"Ahhhh!" screamed the sneaky vulture and he struck out violently at Billy, breaking his stick on the canine's head and shoulders. Felix and Floyd immediately came to their brother's aid, striking frantically at the dog. Finally Floyd slammed the long pole into Billy's midsection, causing the dog to release the leg and clutch his own stomach.

After the brief melee the vultures huddled together at a respectful distance from Billy. Even though the dog was in pain, his sharp ears caught everything they were saying.

"Well, he speaks! At least we know he's part a' the magic," determined Felix, who seemed to have some control over his two brothers.

"I still say he's a spy!" said Festus, glancing at Billy out of the corner of his eye.

"But he ain't got no clothes on. How can we tell what he is?" commented Floyd.

"That shows he's a spy, stupid! By wearin' nothin', he thinks he can confuse us," insisted Festus. The three brothers themselves were dressed in sleeveless plaid shirts that had been patched numerous times.

Felix Vulture moved a little closer to Billy, who was just starting to catch his breath. "Who are you, dog?"

"My name is Billy Bones," panted the dog, "and I was just trying to rest on this rock!"

"Well, you ain't allowed up here! This place is off limits to creatures from the Prairie!" snarled Festus.

"I didn't know that!" insisted Billy, catching his breath. "I only entered your world yesterday. I came through the opening during the summer solstice!"

"Didn't they give ya' no clothes?" asked Floyd, still worried about the dog's lack of identifiable attire.

"Yes, but I guess I must have torn them off when I tried to get back to my farm," explained Billy, still curled up from the pain in his stomach.

"Then how did you get up here without us seein' ya'?" inquired Felix.

"I came through there!" Billy pointed up the wagon trail at the dank mist that ended The Enchantment to the west.

"I told ya' he was a sorcerer!" said Floyd nervously, as he grabbed Felix off to the side. The three big birds huddled together again to try to decide what to do with their prisoner. "Too bad Momma's not here. She'd know what to do," whined Floyd.

"One thing's sure: we gotta get him undercover. I seen that nosy eagle flyin' around here earlier today. The dog needs to go before the council. This is too important for us to decide!" continued Felix.

The vultures took the long pole and with some difficulty managed to slip it under the ropes at Billy's ankles and wrists. Felix and Floyd hoisted the pole on their shoulders and carried the dangling dog to their shabby little hut built into the hillside.

Once inside the hut, Felix gave the uncomfortable dog some stale bread, a partially cooked chicken leg, and some water. "We're takin' you on a trip tonight, so ya' better get your strength up."

Lying on the dirty damp floor, Billy tried to take stock of his situation. Even though he was bruised and uncomfortable, he had begun to accept his fate, not only as a year-long inhabitant of The Enchantment but as a helpless captive of three awkward birds.

While waiting for his trip to Echo Canyon, the dog learned that the vulture's mother was the spiritual leader of the Hill Country. He also discovered that her name was Lucinda and that she was at a lodge in the canyon attending the quarterly meeting of the Tribal Council. After hearing the young vultures speak about their mother with such awe and respect, Billy became anxious at the prospect of meeting her.

Shortly after dark Felix, Festus, and Floyd Vulture fastened two ropes around Billy Bones' neck and tied his hands behind his back. After that they loosened the rope between his ankles so he could walk. Felix chose Festus to head the procession. Apparently it was his job to find the trail that led back over what the vultures referred to as The Blue Mesas.

Luckily the waning moon was still fairly full when the journey to Echo Canyon began. The two stronger vultures, Felix and Floyd, walked on either side of Billy holding the ropes. The climb across the rocks was especially dangerous for Billy, who could not use his hands and had limited use of his feet. Twice he fell on his face and had to roll over and stand up by himself, since the vultures were leery of getting too close.

It was after midnight by the time the odd procession reached the canyon. The steep descent into the valley was again very treacherous for Billy. Fortunately the fires around the different campsites shed some light on his path. When they reached the floor of the canyon, Billy noticed that the ground was strewn with merrymakers who had found places to rest for the night.

At the end of the canyon Billy could just make out a large lodge-type building lit by lanterns hanging on either side of its entrance. Just before he and the vultures reached the lodge, they stopped at a rundown shed and woke a huge elk sitting out front.

"Any more room in there, Arthur? We've got a dog here that's gotta be locked up 'til he goes before the council," said Felix wearily.

Still rubbing his eyes, the elk nodded and took Billy inside where there were several cage-like cells. After he found one big enough for Billy to stand, he removed the restraining ropes, pushed him inside, and locked the door.

"We'll be back to look in on him tomorrow," promised Felix, as he, his brothers, and the elk left Billy Bones alone in the dark. After discovering some straw on the floor, the exhausted dog curled up on it and fell fast asleep.

For two days Billy Bones was held captive in his cell. During that time he came to understand the meaning of Echo Canyon. Besides the gurgling of a stream close by, the most constant sounds were those of the many partici-pants still celebrating the summer solstice.

By the second night Billy was wondering, "Why did I act so rashly when I heard the boy call? Why didn't I give myself time to enjoy the wonders of this place? I've spent more days in this blasted jail than outside in the sunlight. What was I thinking?"

Even in Billy's depressed state, he finally concluded that some overpowering instinct had drawn him into the mist time and time again, some instinct stronger than his reasoning, conscious mind.

Billy reflected back on his brief encounter with Brother Fabian Lynx. Why had he seen the two angry men in his mind's eye when he shook the lynx's hand? Had he just imagined it? And why was he the only animal who saw it? He was positive that he had felt the hatred that the lynx harbored for the two men. It had seemed powerful and all-encompassing at the time, but had he imagined that too? On the other hand, had it fallen to him to convince Winston Wise Owl of the magnitude of that hatred? Or had he already jeopardized The Enchantment's peace by not telling the owl immediately? After all, the lynx had threatened to burn the owl's books.

As promised, Felix Vulture supplied Billy with food whenever he could. The dog soon came to the conclusion that the vulture really had a good heart.

On the bird's second visit he cautioned Billy that he would be tried by the Tribal Council and that Lucinda Vulture would be there. "Momma can tell if you're lyin'. She speaks to the spirit world!" the vulture warned.

Twice, Arthur Elk and several other large animals blindfolded Billy, tied his hands and feet, and carried him to a damp quiet place. After some time passed, they would return and take him back to his cell. Billy surmised that they were trying to hide him for some reason.

Arthur was a massive animal with a rack of many antlers still in the velvet. From the brief conversations with him, Billy discovered that *The Great Book of Rules* did not apply to the Hill Country. Only the section called *The Vulture's Appendix* had any credence.

"How come citizens of the Prairie aren't allowed to come here without permission?" Billy asked Arthur the second day.

"It's 'cause we don't want 'em meddlin' in our affairs," the elk bellowed. "They'd swallow us up in a minute if they thought they could get by with it!"

CHAPTER SIXTEEN

THE TRIBAL COUNCIL

Late in the afternoon of the third day, Arthur Elk and the three vultures came to get Billy Bones for his trial inside the lodge. Felix Vulture gave him an old shirt and a pair of patched trousers with suspenders to wear, so he would not have to go before the Tribal Council in a state of undress. After that his wrists were bound in front of him.

Billy was impressed with the old building. It was made with great beams joined together log-cabin style. Just inside the lodge was a great hall. Seated around the sides of it were many celebrants who stayed to witness the trial. "Why so many?" whispered Billy to Felix.

"They've heard these here rumors that you might be a sorcerer, that's why. They're waitin' to see ya' perform."

Seated in a semicircle facing the door were the members of the Tribal Council dressed in different colored robes. In the center the chief of the Tribal Council, an ancient mountain goat by the name of Omar wore deep purple. On his left a handsome cougar, a large lizard, and a bat wore gold, green, and deep red. On the goat's far right a rabbit with a multicolored robe had a constant grin on his face.

To the rabbit's left was a vacant chair. Between the vacant chair and the mountain goat sat a creature with a hooded black robe. Billy could only see the whites of its eyes and concluded that it must be Lucinda, the vultures' mother. She had a more frightening countenance than Billy had imagined, and he found his courage waning.

"Who has the next complaint?" ordered the goat with quiet authority.

Arthur gave a nod to Felix, who stepped clumsily forward with his two brothers. "We found this shepherd dog here sleepin' on the flat rock close to the Old Wagon Trail."

"None of us seen him climb up there neither!" interjected Festus.

"We asked him why he was trespassin'," added Floyd, "but he claimed he didn't know nothin' about that."

"I thought he was a spy because he didn't have no clothes on, and I said as much," continued Festus.

"Then we asked him how he got to the rock, and he said he entered the mist down on the Prairie between the two lone trees and came out on the west side by the wagon trail," explained Felix.

"And we knowed nobody ever did that!" gloated Festus.

"We thought maybe he was a sorcerer or somethin' and brought him here," concluded Felix.

"Enough of this nonsense! Is that the culprit?" asked the cougar, pointing to Billy.

"Yeah, that's him," said Felix, lowering his head.

"Maybe the dog should speak for himself," suggested the mountain goat in a reserved manner.

The vultures quickly retreated and pushed the dog to the center.

"What's your name, please?" asked Omar Mountain Goat.

"Billy Bones, sir."

"And how do you plead to these charges?" questioned the goat again.

"I've done nothing wrong!" stated Billy, as clearly as he could.

"Then why did you lie to these vultures?" hissed the lizard.

"I didn't lie. I told the truth," insisted the young dog, forcing himself to remain calm.

"Did you tell them you came out of the mist west of the wagon trail?" inquired the bat.

"Yes," admitted Billy.

"Then you were lying! No one's ever done that, especially in one day!" declared the lizard.

"But I tell you, I did," insisted Billy adamantly, "but not all at once. I went in and out of the mist several times."

"Are you a sorcerer then?" asked the bat, rising from his chair and coming closer to peer at the dog.

"No, I know no magic, sir," said Billy, trying to meet the bat's beady eyes.

"While you were in the mist, did you see anything?" questioned the rabbit, who had also vacated his chair and was circling the dog.

"Well…I guess I saw a number of things," confessed the shepherd dog.

"Like gods or ghosts, I suppose!" laughed the cougar, turning toward the lizard.

"No, more like visions," corrected Billy.

"Wait!" exclaimed Lucinda suddenly, standing and removing her hood. "Everyone except Orville and me must leave while we question this dog. If he's had a spiritual experience, then we must test him for the truth. This is a sacred matter!"

All of the creatures in the hall were shocked into silence.

"Lucinda has spoken," said Omar Mountain Goat, breaking the stillness. "We are required by the code to heed her advice. Everyone but Lucinda Vulture and Orville Bat must leave the building!"

"But I protest. The dog is obviously lying!" complained the handsome cougar.

"That is not for you to decide, Gaylord, unless, like Lucinda and Orville, you've recently gained the gift of spiritual insight," said the rabbit.

"Ha!" exclaimed the big cat called Gaylord, as he strolled angrily out of the room. The other council members followed dutifully. Grumbling, the disappointed onlookers also exited, leaving behind the dog, the old vulture, the bat, and the large elk.

"You may leave too, Arthur. The shepherd dog poses no threat to us." Lucinda had risen from her chair and was facing Billy, who was still standing bravely in the same spot. Orville crouched on his chair as if poised to spring at their bound captive. After some contemplation Lucinda pointed a crooked finger at the young dog. "You say you saw visions. Explain them to us!"

Billy Bones felt instinctively that he must be truthful to this demanding old crone. He forced himself to remain calm as he described each vision as carefully and accurately as he could. He started with the young man at the grave and finished with the runaway wagon and the pioneers leaving their treasures.

"And the horses you saw: were they like us?" demanded Orville. Billy noticed the red veins around the pupils of his eyes as they opened wide with excitement.

"I would say they were more like the horses back on the old man's farm where I used to live. They walked on four legs," concluded Billy.

"And did you see anything else? Anything at all?" asked the vulture with a less threatening tone.

"Yes, I saw the shadows of the boy and the old man who were my humans in the outside world. I could hear them call to me, but I couldn't reach them," answered Billy sadly, remembering again the agony he had felt.

"I see," said Lucinda, staring directly at Billy, as if contemplating a reply. For a moment the dog thought he saw her standing in front of a cool, clear lake.

Just as the vulture was about to continue, she was interrupted by the frenzied entrance of two intruders who barred the great doors of the lodge behind them. When the smaller of the two animals spun around, he cried, "Run, Billy! Out the back door! Before they realize what's happening!"

CHAPTER SEVENTEEN

THE TWO INTRUDERS

Billy turned in amazement as the larger of the two animals grabbed him by the forearm and pulled him toward a door in the west wall. He anxiously glanced back at Lucinda, as if he were further compounding his crimes against the council. "But…I should finish my testimony!" he muttered, but the larger creature kept moving him toward the rear door. Just as they escaped behind it, Billy heard Orville Bat take to the air and flap frantically about the rafters.

Victor immediately bolted the door to the Great Hall and guided Billy and Georgie toward the second door. "Be quick! This must take us out back!"

To the escapees chagrin, they discovered that the second door was locked, and no key was hanging near it. After rummaging around for the missing key, the deer tried forcing it open with his shoulder. But even after the dog and the beaver lent their combined weight, it would not budge. Finally Georgie exclaimed, "Let's try one of the windows. Maybe with Victor's help, I can reach high enough to pry one open!"

After Georgie successfully scrambled up onto Victor's

shoulders and studied one of the windows, he realized that they did not open and that metal bars had been secured across their grids. He also noticed that the slope of the mountain outside was on the same level as the window.

"It's no use," whispered Georgie, "these windows are solid, and they're barred on the outside. It looks like were trapped in here!"

"There's got to be another way out," insisted Victor. "We're just not seeing it!"

"Well, if it's behind that back door, then it goes into the mountain by the looks of the ground outside this window," insisted Georgie, who slid dejectedly down to the floor and gazed sheepishly up at the shepherd dog. "Well, at least you can't say we didn't give it a try, Billy."

Victor also slumped down by Georgie and smiled up at the dog. "Sorry, Billy, I guess our plan was pretty lame at that."

"Hey, you came looking for me. I couldn't ask for anything more," responded Billy, speaking for the first time inside the narrow room.

Just as the dog finished his remark, there was a heavy pounding at the door, and Billy recognized the angry voice of Arthur Elk. "The three of you better unbolt this door and give yourselves up. There's no way out of there!"

Billy glanced over at his two friends. "He's right. We might as well go out there and face them. I'm sorry. It's my fault. If I hadn't stumbled into this place, we'd all be back inside the Prairie, safe and sound." He looked over at Victor and then at Georgie. "But you came looking for me.

I'll never forget that no matter what happens."

By the time the three trapped animals stepped outside, a group of celebrants stood in a semicircle around the doorway leading to the cloakroom. Directly in front of the celebrants stood Omar Mountain Goat, Gaylord Cougar, two husky Big Horn rams, and an infuriated Arthur Elk. Billy looked anxiously around for Lucinda Vulture but could not find her. He spied Orville Bat, however, hanging unceremoniously from the rafters. He felt strangely guilty, as if he had broken the vulture's confidence, as well as the bat's, by trying to escape with Victor and Georgie.

"Take these three back to your shed, Arthur. We'll let the Tribal Council deal with them in the morning," ordered Omar in an even tone. "There's no use trying to pronounce any judgments on them today with this crowd." He paused as Arthur, Gaylord, and the two Big Horn brothers tied Victor and Georgie's hands behind them. He then turned back to Billy, whose hands were still bound in front of him. "And send for Deputy Harold Eagle. It's time we got him involved in this."

CHAPTER EIGHTEEN

THE DREAM OF JIMMY STONE

Billy Bones was returned to his old jail cell inside Arthur Elk's shed, and Victor Running Deer and Georgie Beaver were placed in separate cells across the back. The two Big Horn rams offered to stay and guard the prisoners, but Gaylord Cougar left.

"How long will they keep us here?" asked Georgie, as soon as the elk and the two rams took positions outside the door.

"It's my guess they'll put us on trial again in the morning," remarked Billy. "It sounds like they're going to send for somebody called Deputy Eagle."

"I hope so. At least he'll tell my parents where I am," answered the beaver. "And Deputy Eagle's a good law officer. He won't let us rot in here."

"How are you doin', Victor?" asked the shepherd dog in a loud whisper. "You've been awfully quiet over there."

"I'm OK, Billy. It's just that I keep thinking how dumb our escape plan was. We should've at least checked to make sure the lodge had a back door to the outside."

"Well, it surprised me too. You'd think there'd be more than one way out of there."

"Maybe there was," interrupted Georgie. "We don't know what was behind that other door. Maybe there was a tunnel or something."

"Well, there's nothin' we can do about it now," decided Billy.

After a pause in the conversation, Victor spoke again. "Hey Georgie, how are your teeth? Maybe you could gnaw your way out of your cage. It looks like these bars are made of wood."

"They look like they're maple," returned the beaver. "I could do some damage, but it would take a long time, and we'd still have to get past Arthur and the two rams."

"Or dig our way out under the walls," suggested Victor.

"I'm hoping something will happen in the morning. I think maybe Lucinda Vulture and that bat believed my story," said Billy, changing the direction of the conversation.

"Why don't you tell us what happened to you, Billy? How did you end up in the Hill Country?" asked Georgie, starting to gnaw on one of the bars on the far side of his cell.

During the next quarter of an hour Billy related his experience inside the mist and his capture by the three vultures. Toward the end of his story, he glanced over at Georgie, who had fallen asleep. Victor, on the other hand, had turned away at the mention of the human pioneers. Before long Billy also drifted off into a well-needed but uneasy sleep.

Toward morning, Billy's fitful dreams were interrupted by a dream of absolute clarity. The creatures in this special dream, however, were humans rather than animals. They were the same ones that Billy encountered at Land's End when he first entered the mist on his second day inside The Enchantment, except that this time the pioneers spoke to one another. Billy felt himself hovering over them, hearing every word they uttered.

"Hey Jimmy, what's holdin' you up?" called one man, as he left a long line of covered wagons and circled back to the younger man's wagon. The younger man called Jimmy had pulled his heavy wagon into the shade of one of the two trees on either side of the trail. Billy immediately recognized them as the ancient trees on Will Stuart's farm.

The younger man climbed down from the driver's seat and turned to the other man. "It's Grandpa. I think he's takin' a turn for the worse! Help me get him under this tree where it's nice and cool!"

Billy could see that Jimmy was struggling to remain clear-eyed, as he and the other man lifted an old man out of the back of the wagon. "Ben, I promised to take his library of books all the way to Oregon. He plans to use them to found a new school. What am I to do?"

After the two young men laid the old man in the shade of the tree, the man named Ben pulled Jimmy aside. "Remember what the wagon master said, Jimmy. The books are too heavy to lug over the mountains. We're runnin' late, and unless we lighten our loads considerably, we ain't gonna make it through the pass before the snows come."

"But how about Grandpa? It'll break his heart," cried Jimmy.

"You can't burden him with the truth when he's dyin', Jimmy. You'll have to think of somethin' else to tell him," responded Ben.

At this point Ben's young wife brought a dipper of water and gave it to Jimmy, who returned to his grandfather and knelt down beside him. The old man reached for his grandson's hand. "Remember your promise. Books are the lifeblood of a civilization. They must get through," he sputtered in earnest.

"Don't worry, Grandpa. I'll take care of everything," Jimmy said softly.

With great effort the old man turned to Ben. "Look after him for me. I know he's doin' the work of a man, but he's scarcely more than a boy. He's got no one now...."

"We'll see to him. Don't you fret yourself about that, sir," Ben assured him. The old man closed his eyes, and in a few moments let out a breath and was gone. The three young people buried him north of the two great trees and fashioned a cross to mark his grave. On its crosspiece Jimmy scratched the name W. N. Stone.

At that moment Jimmy looked up and noticed the hole in the tree under which they were standing. "Hey, look at this! If we could get my wagon close enough, we might be able to hide grandpa's library in the hollow of this tree!"

Billy watched closely as the three pioneers in his dream stored all of the old man's books inside the tree. When they finished, Jimmy carefully put a canvas over the hole.

"I promise I'll return and claim you," the young man said in a broken whisper, as he followed Ben's wagon back to the wagon train.

At that moment, it seemed to Billy that he could feel Jimmy's sorrow well up in his own chest. He found that he had somehow slipped into Jimmy's body and was looking out over the trail through Jimmy's eyes. As he bumped along, he looked down at his feet, thinking to see paws. Instead he saw the weather-beaten boots of a human pioneer.

Billy Bones awoke with a start. The first rays of the morning sun were just beginning to beam through the cracks of the old shed. He noticed that Georgie and Victor were still asleep inside their cells. He had the urge to awaken them and tell them about his astounding dream but decided against it. "Maybe I'll ask Winston Wise Owl about it, if I ever see him again," he thought. "After all, the books were hidden in his tree."

An hour after Billy Bones' dream and before either Georgie Beaver or Victor Running Deer were stirring, the dog heard a weird disturbance outside the door of the shed. Shortly afterward Lucinda Vulture burst into the room, followed by Arthur Elk and the two Big Horn rams.

"I want you to take the deer and the beaver outside while I talk to this young dog," directed the vulture.

"But we'd have to tie them up and drag them out," complained Arthur. "We'd never catch the deer if he got loose."

"Then do what you have to do, but leave us alone," commanded Lucinda again.

Grudgingly, Arthur and the rams bound Victor and Georgie and began dragging them out of the shed.

"And open up this dog's cage, Arthur, so I can speak to him directly," continued Lucinda.

"No, Lucinda. I can't do that. He might escape," countered the elk.

"Nonsense, he won't go anywhere when I'm here. Now do what I tell you!" ordered the old bird.

Reluctantly Arthur opened the cage, allowed Lucinda to enter, and left the shed.

"Now Mr. Bones, I don't know exactly what happened to you this morning, but whatever it was it shook me to my very core. I imagine it was a dream or a vision. But whatever it was, please explain it to me. For some unknown reason, we are closely connected! I could feel what you were experiencing, but I could not see it myself!"

"But I don't know what…" began the dog moving over to the edge of his cage.

"Please don't waste my time!" insisted the old bird. "You must tell me exactly what you heard and saw before we meet with the council!"

The dog began faking ignorance a second time but then thought better of it. He was astounded that the vulture would have this strange connection with him. He also remembered how he had visualized her standing before a cool clear lake on their first meeting.

"Well, I was having this dream," the dog began. "I was not only seeing the pioneers I encountered in the mist at Land's End, but I was hearing them talk. I also remembered some of their names."

After Billy recounted his vivid and moving dream, Lucinda walked over to him and stared directly into his eyes. "When you are called before the council, you need to tell them exactly what you told me. Do you understand?"

"Yes, madam."

"All right then," Lucinda said in a kinder tone. "We will bring you and your friends before the council soon after it is called into session. And tell your friends not to be afraid. We aren't heathens here, you know."

As Lucinda Vulture swiftly whirled out of the shed as abruptly as she had entered, Billy Bones sat back in amazement. "How could she have known about my dream," he asked himself again. "And what's this connection she's talking about? What do I have in common with this gnarly old bird anyhow?"

CHAPTER NINETEEN

THE AMAZING DECISION

On the morning following Billy Bones' remarkable dream and Lucinda Vulture's even more momentous awareness of it, the Tribal Council reconvened to decide the fates of Billy Bones, Georgie Beaver, and Victor Running Deer. This time, however, Deputy Harold Eagle had been invited to monitor the trial on behalf of the Prairie. Only the eagle, the three animals in question, and the council members were permitted to attend.

After Omar Mountain Goat's opening remarks, Lucinda Vulture stood to discuss Billy's case. Once again in his mind's eye, Billy saw her standing in front of a cool, deep lake. This time, however, he heard the crisp waves splashing along the shoreline.

"This shepherd dog came to us claiming that he entered the mist at Land's End on the morning after he arrived through the magic portal. He then told Orville and me that he was able to survive the great turbulence for many hours. During that time he saw a number of visions concerning the old pioneers that once passed through this land. Finally he reentered The Enchantment at the Hill

Country's most sacred point, the Old Wagon Trail, something no creature has ever done before. Because of the absurdity of these claims, he's charged with either being a sorcerer or trespassing."

Lucinda hesitated and glanced back at Billy and then over at the proud cougar. "Orville and I have found, however, that Mr. Bones' visions were accurate, and he was telling the truth! All the members in this council have seen snippets of these visions, and over the years I have seen them all. But this dog experienced them all in one day. We also know that he could have easily perished inside the enchanted mist. However, it seems The Great Spirit saw fit to guide him safely through it all and here to our Council."

The members of the council began to murmur uneasily among themselves, but Lucinda raised her hand for silence and continued. "Since then, Mr. Bones has had an additional vision of intense clarity. It was so strong, in fact, that I felt it all the way back in my hut on The Twin Peaks." The vulture paused to let the words sink in. "When I confronted Mr. Bones this morning, he told me what he had experienced." She paused again and looked over at the shepherd dog. "Mr. Bones, would you please come before the council and tell us exactly what you saw and heard in your dream?"

Billy Bones, who was sitting with Victor Running Deer and Georgie Beaver on a bench near the double doors, stood and walked over to the semicircle. Although he began hesitantly, he gained confidence as he described the death of W. N. Stone and Jimmy Stone's final promise to return for his grandfather's books. When he finished, he stepped quietly back to the bench and sat down by his two friends.

As prearranged, Orville Bat stood up on his chair at this point, so that he could be seen and heard. "When Lucinda told me about Mr. Bones' dream earlier this morning, we concluded that he is very highly evolved…spiritually speaking. It is our belief that not only should he be given his freedom, but he should be allowed to walk among us as long as he desires. <u>And</u> because of his outstanding spiritual gifts, we recommend that he be invited to become a member of our Tribal Council for the next year…perhaps longer."

Omar immediately stood and declared in a loud voice, "All who agree with Mr. Orville's recommendation please stand."

A stunned silence fell over the council members. Then gradually, one by one, beginning with Maurice Rabbit, the members stood and applauded. Even the cougar finally stood, shaking his head in disbelief.

At a nod from the old mountain goat, the elk walked over to Billy, untied the ropes that bound him, and brought him before the council. The dog had no idea that what he had done was so exceptional and could only gaze at the members of the council with amazement.

While the members were again taking their seats, Maurice Rabbit hopped into the cloakroom behind the west wall, and Omar Mountain Goat stood to speak. "Mr. Bones, on behalf of the Tribal Council, I invite you to become an honorary member of this body for one year.

You will be asked to attend our council meetings during the time of the autumn and spring equinoxes and during the winter and summer solstices. Other than that, you may come and go as you wish." At that point Maurice came forward with a light blue robe. Omar continued, "And as a token of our sincerity, we invite you to wear this robe of truth whenever the council is in session, and we offer you a seat between Lucinda and Maurice." The rabbit helped the astonished dog slip on the robe and escorted him to his place of honor.

Even though the council members now looked upon Victor and Georgie's failed rescue with more compassion, they concluded that the deer and the beaver were still guilty of trespassing. Because of the unusual circumstances, however, the judges decided that retribution should be paid by their mentor, Winston Wise Owl, in the form of a book that the members had long coveted. They reasoned that it was the owl's responsibility to inform Victor and Georgie about the laws of the Hill Country. Deputy Eagle was given the task of informing Winston of the council's decision.

Before the eagle left, he took the opportunity to reprimand the council. "I'm pleased that Mr. Bones is safe and that you've been so generous to him, but we've been searchin' everywhere for him for three days now!" complained the deputy. "I even came to your canyon twice and inquired about the dog. Each time, I received little or no cooperation."

Omar Mountain Goat stood for his reply. "Deputy Eagle, we deeply regret that we couldn't inform you sooner. I can only tell you that Billy's case has great spiritual significance. We had to keep his whereabouts a secret until the council could make a judgment." He paused briefly and then continued. "We did inform you, however, of the presence of Mr. Running Deer and Mr. Beaver so that you could attend this hearing."

Gaylord Cougar leaned back in his chair. "From their testimony I understand that you told them where Billy could be found if he was still alive."

"Aye, that I did, but I also advised them not to come. It was only their affection for their friend that drove them here, which we've all plainly witnessed," declared Harold adamantly.

"And we've pronounced only the mildest of sentences, as you have also witnessed," returned Lucinda Vulture sharply. "Tell Mr. Wise Owl to honor our request, and the two young animals will be released to you at once. He may come tomorrow morning if he so desires."

Deputy Harold Eagle finally conceded that the penalty was indeed light, and he agreed to try to persuade Winston to cooperate. He left the Great Hall without looking back.

After the trial Maurice Rabbit led Billy Bones into the little room west of the Great Hall where Billy's escape had taken place and where the council members kept their robes. As Billy was about to remove his, Lucinda shook her head and motioned for him to enter the room behind the one they were using. She wore the key around her waist along with a number of other keys. The rabbit leaned over and whispered to the dog, "She would like to show you our Sacred Chamber where we keep the human artifacts. We must keep our robes on, and we can't talk inside the room. The Spirit is very strong there!"

Billy and Maurice followed Lucinda into the room. It had no windows, so she lit two silver candlesticks that had been placed on a long oak table in the center. In front of the candles was a large leather-bound book opened to reveal several tintype pictures of human men and women. On the right side it had the words MY BIBLE printed in bold letters and below it the name Cortland Witherspoon, born June 21, 1825, written in longhand.

To the right of the Bible was another leather-bound book, and to the left was a space for a third book. Billy wondered whether the empty spot was meant for the book that Winston was required to bring as payment.

Surrounding the books were numerous articles: music boxes, a violin, and small chests and caskets filled with personal items. Lining the walls of the room were a number of old chairs, side tables, desks, chests of drawers, cupboards, and other items of furniture. On the wall behind the table were large portraits of two rather severe-looking humans and a magnificent painting of a married couple and their three children sitting under a large tree.

"So this was their holy place," Billy thought, remembering how he and Victor and Georgie had tried to enter. "These things belonged to the humans I saw in my visions.

No wonder Lucinda and Orville believed me. They've seen them too, and that's one of the reasons they're kept in this room. They must have a special importance for the inhabitants here in the Hill Country." He looked up in time to see Lucinda staring at him knowingly.

After Lucinda Vulture left the lodge, Maurice put on his regular clothes. Being a painter, he wore a smock and a black beret when the council was not in session. Although he was constantly joking, Billy discovered that Maurice was the perfect foil for Lucinda. The rabbit appreciated her enormous spiritual gifts but also seemed well aware of her shortcomings. "She certainly wasn't cut out to be a mother!" he laughed, when Billy mentioned her sons. "I'm sure the poor birds pretty much raised themselves!"

CHAPTER TWENTY

ECHO CANYON

When Billy Bones and Maurice Rabbit returned to the Great Hall, Arthur Elk was waiting for them. Georgie Beaver and Victor Running Deer's hands were still tied, and they were sitting on a bench near the front doors.

"They've no reason to escape, Arthur," said Maurice finally. "They know they'll be able to return home in the morning when Winston Wise Owl gets here." In his grudging manner Arthur untied the two animals and returned to his shed.

"Come on, everyone. Let's find Billy somethin' nicer to wear!" Maurice called jovially.

A small store was only a few hundred feet from the lodge. Maurice found Billy a white shirt and a dark pair of trousers held up by suspenders. "This'll have to do until you return to your crazy tailor," he said good-naturedly.

Everywhere the four animals visited, they were met with cheers and offers of food and drink. Georgie was especially troubled because he had been raised to believe that most of the citizens of the Hill Country were a disagreeable lot.

One of the most amazing sights that Maurice pointed out to Billy, Georgie, and Victor was the stream that ran through Echo Canyon. It later became a waterfall and eventually emptied into the beaver pond. An unusual feature was that it came from an underground source and burst directly out of the mountain at the end of the canyon just north of the lodge.

That evening Arthur made a campfire for the three outsiders and cooked some trout in a large frying pan. In the meantime, Maurice secured enough blankets for them to spend the night comfortably under the stars.

"What is the mountain at the end of the canyon called, the one that disappears into the mist?" asked Georgie, as the rabbit finally settled himself in front of the fire.

"It's called Spirit Dwells," explained Maurice.

"And how about the stream that flows out of it?" inquired Billy.

"That's called Spirit Moves," continued the rabbit.

"I was told that you believe there are spirits in every-thing. Is that true?" asked Georgie, feeling a little bolder.

"Not exactly," responded Maurice. "We believe in The Great Spirit like you do, but we believe everything has a spirit of its own connected to The Great Spirit. That's one of the reasons we remain separate from the Prairie. Here we can practice our beliefs without judgment."

"But the things found along the wagon trail, how are they sacred?" asked Billy.

Maurice stopped smiling and faced Billy. "The ancients

believed that the gifts of thought and speech we received after the first great rift occurred were somehow related to the human treasures that were found along the wagon trail. They also felt that if these items were lost, it could tamper with the magic of The Enchantment or prove to be catastrophic."

At the mention of the human artifacts, Victor mumbled something and turned his head away from the group. Georgie, on the other hand, changed the subject and questioned the dog again about his capture and his first trial before the Tribal Council. Billy, in turn, learned about the three-day search for him and how Victor and Georgie journeyed to Lookout Point on the night the search was canceled.

"We finally got Deputy Eagle to tell us about the celebration of the solstice here in Echo Canyon," Georgie said excitedly, "and then he told us that the Tribal Council was still in session."

"He admitted that there was a chance you might've been captured and that they were hiding you for some reason," continued Victor.

"So Victor and I got up early this morning and sneaked up here and hid until your trial started," confessed the beaver, "and when almost everyone left the lodge, we tried to rescue you."

"And that was one sorry rescue!" admitted the young deer. Suddenly all the animals around the fire started laughing at the weak plan. Even the serious-minded Victor was caught up in the spirit of the moment and laughed the hardest.

With Victor and Georgie beside him around the camp-fire and the happy Maurice and even the grumpy elk, Billy felt a contentment that he had not experienced since the last morning he had been with the boy. For the first time inside The Enchantment, he slept peacefully.

CHAPTER TWENTY-ONE

THE TERMS OF RELEASE

"It sounds like a form of blackmail to me, Harold!" sputtered Winston Wise Owl after hearing the terms for the release of Victor Running Deer and Georgie Beaver.

"I can only say that it could've been much worse. I suggest you go along with the request if at all possible," advised Deputy Harold Eagle.

"Was this Lucinda Vulture's idea?" asked Winston suspiciously.

"Come to think of it, she did seem a bit anxious to get hold of that book o' yours," admitted Harold.

The wise old owl knew that Lucinda desperately wanted a particular book in his library called *Pagan Religions of the Western World.* She had already managed to obtain the *King James Bible* and *Great Religions of the World.*

Toward evening a secret meeting was convened at the Old Meetinghouse with Counselor Thaddeus B. Turtle, Mayor George P. Beaver, Winston Wise Owl, Deputy Harold Eagle, and Sheriff Walter Lone Wolf attending. The group reached the consensus that Winston should pay the penalty and viewed this as an opportunity to improve relations between the two states.

Early the next morning, Winston Wise Owl flew to Lookout Point to plan the day's strategy with Deputy Harold Eagle, bringing the book with him. After a brief discussion the eagle finally told the owl about the shepherd dog's dream concerning the early pioneers and how Winston's books got stored in the hollow of his tree. "I thought it was only fair that I tell you 'bout the dream when we were alone. I realize that it sounds pretty far-fetched, but the Tribal Council seemed to latch on to it, 'specially Lucinda and Orville Bat."

The owl sat for a few moments and pondered the eagle's story. "You say that Mr. Bones remembered some of the settler's names?"

"Yep, that's what he told them."

At that point the owl quickly rose and started for the door. "Come back with me to my tree house. I have another book that might shed light on Billy's story, and I'll need you to corroborate it before the Tribal Council so they won't think I tampered with it."

Winston could feel the early morning sun blazing on his back as he and Harold entered Echo Canyon. Far below, he could see the summer solstice celebrants lined up on either side of the pathway that led to the Great Lodge. With his sharp eyes he recognized the Tribal Council members standing in front of the lodge door. They had donned their various colored robes for the occasion. The two great birds zoomed down directly over the pathway and landed on the little clearing in front of the lodge.

Deputy Harold Eagle stepped forward immediately. "My companion, Winston Wise Owl, and I request a private session with the Tribal Council to discuss an important concern. As you can see, Mr. Wise Owl brought with him the book you requested."

Winston noticed that the council was taken by surprise. Apparently they anticipated no further conversation.

After a brief but heated discussion among the council members, Omar Mountain Goat approached the two birds. "Your request is granted. Please follow us into the lodge." He then turned to Billy Bones, who was standing by Arthur Elk's shed with Victor Running Deer and Georgie Beaver. "Mr. Bones, put your robe on. You may sit with us."

After the council was seated in their semicircle, Omar nodded for Winston to advance. The owl was unexpectedly moved at seeing Billy's bright face among the council members, accentuated by his sky-blue robe. His initial judgment concerning the dog's spiritual qualities had been validated, especially since Lucinda also recognized them. What really pleased him, however, was that Billy showed no sign of haughtiness or egotism.

"Well, Mr. Wise Owl, we're waiting!" snarled Gaylord Cougar impatiently.

Winston glanced nonchalantly around the semicircle of judges and noticed that Lucinda's eyes shifted constantly to the book on pagan religions that he held tightly in his left hand.

"Thank you for allowing me to speak," the owl began. "As Deputy Eagle mentioned, we have a major concern.

Mayor Beaver has authorized us to initiate a dialogue between you and our City Council. He believes it's time you eased the restrictions you've enacted about entering your territory, especially since no such laws apply to the Prairie."

"That's because we hold no threat to you!" snapped the lizard. "As long as you build your laws around your so-called *Great Book of Rules*, I see no reason that we should consider easing our restrictions!"

"Nevertheless, Lucretia, there must be some room for compromise," responded the owl.

"But with whom? You're no doubt aware, sir, that a much more reactionary mayor and City Council could be elected in a few months," reasoned Omar Mountain Goat.

"And their new adviser, Fabian Lynx, has absolutely no respect for the sacredness of our antiquities, or yours, for that matter," interjected Orville Bat, almost jumping out of his chair.

Lucinda Vulture stood and lowered her hood. "If Brother Fabian Lynx gets enough power and destroys some of the human artifacts, we're concerned that our way of life could be threatened!"

"I'm aware that he has much influence over the members of the New Meetinghouse.

But about the damage he can do, well, I don't possess your spiritual insight," confessed Winston.

"Then I suggest you lean heavily on Mr. Bones here. Perhaps he can help protect you from that scheming lynx. We can do nothing from here except protect ourselves!" screeched the vulture, her eyes widening.

"Speaking of Mr. Billy Bones," continued Winston, looking back at the second book strapped to Deputy Eagle's chest. "I have a little surprise for you. Deputy Eagle told me about Mr. Bones' dream the other night, and I have something here that might interest you and the council," began Winston, as he took the book from the eagle. "I brought Deputy Eagle with me when I retrieved this book, kept in a trunk at the foot of my bed. Now, what was the boy's name who buried his grandfather just north of my tree?"

"Why, it was Jimmy," stated Lucinda, suddenly showing an interest in the second book.

"Well then, read what's written on the inside cover of this book called *Grimm's Fairy Tales*. Go ahead, read it out loud."

"To my beloved grandson, <u>Jimmy</u>. Remember me always, W. N. Stone."

"Why that proves beyond all reasonable doubt...that we were correct!" squeaked Orville Bat, interrupting Lucinda's reading.

"Here, let me see that!" roared Gaylord Cougar, rising and coming over to Lucinda. "Ha! And how do we know you didn't just put it there?"

"Because when Deputy Eagle told me about Billy's dream, I brought him with me to my house, so he could take it out of the trunk himself. Since then I have not touched it," smiled Winston. "I have to tell you, though, I admire you for believing Billy even without this proof. It shows that this council has a wisdom we do not share inside the Prairie."

"Thank you for those remarks and for sharing your information about the human boy's name," concluded Omar, "but most of the thanks go to Lucinda and Orville. They are the ones who recognized Mr. Bones' remarkable gift. Now please go outside and take Deputy Harold Eagle with you. We will give you our decision concerning easing restrictions shortly."

By the time Winston and Harold were summoned back into the lodge, the sun from the east windows no longer spotted their backs but formed golden puddles below the window wells. The owl and the eagle could tell from the flushed countenances of the councilors that much debate had taken place.

Chief Omar Mountain Goat stood to address them. "I'm sorry, but I'm afraid we have to reject your proposal at this time. Mayor Beaver and his councilors could be voted out of office, and under the influence of Brother Fabian Lynx, the new mayor and City Council may not have the same tolerance. Of course Sheriff Lone Wolf and his deputies already have the right to follow law-breakers across our borders. We feel we cannot in good conscience extend any more privileges than that at this time." Omar glanced over at Lucinda, who nodded slightly. "But of course, we still need the book we discussed in order to make the exchange."

Winston frowned. It had not occurred to him that the Tribal Council was so aware of the Prairie's recently volatile political climate and the concern about Brother Lynx.

Finally the owl carefully reclaimed the book of fairy tales that had been passed around to all of the councilors, handed the book on pagan religions to the eagle, and nodded his consent.

Deputy Eagle, in turn, gave the required book to Omar Mountain Goat and addressed him personally. "We accept your conditions, sir, and we'll be takin' your young trespassers with us and Mr. Billy Bones too, that is, if he'd like to return with us."

Omar turned to the dog. "What is your wish, Mr. Bones?"

Billy stood and addressed the councilors. "You've done me a great honor, and I thank you, but I would like to go with my friends for now."

"We ask only that you return to us for the Tribal Council meeting during the Autumn Equinox. We'll have many difficult decisions to make, and we'll need your special gifts." The kindly old goat walked slowly over to the young dog and placed his fingers lightly on the canine's forehead. "May The Great Spirit be your constant guide."

Maurice Rabbit rose cheerfully from his place and slipped the blue robe off Billy's shoulders. "I'll take care of this for you." He smiled and embraced the shepherd dog robustly. "Don't be gone too long!"

"Come visit me whenever you like," said the dog, returning the smile. "And thank you."

When Winston, Harold, and Billy stepped outside the lodge, they found Georgie and Victor sitting in the shade of the old shed.

"Georgie, take Victor and Billy home. Some concerned parents and search party members are waiting for you," commanded Winston happily.

The beaver quickly jumped up and called to the deer and the dog. "Well, come on! I missed my swim practice for the last four days, and I've got a lot of makin' up to do if I'm ever gonna beat Johnny Otter in the summer races!" He then glanced at the young buck. "And you, Victor Running Deer, you've got to start training yourself if you plan to go up against Rodney Wild Deer in the Big Race. Besides, Pa says he's really mean and can't be trusted!"

Winston saw Billy smile and knew he looked forward to building a lasting friendship with the amiable beaver and the earnest deer who had attempted such a daring rescue.

As Winston Wise Owl and Deputy Harold Eagle flew off together, the owl looked back in time to see Victor and Billy running to catch up to the anxious Georgie. "Maybe Billy Bones is finally ready to resume his journey," Winston shouted over at the eagle. "He's an extraordinary animal. I hope he can stay above the fray…especially when it comes to Brother Fabian Lynx and his hatred for anything human. But with Billy's insights and amazing visions related to the humans, I'm afraid he might find himself in the thick of things!

CHAPTER TWENTY-TWO

THE LOST DOG

For three days Will Stuart and his grandson Billy scoured the area around the beaver pond and up into the foothills for their lost dog, Bones. They were especially thorough along the shoreline, where the shepherd dog had in the past spent hours sniffing for various kinds of aquatic animals, and around the Prairie Dog Town, where Bones enjoyed barking and stirring up trouble.

"You don't suppose some wild animal got him?" questioned Billy on the third day, trying to hold back tears. "I mean, the coyotes could've ganged up on him…or maybe that mountain lion. Remember the tracks we found last winter?"

"Of course, that's always a possibility," agreed Will, "but Bones is pretty savvy. I doubt he'd get too close to a big cat like that!"

On the fourth day the boy and his grandfather searched the back roads and little towns close to the farm in Will's old pickup, asking questions and posting signs. Finally on their way home, Billy snuggled close to his grandfather and broached a subject that still troubled him.

"Grandpa, remember when we thought we heard someone calling us on the second morning, when the fog was really thick? Remember? It sounded like a man yelling, 'Wait, Billy, wait! Do you remember?"

"Ah yes, it was probably some large bird screaming… like a horned owl or something. Or maybe it was just the wind whistling through the trees," reasoned Will. "For one thing, it certainly wasn't a dog barking. It sounded too human for that."

"Yeah, it sure wasn't a dog. You're right. It probably was some kind of wild creature. Like a bird…or even a mountain lion. When they cry, they sound almost human…. Or, as you said, maybe it was just the wind whistling through the trees—that can make all kinds of strange sounds. Yeah, that's probably all it was…just the wind…."

PART TWO

ON TO THE GRAND FAIR

— 156 —

CHAPTER TWENTY-THREE

BILLY'S COTTAGE

Four weeks passed since Justin Beaver first offered to help Billy Bones build his new home. Although Billy and Georgie Beaver did most of the work, Justin kept close tabs on them. Billy quickly showed an aptitude for carpentry, and Justin asked him, along with his son, to work on a number of other projects.

Billy chose to build on a site just off the East Wagon Trail, facing the morning sun. Although only a few trees grew there, he settled on a spot near a large cottonwood that would provide shade during the afternoon hours.

Throwing his energy into his work was good therapy for the dog. Until now he had successfully avoided trying to make sense of the experiences inside the mist or the disturbing visions about the ancient humans. All he wanted to do was live simply and enjoy his newly-formed friendships with Georgie Beaver and his parents, his mentor, Winston Wise Owl, the owl's saucy neighbor, Hester Groundhog, and, of course, Victor Running Deer. Therefore he was especially delighted to look up from his work one morning and see Hester approaching Justin Beaver, who was inspecting Billy's newly-built cottage.

"Billy and Georgie work well together, don't they?" commented Hester cheerfully as she padded over to where Justin stood.

"The shepherd has a good eye," bragged the older beaver. "If you notice, he copied your Dutch doors and shutters and borrowed the idea of thatching the roof from Thaddeus Turtle's cottage."

Hester crossed over to where Billy and Georgie had just finished hanging the top door for the second time.

"Miss Groundhog, it's about time you got down here to see what we've been doin'," chided Billy. "And what've you got there?"

"Oh, it's just some of my freshly baked pecan bread, but I don't suppose you'd be interested," returned Hester good-naturedly.

"I don't think I can convince Georgie to take a break, but as for myself, I can't think of anything I'd like better!" laughed the canine.

"Don't listen to him, Miss Groundhog!" exclaimed the younger beaver. "If he keeps smartin' off, don't give him anything."

As Billy started to sit down at a makeshift table just north of the cottage, he playfully bopped the young beaver's head with his knuckles. In response Georgie grinned and ducked as he reached for his first helping of Hester's wonderful bread.

After the dog and the beavers had several slices each and a dipper of cool water, they invited Hester inside. The living area was one large room with a stone fireplace on the north side. The ceiling was pitched high in the center with large beams running across the width of the room. A small loft had been built above the beams on the west wall with a narrow ladder leading up to it.

"It's a charming place!" exclaimed the groundhog.

"Yep, that it is," echoed a voice behind them.

The four friends turned to see Farmer Jason Crow standing just inside the doorway. The crow was chomping on one of the many wheat stalks that he perpetually chewed.

"Jason, how good to see you," cried Justin, as he walked over and shook the crow's hand. "Come over to inspect our work?"

"Well actually I just dropped by to see Mr. Bones here," responded Jason, glancing at Billy. "I'm here representin' Brother Fabian Lynx. He says he invited Billy to attend the New Meetin'house the first day he got here, and he ain't seen hide nor hair of him."

"I've been attending the Old Meetinghouse, Mr. Crow," responded Billy, looking somewhat embarrassed.

"Well, I just need to tell you that Brother Fabian's worried about you. He's been hearin' these strange rumors about you seein' human spirits inside the mist. He thinks maybe you need to talk to him."

"Tell him I appreciate his concern, Mr. Crow, and I'll consider his invitation," said Billy solemnly.

"And that's it?" snapped the crow, obviously expecting a more positive response.

"Yeah, I guess that's it," answered the shepherd dog.

"Well then, I guess that's all I've got to say," cawed Jason, abruptly turning and leaving.

"That was odd, I must say," muttered Hester. "I don't like the sound of this." The groundhog looked over at Justin. "And I don't think he was expecting to see us here."

"I wonder why Brother Fabian didn't come himself?" questioned Justin.

"I guess he wants Billy to make the first move," concluded Hester, turning to the dog. "Do you think you'll accept, Billy?"

"I don't know. Should I?" asked Billy. "I've already talked to Mr. Wise Owl. Maybe I should just leave it at that." He hesitated. Knowing the lynx's hatred toward humans, the dog had no desire to seek his counsel.

"I'm anxious to see what you'll put inside this quaint little cottage," interjected Hester, changing the subject.

"Georgie and I are going to Percival's shop on Monday. Would you like to come along and give us some ideas?" inquired the young dog.

"I was hoping you'd ask," chuckled Hester in response. "You know how I like to be a part of everything. Let's ask Gladys too. She's got a good eye for furniture."

CHAPTER TWENTY-FOUR

THE OLD CORNER CUPBOARD

Early Monday morning, Hester Groundhog, Georgie Beaver and his mother Gladys, and Billy Bones met at Percival Gander's shop. The obliging gander fell over himself trying to show the four animals his latest acquisition. "Come around back. I think I've got just the thing for our young builder. Yes, yes, just the thing!"

Percival Gander led the quartet of amateur decorators around to the basement entrance of his coop and opened the double doors. Billy was amazed at the quantity and variety of furniture that the gander had collected over the years to help young homebuilders. His eye fell on an old corner cupboard just to the right of the door.

"Isn't she beautiful!" sighed the gander, when he noticed Billy's interest. "Yes, yes, one of the best, one of the best."

"But who would give up such a handsome piece?" asked Hester, clapping her hands together. "It must have been left by humans along the Old Wagon Trail."

"Yes, it was. That it was," admitted Percival. "It was passed down to Granny Muskrat who, as you know, died a couple weeks ago. After her death, Brother Fabian Lynx tried to persuade her children to break it up or burn it."

"So how did you get it?" asked Georgie. "Why wasn't it destroyed?"

"Granny's youngest grandson, Alvin, wouldn't let them. He loved this old cupboard. He said that I should choose the new owner. Yes, that I should choose!" Percival glanced over at the young dog. He could hardly restrain his enthusiasm. "And I think our friend here with the rare spiritual gifts should have it. Yes, I do. Yes, I do!"

Gladys, Georgie, and Percival also glanced at Billy, but he could not meet their gaze. He was now viewed as something of a celebrity since he was asked to be a member of the Hill Country's Tribal Council, and he didn't know quite how to handle the popular acclaim.

"I don't really deserve…" the dog began softly.

"But it must go to a worthy home, Billy," said Hester sincerely. "And Percival knows you will honor it, and I believe so too."

"And so do I," said Georgie.

"And so do I," said Gladys.

"And so do I," said a new voice. It was Thaddeus P. Turtle, who had just poked his head inside the double door.

"Counselor Turtle!" exclaimed Percival, looking up suddenly. "What an honor to have you in my shop. Yes, yes, quite an honor! Are you looking for something in particular?"

"Well actually I was seeking out young Billy here. I would like a word with him. I promise to be brief."

While Billy conversed privately with Thaddeus, Georgie and Percival loaded the top half of the ancient cherry cupboard onto a cart that the gander used for just such purposes.

"Be especially careful to keep the doors facing up, yes, facing up. All the panes in that window are still intact. You wouldn't want to break any. No, you wouldn't want to do that!" warned the tailor.

As soon as the beaver and the gander began loading the cart, Hester and Gladys started rummaging through the storage area and found a little pine table, several sturdy chairs, and a chest of drawers that had been crafted by one of Gladys's uncles.

After the turtle left, Gladys could see that the dog was in somewhat of a quandary. "What did Thaddeus want, Billy? Is everything all right?"

"Well…kind of the same thing that Brother Fabian wanted, except he wants me to speak to his gathering next Sunday after his meditations. He wants me to tell everyone about my experiences inside the mist," explained the dog a bit nervously.

"What did you tell him?" asked Georgie excitedly.

"I said I wanted to talk it over with Mr. Wise Owl," answered Billy uneasily. "I said I'd let him know by the middle of the week."

"Go see Winston right now then," urged Hester. "We'll take care of the furniture for you."

"But I can't just leave you with all the work. It's for my place," responded Billy.

"Nonsense," chided Gladys, "Hester's right. You can help Georgie move things when you get back. Now off with you!"

Billy moved silently up the hill to the path. The turtle's request and the crow's invitation had finally forced him to revisit that fateful morning when he had so boldly stepped into the golden mist. Except for Georgie, Victor, and Winston, he had avoided speaking to anyone in the Prairie about his strange adventure.

CHAPTER TWENTY-FIVE

THE CROSSROADS

As Billy Bones moved along the path toward Land's End, a slight breeze rose out of the foothills, causing the dog to shiver slightly even though the day was quite warm.

When the young dog reached the crossroads where the Rogue Deer had collided with Victor on the first day inside The Enchantment, his peripheral vision caught a whirl of motion in the south. This unexpected movement was followed by a familiar voice yelling, "Watch out, Billy!" and an arm and a hand pushed him firmly but safely out of the way.

In an instant, Billy found himself sitting unceremoniously in the middle of the path. "Billy, Billy, you've got to watch where you're standin'!" laughed Victor Running Deer, also remembering the earlier collision with Rodney. "If this isn't a coincidence, then I don't know what is."

"It's certainly becoming a dangerous corner, that's for sure!" gasped Billy, as two friendly pairs of hands helped him to his feet.

"Billy, I'd like you to meet Sandy Antelope and Arnold Big Horn. They're my new runnin' partners since you abandoned me to work on that precious house of yours. They're also planning to enter the Big Race," explained the deer.

Because the three hoofed animals were in training, they only wore trousers held up by suspenders.

As the dog greeted Victor's new companions, he suddenly noticed a number of cuts and bruises about the young deer's face and body. "What in the name of The Great Spirit happened to you? You look like you've been hit by a tree!"

"That's exactly why we're here," said Sandy, trying to explain the situation. "He's had quite a run-in with Rodney Wild Deer and some of his friends."

"Apparently Victor put up quite a fight, but I'm afraid he got the worst of it. We found him lyin' unconscious along Timber Trail a couple days ago," continued Arnold.

"We told him he wasn't to jog by himself anymore," said the antelope resolutely.

"Of course we thought he'd take a couple weeks to recuperate, but as you can see, he's out runnin' again. I think it'll take more than a beating to keep Victor out of the race," concluded Arnold.

"Or away from his sweetheart," grinned Sandy.

Billy had known for some time that Victor Running Deer was totally smitten with Olen Buck's daughter, Melinda. He also knew that Rodney Wild Deer had similar feelings for the doe but that Olen had forbidden any contact between the two. What really concerned Billy, however, were persistent rumors that somehow the devious Rogue Deer was responsible for the disappearance of Melinda's previous suitor, Terry Deer.

"You're right. It looks like we're all going to have to get involved in Victor's training," determined Billy, beginning to catch his breath.

At that moment fate intervened again. Rodney and two of the four coyote brothers who lived along the Old Wagon Trail came sprinting around the corner of the Southern Road. Because the three runners were also shirtless, Billy surmised that they too were in training for the races. They came to a screeching halt when they saw Victor and his three friends.

"Well well, look what we've got here," snarled the Rogue Deer. "I guess we were too easy on you. I thought I told you to stay out of the race!"

"And since when do I take orders from you, Rodney? I suggest you keep going. You were lucky last time because you caught me alone, but this time I'm not outnumbered!"

"And I suggest you watch your back from now on and stay away from Melinda if you know what's good for you!" threatened Rodney, as he turned sharply and headed north on Wheat Walk with Lester and Leon Coyote hard on his heels.

Sandy had to restrain Victor from lunging after the malicious deer and his canine companions. "Hold it, Victor! That just proves what we've been sayin'. You should never train by yourself. Rodney's a dangerous one. There's no gettin' around that!"

"Especially since the Grand Fair's only a month away," added Arnold.

Victor took a moment to compose himself and then turned to the shepherd. "Billy, would you like to join us? It looks like we'll be headin' back south."

"No thanks, not today. I was just on my way to see Mr. Wise Owl."

"Anything serious?" wondered the curious buck.

"I just need some advice. Counselor Turtle asked me to speak to his gathering after meditations on Sunday. He wants me to tell them about my experiences inside the mist."

Billy suddenly stopped talking and gazed over at his old friend. He knew that for some reason Victor did not like hearing about the visions or anything else that had to do with human beings.

"Maybe you ought to forget about that, Billy," said Victor, momentarily looking away.

"I wish it were that easy, Victor," said the dog, somewhat shakily. "I've even asked Winston Wise Owl for advice. He says that if I speak truthfully about my experience, the creatures of the Prairie will realize my visions weren't caused by spells or something evil."

"Well, Brother Fabian Lynx thinks they were!" blurted out the young deer unexpectedly.

The shepherd dog was taken unawares. He suddenly realized that it was probably Victor who had been talking to Brother Fabian.

Finally the dog confronted the deer. "When did you start hanging around him, Victor? How long has this been going on?"

"I didn't go looking for him, Billy, if that's what you're referrin' to," refuted the deer. "Olen and Myrtle Buck have Brother Fabian over for supper from time to time, and a couple of times they included me. I've also gone to the New Meetinghouse with them." Victor stopped speaking and looked down at his hooves. Billy could see that the deer hated explaining himself and that he was making an exception for him. "He says your apparitions are evil spirits left over from the old world." Victor paused again and raised his eyes until they met Billy's. "And I'm inclined to agree with him."

Billy was silent for a moment. When he spoke, his voice wavered slightly. "I don't think either of you are right, Victor. I think the visions show momentous happenings in the lives of humans long ago. Traumatic moments, maybe, but certainly not evil."

"You think that way because the humans never killed your mother, Billy! Well I saw them shoot mine right in front of me! Perhaps if that'd happened to you, you might feel different," cried the young deer resentfully.

Billy was stunned. Victor had never mentioned the brutal murder of his mother to anyone, and now Billy knew, as well as Sandy and Arnold. Billy suddenly realized that the painful memory must have haunted the deer since he was a fawn, festering inside him.

Billy put his hand gently on the deer's shoulder. "Most humans aren't like the ones that killed your mother. I know this from experience."

"You need to talk to Brother Fabian. Find out what they did to him," insisted Victor, trying to regain his composure.

The young deer said no more but turned away and started jogging southward. Sandy looked at Billy sympathetically and shrugged, "I guess we'd better be off too. Maybe you can join us tomorrow."

As Billy watched the three runners depart, he knew in his heart that he and Victor were moving in different directions. He hoped it would not affect the Great Medley that he and Victor and Georgie were planning to enter on the fifth day of the Grand Fair. Georgie would be terribly disappointed if it did.

When the shepherd dog reached the home of Winston Wise Owl, he found him sitting in the shade of his gigantic tree. As usual, he was engrossed in one of his leather-bound books.

"Excuse me, sir, but could I bother you for a moment? I'm afraid I need your advice again," said the dog respectfully.

"Of course, any time for you, my young friend. What seems to be the trouble?"

After discussing Thaddeus's invitation, Billy reminded Winston of the dream he had four weeks ago about the pioneers who left the books in the hollow of the owl's tree.

"I tell you, it was as if I was actually there," concluded Billy.

"Well, I'm convinced that's the way it happened," agreed the owl. "Everything seems to fit anyway. I'm convinced that Jimmy Stone left his grandfather's books in my tree on his way to the Oregon Territory. Yes, it certainly fits."

After rehashing the dream, Billy mentioned the old corner cupboard and how it had come into his possession. When he finished, he decided not to reveal what he knew about Victor and Brother Fabian's new friendship. Even though it bothered him immensely, he felt he could not pass the information on without the deer's permission. For some reason, he also failed to mention the lynx's invitation to discuss the images he had seen inside the mist.

"I'm very concerned about Brother Fabian and his effort to destroy Granny Muskrat's cupboard. I think we should inform Counselor Turtle and Mayor Beaver as soon as possible," concluded Winston. "Let me see if I can arrange a meeting with them tomorrow. We can also discuss your talk on Sunday. We're liable to get quite a crowd you know."

Billy Bones lowered his head slightly. "Then you think I should speak on Sunday?"

"I think the gathering at the Old Meetinghouse needs to be enlightened by your new knowledge of the great mist that surrounds us. As long as you stick to the facts, there shouldn't be any problem. Of course, there'll always be those who'll try to twist your words. That's why it's better to go over all the details first."

"And the dream…?" asked Billy.

"Well, for now let's not make that public to the Prairie citizens," decided the owl. "But I think we can mention it to Mayor Beaver and Counselor Turtle. It's time they heard."

Winston Wise Owl sat back in his chair. He had a mischievous twinkle in his eye. "And maybe we can get the good mayor to open up his castle for us. Yes, I think you would enjoy that. Now go home. I'll let you know about the meeting."

CHAPTER TWENTY-SIX

THE MISCHIEVOUS INTRUDERS

By the time Billy Bones returned to Percival's shop, Georgie Beaver had already hauled both sections of the old corner cupboard to the dog's new home. Since the trips with the old handcart were cumbersome for one animal, the beaver was glad to see the shepherd dog.

It was late in the afternoon before the two friends finally set the last piece of furniture in its space and returned the handcart to the generous gander. In the meantime, Gladys Beaver had prepared an evening meal for them and invited Hester and Percival over as well.

After the meal Billy thanked the gander, the groundhog, and the beavers for their kindness, excused himself, and left for his new home. He and Georgie had slept at the site several times after working late, but this would be the first night that he actually stayed by himself. He was eager for the experience.

Because of a nearly full moon, Billy had no problem finding his way home. When he opened the Dutch door to his cottage however, he instantly heard rustling noises and the sound of scampering feet.

"Who's there?" Billy shouted, peering into the darkened room. The moon's blue brightness cast enough light to allow him to see two feet falling awkwardly out of the back right window. Instinctively he turned and ran out the front door and around to the back of the house. He was just in time to see a short figure scurry clumsily down the bluff and into the blackness of the thicket that ran along the river.

After realizing the difficulty of chasing anyone through the maze of bushes and small trees that grew next to the water, Billy returned to his home. He fumbled briefly for a candle and a flint box that he kept inside the little hutch that he and Georgie built into the wall next to the fireplace. After several tries he lit the candle and proceeded to look around the room to see if anything was missing.

"Blast it! He took the rest of the pecan bread and used up all the jam! That scoundrel!" Billy sputtered out loud after examining the hutch. He then crossed the room to see if the old cupboard had suffered any damage. It looked unharmed. He then moved back to the new chest and opened the drawers. He could see that his white shirt had been mussed up, but again nothing was missing.

"I guess he was after food," muttered the tired dog half to himself. "No harm done."

Billy Bones proceeded to shut his doors and inside shutters except for the single window on the south wall. He wanted to let some moonlight into the room and reasoned that the culprit probably would not return.

By the time Billy crawled into his bunk under the loft, he had pretty much forgotten about the intruder. Instead his thoughts turned back to Victor Running Deer and his changing attitude over the past four weeks.

When Billy, Georgie, and Justin first started constructing the shepherd's house, Victor visited almost every afternoon. With the help of Olen Buck, his wife Myrtle, and his daughter Melinda, the deer's own lean-to had been rebuilt in a much shorter period of time. Billy and Georgie had noticed that Victor seemed somewhat reluctant to enter the Big Race and the Great Medley when they first mentioned it. However, when the lovely Melinda Doe encouraged him, he immediately was won over.

In the first weeks that followed their return from the Hill Country, Billy and Victor would often train together in the early morning while Georgie practiced at the pond. As time passed, however, Billy and Georgie got more absorbed with their building project, while Victor turned his attentions to Olen's comely daughter. Finally the visits between the two groups stopped altogether. Although Billy could now understand some reasons for the deer's hatred of humans, it bothered him greatly that the deer had fallen under the influence of Brother Fabian Lynx.

Just as the young shepherd dog was finally about to doze off, he felt something wispy and irritating fall onto his face. He brushed it off quickly and shifted positions. At that moment another particle of the same substance fell close to his mouth. This time he got hold of it and realized it was a piece of straw that apparently fell from the mattress in the loft directly over him. Then he became aware of something moving ever so cautiously on the same mattress. Billy tried to remain very still until he saw a scrawny leg reach over the edge of the loft and try to find the first rung of the ladder. Slowly another skinny leg followed, and the creature began his careful descent.

When the strange animal's feet got to the rung even with the top of the bed, Billy reached over, grabbed a leg tightly, and wrestled it to the floor. The intruder fought desperately to free himself, but he was much smaller than the dog and could not get away.

Panicking, the little animal found Billy's right hand and bit it. "Ow! Stop that!" screamed the dog, as the intruder freed himself and darted for the window. In one quick movement, the dog tackled the frightened beast and pinned him to the floor once again.

A sudden movement at the open window made Billy glance upward. Because of the moon's glow, he could only make out a shadowy outline and two large eyes of a creature peering into the opening. The figure struggled valiantly to pull himself up over the edge of the window but failed and fell back out of sight. After another mighty effort the animal finally got one leg over the sill and then another until it dropped into the room.

"Oh, no! Not another one!" was all the shepherd could say, as the other trespasser threw himself onto Billy's back.

"Ouch! What've you got on you, pins or something? Stop pokin' me!" cried the young dog, trying to shake off the second invader.

"You let him go! He didn't mean nothin'!" the newest trespasser managed to holler, still trying to catch his breath.

"Well, stop hittin' my head and pricking me with those needles, and I'll see what I can do!" yelled Billy in return, still not willing to surrender the creature beneath him.

Ever so slowly, the last intruder slid off Billy's back and cowered a little way in front of him. Just as carefully, the dog got off the animal on the floor, who gave up fighting him. With one hand tight around the wrist of the creature that had climbed down from the loft, he dragged him over to the table. As he reached for the candle and the tinderbox, he complained breathlessly, "I don't know what your friend's got on him, but I'm stinging all over!"

"He's a porcupine! He can't help it!" said the captive animal, speaking aloud for the first time.

"Well, tell him to keep his distance!" said Billy, still smarting from the pricks. "Now as for you," continued the dog, "if you stay put, I'll let you loose while I light this candle."

Slowly he released the strange little beast, who immediately started to back off. "Oh, oh! What did I just tell you?" warned the shepherd again.

The frightened beast stopped immediately, as Billy tried to light the candle while keeping an eye on both animals. After he finally succeeded, he took two chairs and set them in a row facing the table so he could see them both clearly.

Reluctantly the uninvited visitors sat as Billy paced back and forth in front of them. "All right now, who are you, and what are you doing in my house?" Both animals lowered their heads. "OK, someone needs to talk to me! I'm not going to hurt you."

Finally the creature he had pinned to the floor raised his head. "We didn't think you'd be back tonight. You've been gone so long."

Billy got his first good look at the little animal who had hidden in his loft. The mask around his eyes identified him immediately. "So, you sneaky raccoon, what's your name then?"

"Nolan, Nolan Coon, but everybody calls me Nosey," said the raccoon, as he reached over and lifted the porcupine's chin up. "And this is Needles. He's kind a' shy sometimes, as you can see."

"We didn't mean to steal nothin' or do no harm. Nosey just wanted to look at the new furniture. He's always pokin' his head into things. He can't help hisself!" said Needles reluctantly.

"We live down below the bluff. We've been comin' up here almost every night just to see how things is comin' along," said Nosey, feeling braver.

"So you come up here almost every night, do you?" queried the dog, trying to reach one of the many quills lodged in his back.

As soon as Needles realized Billy's discomfort, he overcame his fear and moved to help him. "Only when you ain't here," he admitted. "I guess we should've said somethin', huh?"

"Why didn't you?" asked Billy, thankful for Needle's assistance.

"We was afraid you wouldn't like us. We're not very important, you know, and well, everybody knows who you are," confessed the raccoon, who by this time had joined the porcupine.

"Well I'll be confounded! If you aren't a pair!" laughed the dog, as he knelt down so that the quills in his upper back could be removed more easily. "If you didn't steal anything, then where's the rest of my pecan bread?"

"Oh that!" said Nosey, glancing over at the porcupine. "Well, it smelled so good, we thought we'd jus' take a taste."

"And before you knowed it, it was all gone," continued Needles, pulling out an especially deep quill.

"Ouch! And that's not stealing?" yelped the shepherd dog, not wanting to let them off too easily.

During this strange exchange in the middle of the night, Billy noticed that the raccoon had on what seemed to be a pair of long johns on his upper body with the arms cut out on and old trousers with numerous patches on his lower body. Needles just had on a pair of pants held up by a single strap over his shoulder. It too was heavily patched.

"By the way, what were you doin' in my loft, Nosey? Were you just trying it out, or have you slept there before?" asked Billy, suddenly suspicious.

"Well..." Nosey looked over at Needles for support, which was not forthcoming. "Well, sometimes when you ain't here, we sort a' spend the night."

"I see, and Needles, I hope you don't sleep in my bed. I'd hate to wake up some night with one of your pins in my back!"

"Oh no, he always sleeps on the floor. He brings an old blanket and curls up over there where your corner cupboard's sittin' now," explained the little raccoon.

"And what's wrong with your place that you've chosen to sleep here?" asked Billy.

"Oh, yours is so grand. Ain't nothin' like our hole in the tree!" said Needles, suddenly brightening up.

"Oh, I see. Well, what are we going to do about this little situation here?" asked Billy, starting to enjoy the confrontation.

"You ain't gonna tell Sheriff Lone Wolf, are ya'?" pleaded Nosey. "We're in enough trouble with him as it is!"

"We didn't mean nothin' bad, honest," said the porcupine, pulling out the last quill from the dog's back.

Billy Bones turned around and looked at the two animals closely. He was already starting to like them in spite of himself. "Well, next time you visit, how about coming to the front door and knocking?"

"You mean we can come back?" exclaimed Needles excitedly.

"Yes, but no entering without permission. Do you understand?" ordered Billy, trying not to smile.

The two night intruders nodded affirmatively but remained in their chairs and made no effort to move. Billy decided that he had better bring the bizarre confrontation to a close. "You can go now. I'd really like to go to bed."

The two little animals looked at each other and then slowly trudged to the door. Before they went out into the night, Nosey Coon turned one last time. "Can I ask you another question?"

"All right, what is it?" said Bones, already exhausted.

"Can we ever stay overnight again?"

Billy eyed them both incredulously. "You want to do what?"

"Stay overnight," repeated Needles. "We won't be no trouble."

"In heaven's name, why?" asked Billy.

"Because it's like stayin' in a castle," they both chimed.

"'Cause it makes us feel good!" said the raccoon.

"Yeah, we ain't never been so happy!" added the porcupine.

The dog scratched his head and yawned. "I'll have to think about that. Maybe when I get to know you better."

The two animals reluctantly exited, and Billy locked the Dutch door after them. He had just crawled into his bed when he heard a tapping at the south window. Somewhat perturbed, he pulled himself up and trudged over to the opening. "What in the name of The Great Spirit do you want now?"

Nosey Coon poked his head through the window, and Needles Porcupine stood back slightly with his finger up to his mouth. Finally the raccoon worked up the nerve to speak. "Me and Needles was just wonderin' if we could stay tonight."

"Would you get out of here!" Billy shouted, and the two rascals scattered into the night.

Billy stuck his head out into the moonlight for a few moments and looked around. Seeing no sign of anything else, he decided to close the inside shutters and lock them.

This left him completely in the dark. As he felt his way back to his bed, he misjudged the direction and smashed into a pole that held the rungs of the ladder. "Ow! Those blasted critters have put a curse on me! I swear they have!"

That night Billy Bones dreamed again. This time, however, it was of the first animals in The Enchantment and of lightning and a great storm. When he finally woke, he was shivering. He reached down and pulled up the blanket that he kept folded at the foot of his bed. He thought back on the two clumsy intruders and how he had chased them away. Now he wished that he had let them stay. He could have used their company.

CHAPTER TWENTY-SEVEN

THE MAYOR'S CASTLE

As Billy Bones crossed the little bridge that led onto the beaver pond's largest island, he spied Winston Wise Owl as he flew over River Road and landed on a small finger of land that led over to Mayor George P. Beaver's double doors. The mayor's home was one of the most remarkable in the Prairie. It was perched on the southern tip of the island. Although it was formed from a mixture of sticks and mud and great beams like Justin Beaver's house, it had two towers on its south side. This gave the dwelling an appearance of an old castle made impenetrable by surrounding it with water.

Overhead, the clouds had taken on a dark ominous color, and it started to sprinkle as Billy hurried toward Winston and the mayor's front doors. At the owl's suggestion, the dog had worn his white shirt and black tie.

"You look very dapper this afternoon, Billy. I hope you don't mind the tie."

"No sir, if it will please the mayor and his wife, it's all right with me," said the dog good-naturedly.

"Good. Then let's go in," suggested the owl.

The mayor's wife, Constance, opened the doors and motioned for them to enter. In front of them was an entrance hall, and beyond that a large room with beamed ceilings. On the stone floor of the first hall was a splendid old Oriental rug. Billy's jaw dropped, and he strained his neck to get a better view of the rest of the great house.

"Both this rug and the old tapestry hanging on the wall in the next room were found along the wagon trail," explained Winston.

When the owl and the dog entered the larger hall and began studying the old hanging, Constance noticed their interest and immediately padded over to them. "Isn't it beautiful, Mr. Bones? My husband's grandfather found it, you know. It was wrapped around Mr. Wise Owl's grand-father clock."

Before Billy could respond, George P. himself approached them. "Good afternoon to you both. Billy, I'm anxious to hear your talk on Sunday. Counselor Turtle and Winston here have informed me that you wish to go over the particulars with us. Thaddeus should be here shortly, so just make yourself comfortable."

The mayor turned and pulled Winston aside, as was his custom; and Constance took Billy by the arm and patted his hand. "Here, let me show you the rest of my house."

Billy soon learned that the southwest tower held a small office. A ladder led down into the water and a hidden passageway to the beaver pond. Above the office was the main bedroom, reached by a circular staircase. The family kitchen and the bedroom of the mayor's father were located in the southeast tower.

"George's father was over one hundred when he finally took to his bed," explained Constance as she guided Billy back into the great room. They found Mayor Beaver, Counselor Turtle, and Winston Wise Owl already seated in comfortable armchairs before a large stone fireplace.

Outside the old dwelling the wind had picked up in intensity, and the rain had become fairly steady, pelting the slanted roof of the great room. After several claps of thunder, Constance excused herself and trod anxiously into the entrance hall, where she locked the double doors. Just as she turned to leave, the gracious beaver was startled by a loud, impatient knocking. With some effort she raised the heavy wooden bar that secured the doors and allowed the visitor to enter.

When Lucinda Vulture stepped into the hall, she immediately began shaking water off her great wings and removed her black hood, which had become soaked. She then dripped by the well-bred Constance with only a nod and moved directly to the area where Billy and the three advisers were.

"I see you forgot to invite me to your little meeting this afternoon, or were you unaware of the severity of Fabian Lynx's action? I have a way of finding these things out, you know!" remarked the vulture sarcastically. She looked almost ludicrous in her damp robe and wet feathers that exaggerated the skinniness of her neck.

The owl, beaver, and terrapin quickly jumped to their feet. Winston was the first to address her. "Lucinda, what an unexpected pleasure! Would you please join us?"

Billy pulled over a straight-back chair and placed it behind the vulture. She sat down stiffly, and the three advisers returned to their armchairs.

Without waiting for a formal invitation to speak, Lucinda turned to the shepherd dog. "Billy, I understand that Granny Muskrat's corner cupboard is in your possession."

"Yes madam, I have it in my home."

The old vulture pointed her gnarled finger at the young dog. "You must guard it carefully! If there's a chance you may lose the cupboard, you must bring it to the Hill Country. It will be safe there."

Thaddeus P. Turtle was somewhat puzzled by the vulture's concern. "Lucinda, do you think that someone would actually break into Billy's house and harm the cupboard?"

"No, not until after the election," she said sternly. "After that, all bets are off."

"You mean you believe that George could actually lose the election?" asked Constance, who had positioned herself behind her husband's chair.

"Yes, I think that's a strong possibility," said Lucinda, mincing no words. "I think we must be prepared for the worst."

"In your opinion, is there anything we can do?" queried the mayor.

"For one thing, you must understand the importance of the human treasures that remain here and in the Hill Country – your tapestry, for instance, and your Oriental rug. You must never surrender these things to Fabian Lynx's new regime! Do you understand?"

"But why? What will happen?" questioned the beaver.

"Because there will be a terrible consequence if you do. Of that I am sure." The old vulture looked earnestly at Billy and narrowed her eyes. "But he will know. Listen to him!"

"Be reasonable, Lucinda," said the doubting turtle. "That's too much responsibility for Billy. He's still only a young dog. He can't possibly know what will happen."

"Ah, but he's an old spirit, Thaddeus P. Turtle—much older than you or I."

"But how can you know such a thing, Lucinda? I know he's done some remarkable things—but to see into the future!"

"Wait, Thaddeus, I think there might be some truth in what Lucinda is saying," said Winston, surprising even himself. "I already know that he has the ability to see into the past." He turned to Billy and continued, "Billy, it's time you told Counselor Turtle and Mayor Beaver about the dream you had in the Hill Country, the one concerning the humans that you saw earlier inside the mist by my tree."

Billy was quiet for a moment, gathering his thoughts. He could feel his heart thumping in his chest. Carefully he related his dream about the young man and the two pioneers who helped him bury W.N. Stone. He told how they hid the books that were in W.N. Stone's wagon in the hollow of what was now Winston's tree house. After that he explained how he could hear them speaking to one another.

"What did you hear, Billy? What exactly did they say?" asked Thaddeus, as he was trying to understand the significance of the dream.

"Well…the boy called the man who died Grandfather and the other man who helped him Ben. I remember that for sure, and that they were going to a place called Oregon. Then this man called Ben explained that they had to leave the books because they were too heavy to carry over the mountains. He said that the wagon train was running late, and they were afraid they wouldn't get through the pass before the snow came."

"And tell them what the boy's name was. Tell them what Ben called the grandson!" said Winston excitedly.

"He called him Jimmy…yes, Jimmy. I'm sure of that."

"But what does that prove? It's still just a dream," reasoned the turtle.

"Yes, that would be true," agreed the owl, "except for this!" At this juncture Winston pulled out a small well-worn book that he had strapped to his body. "I brought this along to show you this afternoon. Lucinda and Billy have already seen it, but the rest of you haven't. However, there's no way Billy could have known about this book when he first had the dream. I keep it in a trunk at the bottom of my bed. See, it's a copy of *Grimm's Fairy Tales*. Look here…here inside the cover. See what it says!" The owl held up the book for all to examine as he read the inscription: "To my beloved grandson, Jimmy. Remember me always, W. N. Stone."

Winston Wise Owl handed the book to Thaddeus P. Turtle, then to George P. Beaver and then to Constance.

Before the turtle and the beavers could marvel at this extraordinary event however, Lucinda turned to the shepherd dog again and said rather sharply, "But you have one more dream to relate to us, don't you, Billy? One that you had last night!"

The young dog was dumbfounded as he glanced over at the vulture. He felt a sudden shiver race through his body. "How did you know? I told no one."

"Because I felt your spirit move even from my hut on the mountainside. Again, I could not see what your dream was, but I knew it greatly troubled you. As I told you before, Mr. Bones, we are kindred spirits you and I. There is no escaping it."

Billy stared in disbelief at the old vulture. He was now certain that she was correct, but he wondered how this ancient haughty bird could be so in tune with his own spirit.

"Well, Billy, what did you see?" she demanded again.

"You're right. I did dream something, but I don't quite understand it. It was violent and yet vivid and moving."

"Go ahead, Billy, tell us what you witnessed in your dream," urged Winston kindly.

"Well…I remember I was walking out of the mist in the Hill Country. I was on the Old Wagon Trail. When I reached the area where I had seen the people with their covered wagons in my previous vision, they were no longer there. Instead, it was much later. This time the animals and birds that lived through the first great rift were lookin' through the items the pioneers had discarded, stacking them up in a great pile. They had their children with them, and the young ones were laughing and playing with the clothes and things. Suddenly a storm arose and great bolts of lightning started to hit the ground. One bolt struck the stack of treasures and caused great destruction and a fire. Then from the east, I noticed a huge bank of dark storm clouds rolling in at ground level. They were movin' extremely fast, and it was very frightening. The creatures grabbed their children and hung on to trees or rocks or anything that could anchor them down. Somehow the parents survived, but they couldn't hold on to their offspring, who were carried away by the storm," said the dog finally. Reliving his dream had made him start to shiver again. He turned his face away from the others.

"I don't understand," said the mayor. "Does this mean that my father is in danger? He was one of the surviving children, you know. Billy, do you remember any of the animals? Was there a beaver?"

"Yes, I believe there was. I don't remember them all, but I do remember a beaver, and a prairie dog, and a mink, and several birds. Let me see, there was a crow—yes, I remember a crow." Billy paused a moment and looked at Lucinda. "And there was a vulture."

The mayor looked at Winston. "Elmer Prairie Dog's grandfather is still alive, and so is Farmer Jason Crow's. They were both sons of the first citizens…and then of course, my father."

Winston put a wing about the mayor's shoulders. "We don't know if it means your father is really in danger,

George. We mustn't jump to conclusions."

"But it does prophesy a catastrophe if we don't protect our human treasures, just as I always feared," concluded Lucinda. "If the election goes against George, you and Thaddeus must meet in the Hill Country with our council as soon as possible. In the meantime, we must all be vigilant and quickly handle any situation in which an old artifact is involved." She turned her attention to Billy. "Speak the truth on Sunday. It's important that the members of the Old Meetinghouse are on our side."

As soon as Lucinda concluded her interest in the meeting, she clutched Billy's arm and whispered to him. "Walk me to the door." Once they were out of earshot, the vulture stared at the dog pointedly. "I know this is difficult for you, but you must remain strong. If you have any more portents, come to the Hill Country and tell Maurice. He'll arrange a meeting with Omar and me. We'll try to help you decipher the message."

The mysterious old bird raised her hood over the back of her head and walked out into the open air. The storm had abated, and the sun was already poking its bright beams through the clouds. She looked back at the shepherd dog, and he thought he caught a kindly glance from her. The moment passed swiftly, however, as she turned abruptly and rose into the late afternoon sky. Billy watched her for some time and then shuddered again and joined the others inside the fine old fortress.

CHAPTER TWENTY-EIGHT

SUNDAY MORNING

The first rays of the sun awakened Billy Bones on Sunday morning. He had purposely left the inside shutters open on the window by the Dutch doors so the beams would land on his pillow. He especially wanted to be up early this morning so he could go to the meetinghouse with a clean body and a clear mind.

After a slice of Hester Groundhog's fresh bread and a glass of water, he made his way down the bluff behind his house and through the thicket to the stream. He had found a good place to bathe and swim and established a suitable path to get there. After he returned to the cottage, he put on his clean white shirt and trousers and waited for Georgie Beaver. The young animal had expressed a desire to accompany him to the Old Meetinghouse, and Billy had been only too happy to accept the offer.

As usual, Georgie got to the cottage with little time to spare. By the time the two friends reached the meeting-house, it was filled to capacity. Gladys and Justin Beaver had saved them a space, and they squeezed over to let Billy sit on the aisle.

Counselor Thaddeus P. Turtle was undoubtedly aware that the audience was large because of Billy's willingness to speak after the meditation. Attendance at the Old Meetinghouse had dwindled since Brother Fabian Lynx had taken control of the New Meetinghouse. The cat's charismatic personality and fiery speeches had attracted many Prairie citizens to his lectures.

After the good turtle finished his remarks, he beckoned for Billy Bones to come forward. At the same time a new group of curious citizens crowded into the hall and took up all the remaining standing room. Among the late arrivals Billy noticed Phineas T. Fox, Farmer Jason Crow and his son, and Olen and Myrtle Buck from the New Meetinghouse. He also recognized Victor Running Deer's two running partners, Sandy Antelope and Arnold Big Horn. Victor, however, was not present.

As Billy reached the front of the hall, Maurice Rabbit, dressed in his many-colored Tribal Council robe, suddenly entered from the counselor's study. The jovial rabbit fairly hopped across the stage in order to greet Billy.

"Maurice, in the name of The Great Spirit, what are you doing here?" was all the astounded dog could manage to utter.

"Lucinda told me you'd be speaking this morning. She told me to bring you this," grinned the rabbit, as he slipped the Tribal Council's blue robe over the dog's shoulders.

The unexpected arrival of Maurice and the warmth of the robe instantly bolstered Billy's confidence. As for Counselor Turtle, he seemed only too glad to have someone from the Tribal Council present, since the rabbit was aware of the dog's actual accomplishments. "We are especially privileged to have Maurice Rabbit with us this morning. As most of you know, he's a member of the Hill Country's council and has been a long-time friend of the Old Meetinghouse. He has graciously consented to introduce our guest speaker."

Maurice Rabbit and Billy Bones stood next to each other. Their wonderfully colored robes made an official and yet festive statement of good will to the overcrowded hall. The friendly rabbit smiled even more as he began to speak.

"As most of you know, Billy Bones here stumbled into the great mist while searching for his previous human family and reentered The Enchantment finally at the Old Wagon Trail in the Hill Country halfway around our little universe. While caught in that dreary haze, he was able to escape all its hazards and dangers. This is a feat that has never been duplicated by any other creature in the history of our existence. Only a being of exceptional spiritual stature could have survived such rigors. After a hearing before the Tribal Council, we also discovered that his visions inside the mist were accurate and truthful. He was then invited to move freely among us and was given an honorary membership on the council for a period of one year. As you can see, he's wearing The Blue Robe of Truth today that is on loan from our council for this meeting." Maurice turned and gestured to Billy. "Members of the Old Meetinghouse and other guests, I give you Billy Bones!"

After this stirring introduction the audience applauded as Maurice left Billy alone in the center of the platform.

During the next quarter of an hour, Billy Bones related his experiences on his second day inside The Enchantment. He heeded Winston Wise Owl's advice and spoke as clearly and precisely as he could, adding no embellishments. Most members of the gathering were grateful that Billy was willing to share his amazing adventure with them. A few, of course, hoping to hear fantastic tales of frightening creatures swirling inside the mist, were somewhat disappointed.

When Billy finished, Thaddeus returned to the stage to act as moderator for a question and answer period with the audience. He chose various members of his own gathering first.

"Mr. Bones, most of the creatures who entered into the mists in the past have been turned around and sent out immediately, suffered mental or physical damage or have never been heard of again. Why do you suppose your experience was different?" questioned a woodland bird who always greeted the dog whenever he passed her home.

"I think I was very fortunate," admitted Billy. "I too was turned back toward The Enchantment. I think that if it weren't for the continual calls from the boy and his grandfather and my desire to return to them, I would not have continued to reenter the mist."

"What turned you around inside the mist?" asked another friendly voice.

"I was continually drawn toward a kind of singing and a great rushing of wind. Then I would find myself headed back into The Enchantment. This happened time and time again."

"Mr. Bones, you said you often heard your masters call to you. Did you also see them?" queried Milton Brown Bear.

"I thought I could see them move just ahead of me. They were almost like shadows."

"Why do you think you couldn't reach them? What do you think they were doing?" continued the bear, who was the only one to see the dog on that fateful day.

"It's my belief that they were looking for me in the other world. Somehow I was able to hear and follow them, but I wasn't able to connect with them."

"How can you expect us to believe such a thing?" shouted Phineas T. Fox unexpectedly. "Why hasn't it happened to anyone else?"

"But it has!" said a voice in rebuttal. When Billy looked for the speaker, Whiskers stood up and faced the fox who was standing against the wall. "On the mornin' after my arrival into this charmed place, I heard the ol' man on the farm call for me."

"Then why didn't you go into the mist like Billy?" shot the fox back to the old cat.

"Because he stopped callin' for me. The boy wasn't with him yet. I think the boy might've looked for me longer," reasoned Whiskers finally.

"I also heard the call," said another voice from the audience. This time it was a nervous Percival Gander, who was trying to work up the courage to confirm his friend's story. "I heard someone calling, 'Bones!' on the morning that Billy was missing…yes, on the morning he was missing.

In fact, that's what woke me up, and that's when I discovered Billy's trousers out in the middle of the road…yes, in the middle of the road!"

The audience suddenly laughed. The mention of lost pants lightened the procedure immensely.

"These visions of yours, why ain't no one else ever seen 'em?" questioned Farmer Jason Crow, who decided to join the discussion.

"But they have!" It was Maurice this time who came to the dog's defense. "All the members of the Tribal Council have seen portions of Billy's vision along the Old Wagon Trail." He turned back to his canine friend. "But none so clearly as Billy."

"You're sayin' that all the members of your council have entered the mist at one point or another?" asked the farmer again.

"Yes, but each was under a different circumstance," stated the rabbit.

"Do you know that *The Great Book o' Rules* forbids enterin' into the mist under any circumstance?" continued the crow. "We're taught that in the New Meetinghouse!"

Maurice turned to the old farmer, who was standing by the fox and the old buck. "We don't follow your *Book of Rules* in the Hill Country, as you well know. Our code states that going into the mist is very dangerous and advises against it, but we're also aware that sometimes a creature like Billy gets caught inside."

Olen Buck, who had been listening attentively, could hold himself in check no longer. "Brother Fabian teaches that the sighting of humans inside the mist is evil and can cause great harm to your mind and body. What do you say to that?"

At this point, Billy Bones walked over to Maurice. He had managed to stay out of the worst part of the debate, but he wanted to answer Olen. He felt that Victor's friendship was somehow at stake.

"I'm not the leader of any meetinghouse, so I'm not fully qualified to answer your question." Billy paused for a moment and then remembered Lucinda's last entreaty to him. "But I have to say, I saw nothing in the visions to suggest evil of any kind. The humans that I recall were simply experiencing a critical moment in their lives."

Another question from the audience stirred much interest. "Mr. Bones, do you believe that these visions are ghosts?"

"No, I don't. I think they're memories that are somehow caught in the great mist that surrounds us. That's all." He looked over at Olen, Phineas, and Jason. "And I do not believe they are evil."

Phineas T. Fox countered immediately. "Mr. Bones, Brother Fabian teaches directly from *The Great Book of Rules*. Are you implying that he and the *Great Book* are wrong?"

Thaddeus Turtle quickly intervened on the dog's behalf. "*The Great Book of Rules* advises and teaches us how to live better lives. Billy had not read the book before he entered into the mist. It was only his second day with us."

"Brother Fabian Lynx also says that ignorance is not an excuse. What's wrong is wrong. Ultimately we all have to pay for our mistakes!" cried Phineas.

"*The Great Book of Rules* was written by our forefathers as a guide to live by. It's subject to interpretation like all great books," retorted Winston, suddenly standing.

"Well, we believe that Billy's committed a crime," said Farmer Jason Crow finally. "I'm sorry, but it's as simple as that."

After the farmer's last pronouncement, he and his son, Olen and Myrtle, Phineas T. Fox, and several other members of the New Meetinghouse left the building. Nevertheless, by far the majority remained to listen to Billy's final statement.

"I'm sorry that my remarks have upset some of my good friends and neighbors. I can relate to you only what I've experienced." Billy looked at Maurice and smiled. "I think that *The Great Book of Rules* and the code of the Hill Country are both correct in advising against entering the mist. I think it's fraught with dangers, but I also think that the visions of these human memories are there to help us understand why we've been given such wonderful gifts. We mustn't forget where they came from, and we must also remember that outside our world only human animals possess these gifts. I believe that maybe we should think about this carefully when we leave today." He smiled again and nodded to the crowd. "Thank you for listening to me."

The remaining citizens stood once again and clapped, appreciating the young dog's wisdom and courage.

Afterwards Winston Wise Owl approached Billy with some concerns he had for the dog's safety. "Well done, Mr. Bones. I'm just sorry about some of the negative reaction you received from members of the New Meetinghouse. I hope you haven't joined me in incurring the wrath of Brother Fabian Lynx."

That night Billy allowed Nosey and Needles to stay with him. The raccoon quickly headed for the loft, and the porcupine curled up before the corner cupboard.

When Billy finally crawled into his bed, he tried not to think of the day's events. Instead, he wanted to focus on the Grand Fair. Whether Victor liked it or not, Billy would visit him in the morning. He would run with the young deer and Sandy and Arnold as long as he could, and then he would take off on his own. In order to run the long distance part of the Great Medley, he knew there were many lonesome hours of training ahead of him.

Even though Needles tended to snore from time to time and Nosey liked to toss and turn, Billy was glad for their presence.

CHAPTER TWENTY-NINE

THE PRACTICE RUN

For the next three weeks Billy Bones got up every morning and jogged a new route around the various trails encircling the town. Sometimes he joined Victor Running Deer, Sandy Antelope, and Arnold Big Horn, but usually he worked out just on his own.

At the start of the fourth week, Georgie Beaver persuaded Victor and Billy to attempt a dry run of the Great Medley. All the legs of the race began and finished at the beaver dam. Billy's long distance route made a wide circle around the pond and the little town. Georgie's leg consisted of a swim around the large island. Victor's job was to run the shorter race around the beaver pond itself.

Georgie speculated that their keenest competition would come from the team that Johnny Otter had put together. The clever otter had talked Rodney Wild Deer and Lester Coyote into joining up with him. Rodney had won the Big Race in the previous five years, and the coyote had won the difficult Overland Race, always scheduled on the first day of competition. Johnny, of course, had defeated Georgie in every water race they ever entered.

When the time came for the practice run, everything seemed to go wrong. The first mishap was on Billy's route. As he turned onto Sleepy Walk west of Main Street, he noticed all four coyote brothers coming directly at him up the trail. When they spied him, they made a hurried blockade with their bodies to waylay the young dog. Billy immediately assessed the situation and increased his speed to break through their obstruction.

"Hey, watch out, I can't stop!" Billy managed to scream, as his momentum knocked Lenny and Leroy out of the way and sent them sprawling over the path. Lester and Leon immediately took up the chase and caught up with the dog before he could get away.

"Hey counselor, seen any ghosts lately?" snarled Lester, as he stuck out his right leg and simultaneously threw a sharp elbow into the dog's face.

"Get off me, you jerk, you've got no right!" countered Billy, stiff-arming the coyote and causing him to topple down on the well-worn trail.

In the meantime Leon closed in on Billy from the right. "You tell your deer friend that we got plans for him! We already warned him twice! He'll never run that medley!"

"Tell him yourself, buddy!" said Billy, suddenly stepping to one side and giving the coyote a quick shove. The unexpected maneuver caused Leon to careen head over heels into the tall grass that grew on the side of the path. Billy stumbled himself, but only slightly, as he hopped over the falling coyote. Regaining his balance, he managed a backward glance and saw the two other brothers standing in the middle of the road scratching their heads. By the time he got back to the beaver dam, he was limping slightly. In spite of his usual good nature, he was really infuriated, and it showed on his face. When Georgie saw him, he asked Billy to stop and explain what happened.

"Go on. I'll tell you about it later!" said the dog, nudging the beaver toward the water.

While Georgie was swimming around the island, Billy filled Victor in on the episode with the coyotes. Unlike the young buck, the dog had never before been accosted while working out. Victor shook his head. "It looks like some of my bad luck's rubbing off on you."

"I know one thing," began the perturbed dog. "I've been trying to decide whether I should enter the Overland

Race too, and this little incident made up my mind for me. After practice today, I'm going to ask Georgie's dad if he'll let me use one of his wagons. That's all I need, plus someone half my size, and I know just the little critter to ask. He'll be only too happy to join me. First thing tomorrow morning, we'll go out west of town and have ourselves another trial run. But this time it'll be up the Old Wagon Trail. Those rotten coyotes have just bought themselves some competition!"

"Wow Billy, I don't think I've ever seen you this mad," exclaimed Victor, putting a hand on the dog's shoulder. "But there's no way you're going to practice over there by yourself. That road runs right by the coyotes' chicken farm. All we need is for you to get ambushed the way I was. I'll ask Sandy and Arnold if they'll go over there with me."

"Maybe it's time we get Sheriff Lone Wolf involved. Isn't that what Olen Buck suggested after your run-in with Rodney, Lester, Leon, and Leroy?" inquired Billy seriously.

"Perhaps you're right," agreed the deer. "It's just that I hate to bring the law into this!"

As Georgie emerged around the western part of the island on his return trip, Victor and Billy thought they could hear him hollering. When he got closer, they noticed that Johnny Otter was bobbing up and down on either side of the exhausted beaver. The otter was splashing water and jeering, "Hey Fats, it's gonna take more than a practice run to beat me! Ain't you givin' up yet? I'll get my sister to swim your leg if you like!"

Even from where they stood on the dam, Victor and Billy could see that Georgie's frustration at the happy-go-lucky otter was taking a toll on his stamina. Billy motioned to the deer to wait on shore as he pulled off his trousers and dove in the direction of the two swimmers. As he came to the surface, he started yelling, "Hey, cut that out, Johnny! Can't you see we're practicin' here? You'll have your chance next week. Now get out of here!"

"Aw Billy, I was just playin' with him!" cried Johnny, as he twisted and swam back to the island. Billy knew that the young otter was not really mean-spirited but only enjoyed the habit of taunting the beaver.

By the time Georgie and Billy got back to the shore, Sandy Antelope had joined Victor for the last leg of the race around the pond. The antelope had asked the day before whether he could participate. He entered the medley with Philip P. Fox, Phineas's younger brother, and Alvin Muskrat, Granny Muskrat's youngest grandson, who had saved Billy's corner cupboard from destruction.

Victor and Sandy ran a fairly even race around the pond. Victor's kick at the end, however, was a bit too strong for the antelope, who was smaller and still had not come into his full growth.

When Victor told Sandy about Billy's run-in with the coyotes, the antelope responded angrily. "Those little devils! They can't be trusted any more than Rodney! I'll let Arnold know. We'll all practice along the wagon trail tomorrow mornin'. See you then!"

After Victor and Sandy left, Billy and Georgie hurried off to find Justin Beaver and see if the dog could borrow one of the carpenter's wagons. The older beaver, one of the main suppliers for The Overland Run, was only too happy to cooperate.

That evening Billy went to see Nosey Coon, who lived below him in the thicket. When Billy rapped at Nosey's door, the raccoon peeked out of his tiny window. "Who's there?" he squealed before recognizing the dog he worshiped. "Oh, it's you, Billy. Just a moment."

After much scurrying about, Nosey opened the door. One of the hinges was loose, so the door scraped annoyingly along the ground. Inside, the raccoon had lit a small candle on his table and had hurriedly pulled the covers over his bed. Out of the corner of his eye Billy could see that the place was in shambles, but he tried not to pay much attention to that.

"I came to ask a favor of you, Nosey. I need someone to help me in the Overland Race next Monday, and I'm required to have somebody about half my size. I think you would be perfect. That is, if you think you'd like to."

"Me? You want me to enter the race with you? Oh, thank you, thank you, thank you!!!" Without warning, the little raccoon leapt into the dog's arms, knocking him over onto the earthen floor. "When do we start? I'm ready right now!"

"Well, how about first thing in the morning?" laughed Billy, picking himself up off the ground. "Let's meet at my place. I already have the wagon. We'll need to go across the stream and practice going up the Old Wagon Trail."

"Just exactly what do I have to do?" asked Nosey, wide-eyed with excitement.

"I have to pull you in the wagon up the Old Wagon Trail to the High Pass. Then I leave you and the wagon and run up to Eagle Butte. When I get to Deputy Eagle's cabin, I grab a mail pouch and carry it back down to the wagon trail. At that point I give the wagon a push with you in it, of course, and jump in myself. Then we both roll back down to Dry Gulch. From there I pull you and the mail pouch across the stream and on to the finish line at the foot of Main Street. How does that sound?"

"Wow! That sounds great! Can I tell Needles? Can I tell him right now, huh?" pleaded the little creature, grabbing at the dog's shirt.

"Sure, of course!" agreed the shepherd.

Before Billy could turn around, Nosey scampered out the door and across the way to Needle's place. His dwelling was even smaller than the raccoon's. It was only a little hollow at the bottom of a stump that the two animals had expanded and covered with a heavy tarp.

After much excited conversation, Billy left the two happy creatures for the night. "I'll see you shortly after sunrise!" Nosey called, as Billy made his way up the bluff. The dog was sure that he would.

CHAPTER THIRTY

THE THIRD AMBUSH

Early the next morning, Billy glanced out the window. True to his word, Nosey Coon was sitting on the step outside the Dutch doors. The shepherd dog surmised that the raccoon had probably been waiting there since the crack of dawn. When Nosey heard Billy moving about in his kitchen, he knocked on the upper door.

"Hey Billy, you up yet?" the raccoon called in a loud whisper. He cracked open the top door just wide enough to peek in. "Billy, is that you?"

"Good morning, Nosey," said the dog, suddenly swinging the top door all the way open.

"Hey, you scared me!" chuckled the little creature. "I thought I heard you movin' around in there. When do we start?"

"We've got about an hour before we meet Victor down at the river. Come on in, and I'll find us some breakfast," yawned the shepherd dog, still stretching his arms and shoulders.

Victor Running Deer was waiting at the ford that crossed the stream, and Sandy Antelope and Arnold Big Horn joined them at the foot of Main Street.

"The three of us will jog up and down whatever stretch you're practicing on, Billy. That way we're never too far in case you need us," said the young buck, laying down the ground rules.

As expected, the practice run proved uneventful until Billy and Nosey got to the vicinity of the coyotes' poultry farm. Suddenly from behind two large boulders on the south side of the trail, the team was pelted by a number of small rocks.

Before Billy could protect himself, a stone struck his right shoulder. He turned at once to the little raccoon and hollered, "Run down into the gulch! I'll grab the wagon!"

As soon as the two racers started for the old creek bed, three of the coyote brothers came charging down the hill from the opposite side. Just as they crossed the road however, Victor, Sandy, and Arnold came bursting around the corner and set upon the attackers. Seeing their change of fortune, the assailants reversed and retreated back to the boulders. Lester and Leroy managed to escape, but Leon could not outrun Victor and was quickly taken down and pinned to the ground.

"That's the last time any of you will ever pester us again!" cried the enraged deer, as he brought his fist down on the coyote's cheek.

Sandy and Arnold reached the two combatants in time to keep Victor from hitting Leon a second time. As they started to pull the deer off the frightened coyote, he continued his verbal assault. "This is the third time you've tried to ambush one of us, and that's three times too many!

You tell the rest of your brothers that I'm gonna report this to the sheriff! I have four witnesses in case you're wondering whose story he'll believe!"

With one more departing kick on the unfortunate coyote's seat, Victor and his two companions went in search of Billy and Nosey. When they found the pair, Billy was down in the gully trying to help the little raccoon climb over the bank where the wagon was sitting. Sandy and Arnold grabbed hold of Billy and pulled him up as well.

"Are you all right?" asked the concerned antelope, brushing the top of the dog's head.

"Just a little sore in the shoulder where one of those coyotes got me with a rock. Otherwise I think I'm fine," grinned the shepherd. "But I think Nosey and I better practice our downhill from here."

"Sounds good to me!" agreed Sandy, who was already helping Nosey put the wagon back on the trail. "We'll meet you at the bottom."

When they got back to the south end of Main Street, Victor and Billy were chosen to contact Sheriff Walter Lone Wolf immediately. Fortunately the good sheriff was in his office next to the old saloon.

When the wolf heard the details of the three assaults, he turned to Victor. "Sir, if you'd reported the first incident to me, maybe we could have avoided the second two, especially since there was so much injury involved. I will be bringing Rodney and those four coyote brothers into my office as soon as possible for questioning. I'll be asking you and your friends to come back and press charges."

CHAPTER THIRTY-ONE

A COMPROMISE OF SORTS

“ “There are a few complications here,” confided Sheriff Walter Lone Wolf to Billy Bones on Friday morning.

“Calhoun is terribly concerned. The City Council doesn’t meet until after the Grand Fair. Since his sons and Rodney must remain in my custody until after their hearing, they won’t be able to participate in the races.”

Billy had already learned from Sandy Antelope that Calhoun Coyote had inherited the largest chicken farm in the Prairie and was very influential in the small community. He had also discovered that the farmer always allowed his sons to do whatever they pleased as they were growing up. When they got into mischief he would say, “Well, you know how young pups are,” and pass it off as nothing serious. Now, however, they were young adults and beyond his control. Only the youngest, Lenny, seemed to feel any responsibility toward the farm.

Victor Running Deer, Sandy Antelope, and Arnold Big Horn arrived at Walter’s office a half hour after the dog and learned about the dilemma. Calhoun Coyote, for his part, had secured the services of his adviser, Brother Fabian Lynx. Upon entering the room, the handsome cat went immediately to the four accusers and began shaking their hands. When he got to Victor, he put a left hand on the deer's shoulder and spoke as one old friend speaks to another. "Victor, Mr. Coyote is beside himself. There must be a way to solve this." The young buck only smiled slightly, nodded his head, and looked away.

When Brother Fabian finally got to Billy, he did not offer his hand immediately. "Well, Mr. Bones, I haven't talked to you since you wandered into the mist and saw those human spirits. I thought maybe you'd accept my invitation to visit. I was hoping we'd be of like mind concerning these illusions of yours. I'm afraid we're off to a bad start."

After Brother Fabian spoke, he reached out and shook Billy's hand politely. At the touch of the lynx's hand, the vision of two cruel humans flashed again across Billy's mind. As the dog started to withdraw his hand, the lynx held on tighter and said with suspicion, "Mr. Bones, you know something you're not telling me. What is it?"

Billy slowly responded, "I know that humans were very cruel to you. I'm very sorry, that's all."

Brother Fabian stared at Billy for a moment. "We're not through with this yet, Mr. Bones!" The lynx started to say more but changed his mind and abruptly moved to one of the two chairs in front of the sheriff's desk. Calhoun sat in the other, and the strange meeting began.

Sheriff Lone Wolf was anxious to get started but tried to remain professional. "I have enough evidence to bring Rodney Wild Deer and at least three of Mr. Coyote's sons before the council on charges of assault and battery."

"If I may interrupt, sheriff, you know my sons. They were just letting off some harmless steam. If these creatures are afraid…!" exclaimed Calhoun, disturbing Walter's train of thought.

"Please, Mr. Coyote, let me finish," continued the wolf. "Mr. Running Deer here was attacked by Rodney, Lester, Leon, and Leroy and left unconscious along Timber Trail."

"But anyone could have…" said Calhoun again, breaking into the sheriff's explanation.

"Lester, Leon, and Leroy are also charged with stoning Billy Bones and Nosey Coon while they were practicing on the Old Wagon Trail, and all four of your sons tried to stop him while running along Sleepy Walk the day before!" spoke the wolf over the old coyote's objection. "Victor, Arnold, and Sandy were all witnesses to the stoning attempt near your farm. There's no question in my mind that by law I must keep Rodney, Lester, Leon, and Leroy incarcerated until after the trial, unless, of course, we can come to some other agreement. I don't feel I have enough evidence to keep Lenny, however. He may return with you, Mr. Coyote, with a warning that I will not be as lenient a second time."

Out of desperation Calhoun Coyote turned immediately to his adviser. "Brother Fabian, will you say something? Obviously the sheriff is not going to believe…."

"Just a minute, my friend, I don't think you were listening carefully," soothed the large lynx, who had regained his composure. "I believe Sheriff Lone Wolf is willing to consider a compromise, at least until the Grand

Fair is over."

Sheriff Lone Wolf gazed at the crafty cat for a minute and then back to the deer, the dog, and the other witnesses. "That depends on Victor and Billy. They both must be willing to accept your solution."

"Solution? What are you talking about, sheriff?" questioned Billy.

"Brother Fabian has an idea for a compromise," explained the sheriff, looking to the lynx for clarification. "Perhaps he should discuss it with you."

Brother Fabian Lynx stood up and cleared his throat. His robe of office was still immaculate, and his teeth were dazzling white. "I thought that perhaps during the week of the fair you would allow Mr. Coyote and me to take custody of his three sons and Rodney during the daytime. In the evening, of course, they would be returned to their jail cells. They have promised to be on their best behavior." The wily cat paused and smiled. "That is, unless you prefer not to run against them."

"That has nothing to do with it," said Billy directly. "They have forfeited their right to compete. It's as simple as that."

"Well, maybe you should ask your friend if he agrees with you." Brother Fabian turned and faced Victor. "Victor, how would it look to Melinda if you were responsible for keeping Rodney out of the races?" The unexpected mention of Melinda caused the lovesick deer to lower his eyes as the cat continued. "You really have no choice, have you?"

"That's not fair bringing her into it!" barked Billy, surprising even himself. He suddenly knew that the deer had admitted more to the lynx than he first realized. "It's not fair to put Victor under that kind of pressure."

"Wait, Billy, he's right," said Victor unexpectedly. "No matter what Rodney's motives were, I can't be the cause of his not entering the races. I could never live with myself."

"Or maybe Melinda wouldn't approve. Is that what you're worried about?" blurted the shepherd dog without thinking. "I believe you should give her more credit…."

"That's none of your concern," muttered the buck, lowering his head and turning away.

"If it means that much to you…" responded the dog immediately, but the damage had already been done. Pausing, he turned back to the sheriff. "Exactly what options do we have?"

Walter Lone Wolf looked uncomfortable, as if he never should have agreed to open the discussion in the first place. "Well…you could leave things as they are. You could agree to the compromise suggested by Brother Fabian, or you may, of course, not press charges at all."

Billy glanced at Arnold, who was shaking his head. "If you let them get by with this, Billy, it'll be only a matter of time before they try somethin' else."

Billy then turned to the antelope. "Sandy, what do you think?"

"I'm sorry, I can't advise you," said Sandy softly. "It's just that Victor's your friend…."

Billy Bones walked slowly over to Walter Lone Wolf and put his hands on the desk. "Sheriff, if we decide to go along with this compromise, when would it start?"

"Tomorrow, so they can sign up for the events they want to enter. After that I'll hold them here until Monday morning, when the coyotes have to compete in the Overland Race."

"Fine," said Billy, as he walked toward the door. "Then I guess it's settled."

Before Billy could leave, the sheriff glanced over at Brother Fabian and Calhoun and spoke rather curtly. "Brother Fabian, Mr. Coyote, come back tomorrow morning, and I'll release Lester, Leon, Leroy, and Rodney into your custody. Take Lenny with you tonight."

"Give us a little time to explain the situation to Rodney and my sons," requested Calhoun, "and then we'll leave."

"All right. Just make them realize the seriousness of their offense. I'm takin' a big chance here," said the sheriff, frowning.

As Billy stepped quietly out the door, he was concerned about the compromise. He knew that the sheriff had tried to be fair, but he also knew that the good wolf had fallen under the sway of the charismatic cat far too easily.

CHAPTER THIRTY-TWO

THE SIGNING IN

On Saturday morning tables to register for the Grand Fair competitions were already set up in front of City Hall when Winston Wise Owl arrived. The owl always served as a marshal in the sports divisions and looked forward to it all year. Because of all the rain, the bushes and flowers around the grand building were especially lush and colorful. Most tables were for crafts, baking, cooking, sewing contests and the like, but two tables were set aside for athletic contenders. As usual, the Overland Race on Monday, the Big Race on Wednesday, and the Great Medley on Friday were the biggest draws.

From behind his table Winston could see and hear the construction of various booths that would be used by vendors and candidates running for mayor and the City Council. He loved the festive feeling it aroused and for the moment let it override the foreboding he felt about the upcoming elections.

Rodney Wild Deer and the four coyote brothers, under the watchful eyes of Brother Fabian Lynx and Calhoun Coyote, arrived early and approached Winston's table to sign in. Just as Rodney was registering for the Big Race, Victor Running Deer showed up with Melinda Doe on his arm. The doe's father, Olen Buck, and Sandy Antelope and Arnold Big Horn followed behind them. About the same time Billy Bones and Georgie Beaver entered from Court Street, with Nosey Coon and Needles Porcupine scampering after them.

Winston Wise Owl noticed the proud doe immediately. She held her pretty head high and walked with such assurance and grace that all knew she was the unmistakable queen of the morning. She wore a white blouse with a ruffle around the neck, a long scarlet skirt, and a straw bonnet with a matching ribbon of scarlet tied around her chin.

Winston considered Melinda Doe an enigma. He was sure she loved her father dearly, and she seemed to care for her father's choice for her life mate, the handsome Victor Running Deer. But, it also seemed to the owl that she had a strange and unmistakable attraction to Rodney Wild Deer with his loose long-sleeved shirt, red bandanna, and barbarous lifestyle. "Perhaps she can't even explain this fascination to herself," he thought. He was certain, though, that pitting Victor and Rodney against each other in the Big Race and the Great Medley had intrigued her, especially when they were both competing for her affection.

When Victor left Melinda, he walked resolutely up to the table and found himself immediately behind Rodney. When the rogue turned, each deer stared directly into the eyes of the other, but neither spoke. Finally Rodney broke the stalemate with a wry smile and swaggered purposely across to the doe. Her eyes were flashing with excitement as he spoke, "I'm runnin' this one for you, Melinda my dear. Then you'll know without a doubt who's the best buck around!"

As Rodney bent to kiss the doe's hand, Olen grabbed his left arm and jerked him away. "I thought I made it perfectly clear that my daughter is off limits to you!"

The rogue buck turned and glared at the old stag but held himself in check. Winston surmised that Rodney knew he was walking a tightrope with the law and did not want to ruin his big chance to show his superiority over Victor Running Deer.

Victor, for his part, also leapt to Melinda's defense but backed off when his true love did not shy away from Rodney's advances. Winston was aware of the hurt in the young deer's eyes.

When Billy Bones and Nosey Coon signed up for the Overland Race, the owl was anxious to speak of the compromise. "I see that Rodney and the coyotes are still in the races. Sheriff Lone Wolf tells me you were not particularly pleased but that you allowed it."

"No, at first I was against it, but Victor…." Billy did not know quite how to continue.

"I think perhaps the competition between the two deer was inevitable," sighed Winston, continuing the dog's unfinished thought. "I only hope that Victor wins and Melinda Doe doesn't get too deeply involved."

"I think you're too late on that account," declared the dog, glancing in the direction of the young doe, still basking in the adoration of the two deer and the many spectators.

By the end of the morning nearly all the contestants from the Prairie and a number of players from the Hill Country had registered for the competitions. Winston noticed in particular that Gaylord Cougar entered the Overland Race with Billy's friend, Maurice Rabbit, as the rider. The owl knew from past experience that the huge cat would be a formidable opponent, giving Billy and the coyotes some real competition.

CHAPTER THIRTY-THREE

THE OVERLAND RACE

Billy Bones was surprised to see many Prairie citizens on hand for the start of the Overland Race in spite of the strong gusty winds on Monday morning. Some stood behind the competitors at the lower end of Main Street, but most lined the road that branched south toward the Old Wagon Trail. The route had been widened to accommodate the twenty wagon teams signed up for the race that traditionally opened the Grand Fair. As the broadened street approached the stream at Dry Gulch, it tapered off to a point where only six wagons could pass comfortably at one time. The route narrowed again to only four wagon-widths at Lonesome Road and then to two wagon-widths just below The Twin Peaks.

Billy could never remember being so nervous and excited at the same time. He felt his heart beating in his mouth. As for Nosey Coon, he was in his glory. The little raccoon kept hopping in and out of the wagon, glancing around at the other contestants as if to say, "Hey, look at me! I'm riding with Billy Bones! Do you see me?"

Billy and Nosey drew the fourth position along the starting line. Leon Coyote and his rider, Wiley Weasel, captured the third spot, and Gaylord Cougar and Maurice Rabbit the fifth. After a discussion with Sandy Antelope, Billy learned that the only other real challengers were the remaining coyote brothers and Arnold Big Horn. Because of his size, the ram had found it difficult to find a creature half his weight and still small enough to pull in the little wagon. Finally he had settled on Georgie Beaver, who was just heavy enough to qualify.

Before the contestants went to their starting marks, Farmer Jason Crow asked them to make a semicircle in front of him so they could hear him spell out the rules above the whistling of the wind.

"Winston Wise Owl and Deputy Harold Eagle have agreed to marshal the race from the air, and a number of our other good citizens have taken strategic positions on the ground. We ask specifically that you do not touch each other with your hands or purposely run into each other with your wagons. You may go outside the path 'cept where the trail narrows or on the High Pass, where it's too dangerous. If a foul is declared by one of our marshals, your team will be disqualified," the crow cawed loudly. "You got that now? There ain't no exceptions! Now go to your marks."

"Anything I should remember?" asked Billy, as Sandy loped by him on the way to give Arnold a last vote of confidence.

"Don't let the coyotes get too far ahead of you, and keep an eye on the cougar. He's a strong devil," chuckled the antelope. "Oh, and watch out for Arnold. He's amazing in the mountains!"

Because of the swirling wind and the dust blowing around the little wagons, Billy had to strain to hear the whistle that Farmer Jason Crow held in his beak. He was also trying to remember and decipher what Winston Wise Owl had whispered to him earlier in the morning: "Run your own race. Stay your ground."

True to Sandy's prediction, Billy, Arnold Big Horn, Gaylord Cougar, and the four coyotes took an early lead. As they neared the first crossing at Dry Gulch, Leon Coyote pulled ahead and crossed the stream first as the little weasel waved shamelessly at them from the back end of the wagon. Billy and the other five front-runners hit the water at about the same time.

Remembering what Sandy had advised, Billy picked up his own pace so that Leon would not get too far ahead of him. By the time Leon and Billy got to the narrows at Lonesome Road, they had opened up a fairly substantial lead ahead of the rest of the pack. The dog realized that he was traveling at a much faster rate than usual, but Leon was continuing to stretch his lead.

Billy finally took time to look back at the others when he reached the long stretch below The Twin Peaks. He saw that the contestants behind him circled all the way back to Lonesome Road.

"How are we doin', Billy?" asked Nosey, leaning forward in the wagon. He had become more and more excited as the two leaders drew steadily away from the others.

"I don't know if I can keep this up!" panted the dog, as he saw the stubborn coyote some ten feet ahead of him.

"Look back again and tell me what you see!"

"It's Lester and Leroy!" exclaimed the raccoon. "They're about thirty feet behind us, but they seem to be gainin' some."

"Who's behind them?"

"It looks like their little brother Lenny and then Gaylord and Arnold." The little raccoon leaned forward again. "I think Georgie's gettin' too heavy for Arnold. They've moved back a bit."

When Leon reached the High Pass and dropped his wagon tongue, the shepherd observed that the coyote was definitely on his last leg. Wiley Weasel, still sitting in the back of the wagon, pointed at Billy and began laughing, "You're such a fool, dog! They got you! They really got you!"

As the exhausted dog listened to the weasel's taunts, he finally realized what Winston Wise Owl had meant by "run your own race." In disgust, he left his own wagon and followed Leon up the trail. When they finally recrossed the stream and started up the embankment, Billy saw his chance to pass the coyote. At that instant however, Leon let out a loud scream and fell directly back on the startled dog, knocking them both into the shallow stream.

As Billy tried to slide out from under the fallen coyote, he was careful not to use his hands. At that same moment he could feel the splashing of feet on either side of him as Lester and Leroy passed around him and started up the slope.

"Start out a little fast, sucker?" yelled Lester, looking back for an instant.

Suddenly from behind him, two strong hands reached down and picked him up. He glanced around just in time to see Lenny Coyote.

"Go!" the youngest coyote brother cried. "You can still catch them!"

"Foul!" yelled the voice of a marshal from the sky. It was Deputy Eagle. "Sorry, Lenny, but I've got to disqualify you. Can't use your hands!"

Billy looked again at the young coyote, and a feeling of great respect flooded his heart.

"Go! Blast it!" Lenny insisted again, giving Billy a final push.

Billy Bones gritted his teeth and quickly pursued the two remaining coyotes up the hill. The short respite and losing the wagon weight gave the young shepherd dog a second wind. As for Leon, he sat in the creek bottom, laughing and shaking his head. "They've got you now, dog! You'll never get by those two!"

After much struggle and determination the three leaders managed to reach Lookout Point only fifteen feet apart. They retrieved their mail pouches from the deputy's office just as Gaylord crashed into the little room. As they were about to start back down the mountain, Arnold came bounding around the last curve. He had already made up half the distance that he lost to the leaders on the first stretch, and they could see by his pace that he would still be a threat.

Billy tried from time to time to get by Leroy and Lester on his way back down to the Old Wagon Trail, but the two coyotes protected the width of the path with their bodies and would not let him pass. In back of him, he could hear the cougar and the Big Horn close on his heels.

When the three leaders reached their wagons, the two coyotes and their riders managed to push off first, and the harried race to the bottom began. Billy and Nosey were slightly heavier and tended to go downhill a little faster than the coyotes, but again on the upper slope the narrow trail between the peaks and the gulch gave them little room to pass.

"We'll have to make our move when we go by Sand Hill," hollered Billy to Nosey, who was hanging on for dear life. They had never tried the downhill section from so high in the pass, and both animals were wide-eyed with their amazing speeds.

Suddenly the path widened as the wagons passed the coyotes' chicken farm, and Billy decided to leave the trail for the broader plain on the right. He knew he would have to pass Lester and Leroy before they came to the narrow boundaries at Lonesome Road. The coyotes, however, anticipated his plan and moved right with him, keeping both of their wagons just ahead of him which, of course, moved the dog farther and farther to the right.

"This way, Billy!" cried Maurice from the open path to the left, as the heavier cougar and rabbit went sliding by the three leaders, closely followed by Arnold and Georgie.

The coyotes instantly realized their mistake and headed back toward the path, giving Billy a chance to slip by them just before they arrived at the shortened boundaries of Lonesome Road.

By the time Billy and Nosey reached Dry Gulch for the last crossing, they saw that disaster had struck Arnold and Georgie. Their combined weight caused the little wagon to break a wheel as it hit the bottom of the stream bed, and the other wheel got stuck hopelessly in the mud.

When Billy saw the predicament of his two friends, he jumped out of his own wagon and prepared to assist them. At the same moment Arnold yelled, "Don't help! You can't use your hands! Get out of here! You still have a chance to get second!"

The brief delay cost the dog dearly. The athletic Lester Coyote shot past him and was pulling his little groundhog up onto dry land.

"Go!" cried Billy suddenly at the top of his lungs, as he gave the wagon a mighty tug, almost throwing the frenzied little raccoon back out into the stream.

As the New Meetinghouse loomed off to the right, Billy could feel every muscle in his body rebel. His legs felt rubbery, and several times he almost collapsed.

"Go, Billy!" a familiar voice from the sideline cried. "You can make it, Billy!" It was Victor. He was running alongside the road, urging the exhausted dog onward. As Billy tried to summon strength to continue, he noticed the tough coyote struggling just ahead of him.

"Hang on, Nosey!" the shepherd yelled, mustering all his remaining energy. He could see that Gaylord and Maurice had already crossed the finish line, and he was edging closer and closer to the coyote.

Just then Lester turned and saw the dog. "I've got you, counselor! I've got you!" As the coyote twisted back around, the sudden action caused his tired legs to trip and stumble just short of the finish line. At that moment, Billy crossed the line ahead of him.

As the dog looked back to see the condition of the unfortunate coyote, he witnessed an amazing sight. The powerful Big Horn was dragging Georgie in a wagon with only two wheels across the finish line before Lester could regain his feet. The three friendly wagons had managed to shut the coyotes out of all three places. Billy felt a sudden rush of joy. He was satisfied that Gaylord and Maurice had won and that he and Nosey had managed to come in second. He was even more pleased, however, that his good friends Arnold and Georgie had come in third. Only later when he remembered the helping hands of the youngest coyote brother, Lenny, did he feel a twinge of remorse.

CHAPTER THIRTY-FOUR

TUESDAY MORNING

The old tall case clock on the landing struck six times before Winston Wise Owl left his bedroom on Tuesday morning. At six-thirty he climbed down from his house and crossed the path to Hester Groundhog's humble cottage. Tuesday morning was traditionally the day that the baked goods were judged, and he had promised to escort her to the large tent erected across from City Hall.

Hester had risen before dawn and started the fire that would heat her oven. She planned to enter her baked buns and pecan bread that Billy Bones, Georgie, and Justin Beaver had so greatly admired.

By the time Winston knocked at her Dutch doors, Hester had removed her everyday dust cap and replaced it with a lovely white bonnet with green ribbons sewn into it that could tie under her chin. Before they left for the fair, the groundhog offered her old confidant a taste of each of the baked goods and some tea, strawberry jam, and butter.

"Was Billy unhappy that he didn't win?" asked the groundhog about the Overland Race.

"I believe he would've preferred to, but I think that under the circumstances, he was glad to get the red ribbon."

"Knowing Billy, I think you're probably right." She looked up from her cup of tea and frowned slightly. "Do you think he still thinks about his old master?"

"I'm afraid I still see a twinge of sadness from time to time," admitted the owl. "And I'm concerned about him. He doesn't bend easily."

"I know someone else who doesn't bend easily. I think you'll both have to be very careful if the election goes badly!" admonished the good groundhog.

"Well, whatever happens, we must be on our way if we're to get your buns and pecan bread to the fair on time."

After Winston dropped Hester off at the large tent that held all the baked goods to be judged that morning, he walked a block north to the schoolyard where the field events were taking place. On his way he passed many brightly decorated booths and tents along the great court-yard. He especially loved the various colored flags that helped attract visitors to each concession.

The old owl spent a good part of the morning going back and forth between different events. He found the long jump and the log toss to be among the most fascinating. In the long jump Arnold Big Horn managed to defeat his two brothers who still lived in the Hill Country. However, they came in second and third, making it a clean sweep for the Big Horn family.

Milton Brown Bear won the log toss but was closely challenged by Bison Bob and Arthur Elk, the giant guardian of the Tribal Council's sacred lodge. "Sheriff Lone Wolf has asked Bison Bob and me to be special deputies again during the next few days of the fair," the bear confided to Winston. "He said he's especially concerned about the Big Race and the Great Medley in which Victor Running Deer and that scoundrel, Rodney, will be involved. It's become the talk of the fair. Nothin' like a little drama to spice things up, I always say."

"It's almost as exciting as your upcoming elections," admitted the old elk, who had joined the discussion. "Everywhere I go, I'm handed all this propaganda, and I can't even vote!"

At noon Winston met with Hester Groundhog and Mayor George P. Beaver at Chester Hawk's booth. The young hawk and his wife Fanny had established a reputation for the finest chicken pot pies at the Grand Fair.

"Congratulations, my dear," said George P., as he greeted Hester. "I see you've won two more blue ribbons this year. You better be careful, or you'll make all the other contestants jealous, and they'll stop entering the baking competition altogether."

"Thank you, mayor, but I think there were plenty of ribbons to go around this year. I see your sister-in-law won again for her hot cross buns."

"Yes, Gladys also has the talent!" agreed the beaver.

"I noticed that the moderate candidates for City Council were all at their booth this morning," remarked Winston, changing the subject. "The corner of Court and Main near City Hall seems to be a good spot."

"We're doing all we can, Winston, but Elmer Prairie Dog and his crew are all over town. You know, Brother Fabian Lynx even drafted the guides from the New Meetinghouse to work for his hand-picked candidate. He tells them it's for a higher cause!" complained the concerned mayor. He turned and looked out over the many visitors that crowded in front of Elmer's General Store, where the strict constructionists had set up their booth. "I hate to say this, Winston, but I'm really worried. I think maybe Lucinda Vulture was right. There's a good chance I could lose this time."

"Well, we still have the debates on Thursday," answered Winston. "Let's hope that common sense prevails. Elmer Prairie Dog doesn't exactly inspire confidence."

CHAPTER THIRTY-FIVE

THE BEAVER'S CHALLENGE

After a leisurely lunch Winston Wise Owl, Mayor George P. Beaver, and Hester Groundhog wound their way over to the beaver pond. The mayor had promised his nephew, Georgie Beaver, that he would attend The Open Swim at two o'clock. This was the culmination of the water events and consisted of swimming from the dam out to the large island and back.

Winston was amazed at the number of spectators. They were lined up on either side of the pond and all across the beaver dam. He was especially pleased to see Billy Bones, Victor Running Deer, Sandy Antelope, Arnold Big Horn, Nosey Coon, and Needles Porcupine lined up behind Georgie and Alvin Muskrat on the dam, ready to cheer them on. He knew that a lot of Georgie's newfound popularity was because of Billy Bones, who seemed to inspire the best in almost everybody.

"We should've gone to my place," said George P. "We would've had a perfect view from my window. I'm sure that's where my wife is standing."

"Now you tell us," moaned the little groundhog, who was still trying to find a good place to stand.

"Here, Hester, take my place," said Winston somewhat nervously. "I think I'll try that branch up there." Without another word the old bird flew to a nearby tree that offered an unhampered view.

As expected, Johnny Otter got off to an easy lead on his way out to the island, followed by Conrad Van Mink, Alvin Muskrat, and then the hardworking Georgie Beaver.

About halfway to the island, Alvin passed Conrad, but the otter remained well out in front, and Georgie was still fourth but moving at a nice pace. On the trip back from the island, Georgie quickly passed the mink and by midway drew up even with the muskrat. Johnny, although still in the lead, had slowed down considerably.

Shortly after that, Georgie went by the tired Alvin Muskrat and started to gain ground on the cocky otter. Watching from his bird's eye view, Winston almost fell off the tree limb as Georgie started to catch up to Johnny. He could not believe that the little fellow could muster such a kick at the end. He had paced himself well. The otter, on the other hand, seemed completely spent but held on just long enough to touch the dam a second ahead of the beaver. He was so exhausted, in fact, that he could only roll over on his back and breathe heavily. Georgie, on the other hand, was pulled out of the water by Billy and Victor as if he had been the victor.

"Great swim, Georgie; a little farther and you would've had him," said Billy as he patted his friend on the back.

"Nice swim, little guy," said Victor, hoarse from yelling.

"That was a smart swim, Georgie," said Alvin Muskrat, who had managed to hold on for third. "I went out too fast when I saw Johnny. I thought I'd never make it back!"

When Johnny Otter got out of the water, it took him a while to go over to the beaver that had so often been the butt of his jokes. "I gotta admit you're gettin' better, Georgie, but you ain't there yet!"

Winston looked down from his perch at the happy-go-lucky otter who, for the first time, had a worried look on his face. "I bet Johnny'll pace himself more carefully on Friday," he mused.

CHAPTER THIRTY-SIX

THE BIG RACE

Farmer Jason Crow and Justin Beaver had been put in charge of starting the many races on Wednesday and judging their outcomes. Winston Wise Owl, who was one of the acting sky marshals along with Deputy Harold Eagle, was pleased with this decision. The owl knew that both creatures were fair and honest and would not be swayed by any favoritism. Milton Brown Bear and Bison Bob, the temporary deputies, would also be stationed strategically up and down Main Street, and various other ground marshals would be posted at every main road around the track. Although everyone in town was familiar with the route, Winston knew there were always a few who, for some reason or other, would stray into the path of the oncoming runners. It was the worst nightmare for the owl and the athletes.

Mayor George P. Beaver built special bleachers in the block south of City Hall facing Main Street for his council members and their families to enjoy the races. Not to be outdone, Elmer Prairie Dog countered with larger bleachers on the sidewalk east of his General Store for his slate of candidates and their families. Included in Elmer's group of guests was the serious-minded Olen Buck, who was running for election in the Southwest District, his wife Myrtle, and his daughter Melinda. Most of the rest of the spectators stood along the southern half of Main Street.

The path of the main contest, called the Big Race, began at Court and Main and headed south on Main Street until it reached Wooded Walk. It then turned left and formed a huge circle around the town with Wooded Walk on the east and Sleepy Road on the west. When the path returned to Main Street, it headed north again to Court Street and the finish line. The earlier shorter races for various smaller contenders also ended at Court and Main, so the dignitaries in the stands always had the best views.

Winston arrived early on Wednesday morning to help Jason Crow position the ground marshals. He noticed that Melinda Doe and her parents had already arrived and were sitting in the third row. "Isn't that just like Melinda," he thought to himself. "She's positioned herself so everyone can see her, especially Victor Running Deer and Rodney Wild Deer!"

Fifteen minutes or so before the Big Race, Winston noticed that most of the fourteen runners who had signed up for the race were warming up north of Court Street. As usual, most of the contestants were hoofed animals, since the distance around the little community favored their speed. Victor Running Deer, Sandy Antelope, and Arnold Big Horn had arrived together. After Rodney Wild Deer arrived under escort, he kept to himself and did not confront Victor or talk to any other contestants.

As the animals were called to the starting line, Winston breathed a sigh of relief. Everything appeared to be in order, and it seemed that the contest would begin without incident. Before Victor went to the line, however, he suddenly walked over to where Melinda was sitting in the grandstand. In response to the unexpected gesture, the crowd grew strangely silent in anticipation of what might transpire.

"Melinda, may I wear your scarf for good luck?" the young buck requested boldly.

As if on cue, the doe rose, smiled, and handed Victor the blue scarf that she had been wearing around her neck. Victor placed the cloth around his neck, and a tremendous roar of approval rang out from the spectators who were close enough to follow the unusual display of affection.

As Victor headed back to his place in line, Rodney suddenly jumped out in front of him. His eyes were filled with hate, but his voice was even. "Well, that was a pretty little play you just put on, my clumsy friend. I hope you'll allow me equal time?" And without waiting for a response, Rodney strolled over to the bleacher where Melinda was still standing. He bowed to her gallantly and with a loud clear voice exclaimed, "Since you've no more scarves to give out, perhaps you'll do me the honor of lettin' me escort you to the New Meetinghouse next Sunday for meditations if I should win this race, which of course is exactly what I plan to do."

The crowd gasped, and Olen stood up to defend his daughter. "Rodney, is there no limit to your audacity?"

"Wait, Father," said Melinda without a blush, "I think we can accommodate Mr. Rodney Wild Deer on this, since there's little chance that he will succeed."

The Rogue Deer responded by smiling wryly and returned to his starting position on the left of Victor. Almost all the good citizens within earshot clapped and screamed their delight at the unfolding melodrama.

"It's all over now, loser!" Rodney managed to whisper under his breath, as Farmer Jason Crow began to admonish them.

"If you're both quite through grandstandin', do you mind if we get started with this here race? I should disqualify you both for holdin' things up! All right, are you ready? On your marks…get set…go!" The crow blew his whistle as loudly and shrilly as he could.

Winston took flight shortly after the contest began. His job was to follow the participants as they circled the town to the east and then fly back to the roof of the General Store and watch the finish. Deputy Harold Eagle would take to the air soon after the contestants reached Sleepy Road and follow them back to Main Street. The competitors had been warned not to touch the other runners with their hands, but because of all the overhanging branches covering the trail, especially on the eastern side, it was almost impossible to enforce the no-hands rule.

During the run down Main Street there was much jockeying for position. By the time they reached the turn onto Wooded Walk, Victor had managed to take a slight lead, with Sandy close on his heels. The young buck might have gone out a little fast, but on the east side he relaxed and soon was striding nicely. Suddenly without warning, misfortune struck. A low-lying branch swept down, caught the young deer's antlers, and jerked his neck back. This in turn caused him to fall against Sandy, who was running close behind him. The antelope managed to break his fall, but Rodney and a number of other racers were able to push past them. Both Victor and Sandy knew that if the Rogue Deer got too far ahead, it would be almost impossible to catch him.

Winston witnessed the accident from the air. He thought he saw a little creature scatter out of the overhanging tree, but because of the thick foliage he could not be sure. He decided to continue following the race in case something more disastrous occurred. He hoped one of the marshals on the ground had spotted something or that someone who lived along the route would come forth with some information.

Deputy Harold Eagle, following his schedule, picked up the race as it crossed Main Street in the north. Winston observed that the deputy was visibly surprised to see the Rogue Deer so far ahead and momentarily circled back to see where Victor and Sandy were.

By the time Victor and Sandy reached the west end of Court Street, they had passed all the other contestants except the steady Arnold Big Horn and Rodney, who still held a substantial lead. As Winston headed for the roof of the General Store, he heard Arnold call to his friend to go around him.

"You'll have to catch him, Victor! This is all that I can muster!" yelled the determined Big Horn. "You've got to do it, or we'll never hear the end of it!"

From his perch on the roof, Winston Wise Owl could see most of the race on Sleepy Road because of the surrounding open prairie. He admired the determination of the young deer trying so desperately to catch his rival. He knew, barring a miracle, that there was little chance of it, especially if Victor had used all his energy to catch Rodney on the backstretch.

Just when Winston believed all was lost for Victor Running Deer, a fluke changed the tenor of the race. Elmer Prairie Dog's grandfather, who had become nearly deaf over the years, had been picking apples in the little orchard at the south end of Sleepy Road. Forgetting about the race, he innocently walked into the pathway of the oncoming runners. Unfortunately he looked up too late to see Rodney and spilled the fruit all over the path in front of him. The surprised deer could not avoid the apples and stepped on several, breaking his stride and almost falling. In his anger he shoved the shriveled old rodent to the ground and continued the race, but precious time had been lost.

When the ancient prairie dog fell, Winston quickly took flight and circled the area. It seemed to the owl that Victor was about to stop and help the rodent when a voice behind him changed his mind. "Leave the old fellow, Victor, I'll get him. You and Sandy catch Rodney. You've got a chance now." It was the steady Big Horn.

When Winston watched Victor turn the tight corner back onto Main Street, the owl realized that the prairie dog and the apples had slowed Rodney down considerably. However, Victor had also been drained from his surge on the west side. When he finally caught up to Rodney, he could not master enough energy to pass him. The two bucks continued to match each other stride for stride until they reached the finish line, as the roar of the bystanders echoed in their ears. Sandy, for his part, could not quite catch the pair and came in a respectable third.

Farmer Jason Crow and Justin Beaver met for a few moments after the race in order to decide the outcome. The stunned crowd stood quietly, and the dignitaries in the stands remained on their feet. Melinda Doe seemed confused that a clear champion had not emerged from the contest but was maintained her composure.

When Jason finally came out of the huddle with Justin, he stood in the center of the street and announced, "For the first time in the history of the Big Race, we've got a tie! We find both Victor Running Deer and Rodney Wild Deer winners of this year's event! Blue ribbons will be awarded to both contestants, and a white ribbon will go to Sandy Antelope for third."

At the ceremony afterward in front of City Hall, it seemed to the old owl that nearly the whole community gathered to watch the victors get their awards. Because of the unusual exhibition before the race, Mayor George P. Beaver gave Melinda Doe the privilege of putting the ribbons around the winners' necks. She did so with great aplomb, her head high, her eyes shining with the glory of the moment.

"Certainly on this day, Melinda's star is shining very brightly," smiled Winston to himself. "It should carry over to Friday at least."

Victor looked around for Melinda again after the ceremony. She was with her father and Brother Fabian Lynx. "May I have my scarf back?" she asked calmly, to his surprise, as he approached her.

"But I won," said Victor, feeling somewhat wounded.

"But you did not defeat him. That's a different matter altogether, don't you think?"

"There's still the Great Medley," he mumbled, lowering his head.

At that same moment, Rodney stepped between them. "Excuse me, my dear Melinda, but I think we've got a date. It looks like I'll be seeing you on Sunday mornin'."

"I said I would go with you if you won, but Victor tied you."

"Doesn't matter, my love. Ask Jason Crow, he'll tell you. A tie means a victory for both of us."

"She isn't going anywhere with you, Rodney. Besides, Sheriff Lone Wolf will still have you locked up on Sunday morning," reminded Olen Buck, again trying to shelter his daughter.

"Ah, but Brother Fabian got permission for me to attend, as well as Lester, Leon, and Leroy. We're bein' rehabilitated, you know," smiled the conceited rogue.

"Well in that case, Daddy, it seems I'll have to go with him," declared Melinda. "I did promise after all." She then turned back to Rodney, who had a smirk on his face, "… but only this once, mind you!"

"But Melinda, you always go to the meetinghouse with me," said Victor, not quite comprehending the new state of affairs.

"Then you should've defeated Rodney," said the doe coolly, as she turned to Olen. "I think it's time to go home now."

"Will you come to see the Great Medley?" Victor called after her.

"Of course," she nodded, "but I have no more scarves to hand out!"

Winston Wise Owl and Billy Bones listened to the whole interaction from a distance. After a moment, the dog turned to the wise owl. "I wish Melinda weren't so pretty. I'm not sure she's the best thing for Victor."

"Well right now I'm afraid she holds the key to his heart. But you can be sure of one thing," concluded the owl.

"What's that?" inquired the shepherd.

Winston glanced over at Victor, sitting at a bench in the courtyard with his head in his hands. "There'll be no tie next time!"

CHAPTER THIRTY-SEVEN

LOOKOUT POINT

Billy Bones was awakened on Thursday morning by an urgent knocking on his door. He quickly rose, slipped on his trousers, crossed the room, and swung open the top Dutch door. A smiling Georgie Beaver stood there, just outside the entrance. He had a small basket covered with a cloth under his arm.

"It's about time you got up," the toothy beaver teased. "Mom packed us a lunch so we can go up to Lookout Point and see the finish of The Flight for Large Birds. It's the last air race of the morning before all the debates start. Come on! It's great fun!"

By nine o'clock in the morning Billy and Georgie had managed to climb Eagle Butte to the famed Lookout Point, where the whole Prairie and a large section of the Hill Country could be easily surveyed. When the two friends got to the large plateau, the shepherd dog realized that a number of other citizens had similar plans. Among their friends the first ones Billy noticed were Sandy Antelope and Arnold Big Horn. They were leaning against the stone wall that had been built along the east side, at the point where the drop-off was most dangerous.

"Good morning, Sandy, Arnold. I see you two have recovered from yesterday's run," said the dog good-naturedly, as he put a hand on the antelope's shoulder. "Where's Victor, or didn't he come along with you?"

"We checked with him before we left. He said he wanted to work in his corn patch, but I got the idea that he just wasn't interested in the fair today," said Sandy seriously.

"I was hopin' he'd get out and about today. I think it would be good for him," stated the shepherd, as he glanced back at Deputy Harold Eagle's cabin just in time to see Lenny Coyote walk out the office door. "Excuse me for a moment. There's someone I need to talk to."

Billy caught up with the youngest coyote brother as he was about to join his father, Calhoun Coyote. "Lenny, may I speak to you a moment?"

The coyote turned and looked at Billy curiously. "Yeah, what is it?"

"I just wanted to thank you for helpin' me out in the Overland Race. I'm sorry you got disqualified for it."

Lenny lowered his head slightly. "That's OK. It just seemed like the right thing to do, 'specially since my brothers talked me into blockading you on Sleepy Walk during your practice run."

When Calhoun noticed that Billy was talking to his youngest son, he moved quickly to intercede. "You got nothin' to say to him, dog. Now get along with you!"

Billy looked at the older animal and tried to remain calm. "I just wanted to thank him, sir. He did a very brave thing."

"What are you talking about? He caused his own brothers to lose, didn't he?" scowled the old coyote. "I think you better stay away from him. He's disgraced himself enough!"

"I'm sorry you feel that way, sir," insisted Billy, "but I don't think he disgraced himself at all. I think he honored himself and you for trying to do the right thing."

"Honored me? You must have a different idea of honor than I do!" shouted the coyote indignantly.

"But they sabotaged me, sir," said Billy, facing Calhoun squarely. "Leon purposely fell back on me to let your other two sons pass. I'm sure Lenny saw the whole thing, or didn't he tell you?"

"Why, that's preposterous! Lenny, is any of this dog's babble true?" asked the coyote.

The younger coyote lowered his head but did not speak.

"Well, son, I'm waiting. Is there any truth in what this dog is saying?"

"Yes, sir."

"You mean to tell me that my other sons deliberately tried to take this dog out of the race by foul means?" Calhoun inquired again. "I want the truth now!"

"Yes sir, that's what they did."

"And were your brothers guilty of trying to disable this shepherd dog earlier while he was practicing on Sleepy Road, and did they throw stones at him near our farm?"

"I'd rather they told you that, Dad. I wasn't there when they threw stones."

"But you were with them on Sleepy Road?" pressed the old coyote.

Billy Bones looked over at Lenny. He could tell that the young coyote was in a quandary. He had always remained silent about his brothers. It was an unwritten rule to do so.

"I'm sorry, Lenny, I didn't mean to get you into trouble with your family," said Billy sincerely. "You don't have to answer on my account."

"No, it's time I spoke up for myself," answered the youngest coyote. He gazed at his father, who had a wounded look on his face. "What Billy Bones said to Sheriff Lone Wolf was all true, Dad."

"I see," mumbled Calhoun Coyote slowly looking at Billy. "It seems I may have been in the wrong here. If you'll excuse me…." And without saying more, the old coyote turned and walked sadly down to the wall by the edge of the point.

"Would you like to join me and my friends while we watch The Flight for Large Birds?" asked Billy, smiling.

Lenny smiled back but shook his head. "No thanks, but maybe I'll catch up with you another time." The young coyote looked over at his father, standing alone by the overhang. "I think I'd like to see the race with my dad."

As Billy watched Lenny stroll back to Calhoun, he was even more impressed with the coyote's character. Just then, Farmer Jason Crow and Winston Wise Owl landed in the center of the plateau. They were the sole judges for the last event, since Deputy Harold Eagle always participated in the final air race.

For the race of The Flight for Large Birds, various colored flags were flying on poles placed around the

Prairie. Each large bird was assigned a color. All the contestants were required to swoop down in each of the three designated areas, snatch up the flag that bore their color off the poles, and fly them back each time to Lookout Point. The first bird to bring all three flags back would be declared the winner.

"Have you come to root for us, or are ya' still mad at us?" said a voice behind Billy, as the large birds were gathering for their flight. When the shepherd dog turned, he saw the three vultures that tied him up and took him to the Tribal Council in the Hill Country over a month ago.

"Felix, Festus, and Floyd, don't tell me you're going to try your luck against Deputy Harold. I hear he's pretty hard to beat!"

"That sounds like Momma. She says we're too lazy to practice and that we ain't got a chance against the deputy," said Floyd, grinning. "But that don't stop us none!"

"Yep, we try every year anyway. Maybe one day we'll get lucky!" commented Felix, as the double whistle signaling the start of the race sounded.

As predicted, Deputy Harold Eagle soon outdistanced all of his competitors. By the time the eagle returned with the second flag, he was a whole leg ahead of the pack, and when he returned with the last flag, not another bird had reached the poles in the wheat field near the Southern Road. Only Chester Hawk gave him any competition on the first flight, but even he soon lagged far behind.

After the competition Billy and Georgie hiked up behind the deputy's cabin and found an even higher spot to sit and eat Gladys's lunch. They knew they should watch the debates that would be raging up and down Main Street in the afternoon, but neither animal was in a hurry to do so.

CHAPTER THIRTY-EIGHT

THE SILENT VISIONS

By the time Billy Bones and Georgie Beaver reached Main Street, the community inhabitants were already listening to the various candidates for City Council and arguing among themselves. Georgie was concerned about his uncle's slate of candidates and immediately went in search of his father.

After the beaver left, Billy spotted his old friend Whiskers sitting on his usual bench in front of the General Store. On the corner steps close by, Elmer Prairie Dog had just introduced Olen Buck, who had put on a green silk tie and dark coat for the occasion. The old stag was outdrawing the east side of the street by a margin of two to one.

Billy noticed the lovely Melinda Doe and her mother Myrtle among Olen's audience members. As the dog passed near the two, Melinda called over to him. "Mr. Bones, have you seen Victor today? No one seems to know where he is."

The shepherd dog turned abruptly to the doe. This was the first time that Melinda had deigned to address him directly or pay him any mind for that matter—even though they shared a close relationship with Victor.

"I understand he's at home tending to his corn patch. I imagine he's trying to concentrate on the medley tomorrow," he answered politely.

"Oh I see," responded Melinda rather curtly, turning her attention back to her father.

As Billy made his way over to the bench and sat down, the old cat looked up and grinned. "Ah, my friend Bones, I saw the end of your race. Quite a thrill, I must say! I understand you had a little trouble on the downhill."

"We had some pretty scary times on the upper part, too," laughed the young dog. He glanced over at Olen Buck. "What've you heard so far on this side of the street?"

"Well, there seems to be a lot of talk about moral responsibility."

"What exactly do they want to change anyway?" asked the shepherd dog, as he noted the smaller crowd across the way.

"They want the City Council to make it a crime to break any rules found in *The Great Book o' Rules*," explained Whiskers, looking over at Olen's back. "I'm surprised the old stag is goin' along with it."

"And what about Fabian Lynx? Have you seen him hanging around this afternoon?" inquired Billy, looking up and down Main Street.

"He was here earlier shakin' hands, but he's lettin' his hand-picked candidates do all the debatin' today," smiled Whiskers, nodding his head.

"Well, I guess I'll go find Georgie again. He wanted us to watch the mayor's debate together," said the dog, as he stood up and stretched. "Will we see you there?"

"Yes, I'll probably mosey over when Olen's through."

After Billy managed to make his way around the crowd, he discovered Georgie having a very animated quarrel with Patsy Prairie Dog, Elmer's daughter. As he got closer, he could hear the angry voice of the female rodent over the surrounding crowd.

"After my father is mayor, you won't be so high and mighty any more, Mr. Smarty-pants!" screamed Patsy. "Always walking around like...." Something abnormal about the two little rivals caused Billy to halt a few yards away from them. He suddenly realized that he could no longer hear her tantrum. The two of them were standing toe to toe yelling in one another's face, but the dog could hear no sound. Just as suddenly, he thought he could see a yellow light around them that seemed to frame them in the moment, separating them from the rest of the crowd. As he continued to view the strange phenomenon, they appeared to be shrinking in size, as if they would eventually disappear altogether.

Billy started to back away and look around. No one else seemed to notice or react to anything unusual. He suddenly turned, closed his eyes, shook his head, and put his hands to his face. When he finally looked back again, Georgie was coming toward him. Patsy and a number of other bystanders were also staring at him oddly.

The concerned beaver asked, "Are you all right, Billy? I heard you yell and hold your head."

"I guess so," mumbled the dog. "I'm sorry. I didn't realize that I screamed."

"Well, you scared me. I thought maybe you'd been hit or somethin'."

Billy gazed uncertainly at the young beaver. "I just thought I saw something, that's all. I guess I was mistaken."

The shepherd dog glanced around and realized that a crowd had gathered. Even Olen Buck had stopped speaking and was trying to determine what caused the commotion.

"Come on, Billy, let's go over to City Hall and get a good place to stand," suggested Georgie, seeking to ease the dog out of the uncomfortable situation.

By the time the two friends walked the short distance over to the front porch of the beautiful old hall, Elmer

Prairie Dog was going through some last minute notes and suggestions with Brother Fabian Lynx, who had reappeared on the scene. Mayor George P. Beaver arrived a few minutes later with Winston Wise Owl and Thaddeus P. Turtle. Billy was sure that the old bird and the terrapin had also been in a session with the mayor.

After their opening remarks each candidate had to answer some prepared questions by moderators, Farmer Jason Crow and Justin Beaver. Billy Bones was intrigued with Elmer Prairie Dog's answer to a question concerning the artifacts in the community.

"Your counselor at the New Meetinghouse has suggested that having human artifacts in your home is a crime and that they should be taken away from citizens who now have them. He says it's spelled out in *The Great Book of Rules*. How do you feel about that?" asked Justin.

For a few awkward moments, the prairie dog stood and looked uneasily out over his audience. Finally he spoke. "Well of course, it would have to go to the council for a vote, and then I would…well, that is, I would…well, have to sign it into law."

"And what do you think of all this, Mayor Beaver?" asked Jason, who was somewhat intrigued by the idea.

"I don't think that such an interpretation should be made in the first place. I think it would be outrageous to break into citizens' homes and take their possessions as if they were common criminals," declared George P. Beaver.

"As I understand, this would affect you personally, would it not?" countered the crow.

"Yes, you well know it would."

After the debate Jason's son Gerard came up and stood by his father as the old farmer talked to Elmer. When the young crow saw the shepherd dog, he shyly waved. As Billy returned the salute, he noticed that something strange was happening in the vicinity of the crows. For one thing, the noise around the dog suddenly ceased. He could see the older crow talking with the prairie dog, but he could not hear them. He only saw their lips move. The yellow circle also materialized, but this time it was around Gerard, who was becoming smaller and smaller. Billy felt himself starting to panic as before, but instead of crying out, he twisted around and shook his head. Georgie was quick to notice Billy's unusual motions and instantly grabbed the dog by both arms.

"Something's wrong, isn't it, Billy? Do you want me to get Dad or maybe Mr. Wise Owl?" asked the young beaver.

Billy looked back at Jason and his son, but everything had now returned to normal. To make sure he was all right, he even looked back at the two crows a third time and then around at the disappearing crowd.

"I'm sorry, Georgie, I seem to be all right again. It's just that I…I…." Somehow the dog could not tell the little beaver what he had seen, perhaps because it also involved him. He decided he would keep the visions to himself and maybe tell Lucinda Vulture about them at the Autumn Equinox…if he could wait that long.

Even after Billy returned to his little cottage, he could not shake the memory of the two silent visions from his mind. He wondered whether they were relevant, perhaps harbingers of things to come, or just strange delusions. He finally decided that the best thing to do under the circumstances was to go to bed early so he could be ready for the Great Medley in the morning.

When the young shepherd dog finally got to sleep, he dreamed again of William Stuart III and his grandfather. In his dream the dog kept trying to tell the young boy how he felt about being back on the farm, but for some reason he could not find words to do so.

CHAPTER THIRTY-NINE

THE GREAT MEDLEY

By the time Winston Wise Owl touched down on the beaver dam on Friday afternoon, Wendell Red Breast was already waiting for his orders. The amiable robin was running for City Council for the third time. He was well liked among his constituents in the North Central District, and along with Cornelius Van Mink in the Northeast was not in immediate jeopardy of losing his job. Nevertheless, due to the unsettled climate of this year's election, he had happily agreed to be a marshal during the Great Medley.

"Good morning, Wendell." greeted the old owl as he approached the robin. "Were you pleased by the debates yesterday?"

"Ah, good morning to you too, Winston," chirped Wendell. "I must say that the mayor came off looking well, especially on the invasion of privacy issue. I hope the citizens were listening."

Before Wendell could comment further, Deputy Harold Eagle and Farmer Jason Crow arrived from opposite directions.

"I asked Mr. Red Breast to join us," explained the crow. "Considerin' his size, I thought it would be easier for him to fly under them trees along Wooded Walk on the last leg of the medley. There might be some real antics along there if we don't keep a tight lid on 'em."

As the contestants started coming onto the dam, Winston Wise Owl noticed that Billy Bones and Victor Running Deer arrived together. Winston was disturbed that Victor had not come to him for advice since he began going to the New Meetinghouse with Olen Buck's family. He hoped that Billy was influencing Victor, especially if one day the young deer would be forced to choose sides.

When Calhoun Coyote and Brother Fabian Lynx arrived with Rodney Wild Deer and the three coyotes, Winston observed to his satisfaction that Sheriff Lone Wolf was close behind them. Besides the three coyote brothers and Billy Bones, Philip P. Fox, his cousin, and Arnold Big Horn's younger brother were entered in the first long-distance leg. During the second leg, Georgie Beaver, Johnny Otter, Alvin Muskrat, two minks, and two of Georgie's cousins would swim around the island. In the final sprint around the pond, Victor Running Deer, Rodney Wild Deer, Sandy Antelope, Arnold Big Horn, Arnold's older brother, and two smaller deer from the Hill Country were entered. Winston considered the canines to be fairly even in ability and the antelope and the deer fairly close in speed. The owl thought the race would be won or lost in the water.

"Let's do this in the name of friendship!" declared Georgie Beaver, after finding Billy Bones and Victor Running Deer. "We worked hard for this day, and I think we've got a chance to pull it off. Whatever happens, don't give up. That's what I say!"

"I'm with you, Georgie," agreed the dog.

"And I also!" said Victor, as he looked across the dam to the southwestern corner of the pond. Olen and Myrtle Buck had just arrived with Melinda. The young buck quickly looked away as the doe tried to catch his eye.

"It looks like Victor's not going to play Melinda's little game a second time," Billy thought to himself. "Well, it's none of my business."

Shortly before the race started, Billy noticed Lenny Coyote motioning to him from the east edge of the dam. The coyote was partially hidden behind a temporary partition constructed to keep participants from accidentally falling down the dam's steep embankment.

"Lenny, what is it?" he whispered.

"I just thought I ought to warn you," the coyote cautioned, looking over at his brothers. "They've got some obstruction planned for each leg of the race. I saw my brothers talkin' to two of their no-good underhanded friends, Wiley Weasel and Rattlesnake Pete, and that doesn't bode well for you. Believe me! Be on the lookout and tell your friends!" He turned to leave and then looked back. "I'm sorry. That's all I know."

"Thanks. I'll tell them. Now I'd better get back to my place before your brothers see you talking to me," warned the shepherd dog, just before the double whistle sounded.

When Billy returned to his warm-up, he discovered that both Georgie and Victor had observed his conversation with Lenny. Luckily the coyotes on the other side of the dam had not. "What did Lenny have to say, Billy? Are we in trouble?" inquired the wide-eyed beaver.

"He wanted to warn us that his brothers have something planned for each of us and to be on the lookout. That's all he knew," confided Billy quietly.

"That's better than nothin'," said Victor, looking over at the Rogue Deer. "I imagine Rodney's in on it too, but we can't do anything about it now except be on our guard. Come on, Billy, they're linin' up for the start!"

The beginning of the race was fairly clean, but it soon became chaotic as the runners jostled for position on the narrow dam. As the contestants headed east on Beaver Dam Road, Billy noticed that Arnold's younger brother took the lead, as expected. He was closely followed by Lester, Leon, and Leroy. Billy and the two foxes were content to run just behind the coyotes for the first part of the race. The dog was aware that when he made his move, the coyote brothers would try to keep him from passing, but he felt confident that he could eventually get around them.

As the race moved northward onto Timber Trail, the Big Horn sheep opened up a considerable lead. Billy knew that the sheep's plan was to gain the advantage and then try to hold it. However, by the time the winded animal reached the bridge leading back toward Main Street, the coyotes had gone around him, and soon afterward the dog and foxes did the same.

Along the open Sleepy Road, Billy could see that Leroy was having difficulty keeping the pace. When the young coyote fell back a little, the shepherd dog immediately took advantage of the situation and moved in behind Lester and Leon. Shortly after, Philip P. Fox did the same, and the race became a four-animal event.

Billy Bones was glad to see that Deputy Eagle was flying just above them. He hoped that the large bird would follow them at least as far as the ford that led over to the Southern Road. The shepherd dog felt that the water would provide enough diversion to let him slide by at least one of the coyotes.

When the time came to cross the stream, Lester and Leon spread out slightly to keep Billy from going around them. The dog saw the chance he had been waiting for and with a great spurt of energy dashed between the two coyotes. Lester reached out to grab the dog, but the good deputy was hovering just above him.

"Keep those hands to yourself, Lester!" the eagle screamed, as Billy splashed his way through to dry land.

From that point on to Beaver Dam Road, Lester tried desperately to keep pace with Billy, but the larger shepherd dog maintained his advantage. Philip P. Fox, who had also profited by the dog's actions, moved quickly into third place behind Lester.

Gradually Billy Bones widened his lead until he could see the opening to the dam and Lenny and Victor by the edge of the entrance urging him on. The dog was ecstatic that he would be able to give his good friend Georgie such a good lead. Unfortunately in his euphoria, he had forgotten Lenny Coyote's warning and let down his guard.

Suddenly across the path ahead of the shepherd dog, a rope just high enough to trip him tightened across the trail and sent him flying head over heels.

"Get up, Billy," yelled Lenny, as he flew down the embankment chasing the perpetrator of the cruel derailment.

As the disconcerted shepherd dog tried to regain his feet, all he could think of was Georgie's remark, "Whatever happens, don't give up!"

As Billy started to limp in, Lester and Philip were able to easily catch and pass him. At that instant, he realized that the chance Georgie Beaver had lived for was quickly passing by. From somewhere deep within him he gathered the courage to overcome his pain, and he broke into a run. By the time he reached the young beaver, he was only ten feet behind the coyote and had drawn even with the fox. He hoped that he had given Georgie enough to work with. The outcome was now in the beaver's hands.

Winston Wise Owl was amazed at Billy's valiant recovery. Circling down over the dam, the owl watched Lenny Coyote rush off after the culprit who had tripped the dog and then watched Wendell Red Breast veer off close behind both of them. He hoped that Georgie and Victor would be more vigilant. He knew that another ambush was not out of the question.

Georgie Beaver and Alvin Muskrat swam confidently together. Winston noticed that Johnny Otter, in his exuberance at being ahead, had once again started too fast. By the time the three animals reached the first bridge, Johnny had increased his lead. As they rounded the far end of the island, however, the situation reversed when both the beaver and the muskrat started gaining on the otter.

Just before they reached the bridge on the west side, Winston saw the trap out of the corner of his eye. Someone had dropped a net on the opposite side of the bridge just after Johnny passed under it. The ropes effectively blocked the entire entrance to the other side.

"Dive!" the owl yelled to the beaver and the muskrat, as he soared down close to their heads. "Someone's set a trap. You'll have to go underneath!"

The amazing agility possessed by both swimmers allowed them to go beneath the net without losing much time. When the beaver and the muskrat reached the surface on the other side, Winston could see that Johnny was quickly tiring from the longer swim. It looked like Georgie's weeks of training were paying off, as he soon outdistanced Alvin and was gaining considerable ground on Johnny.

By this point in the competition, both sides of the pond were teeming with spectators. The roaring of the crowd was tremendous as Georgie started to catch up to Johnny. When he passed the otter just before reaching the dam, the sound was deafening. The old owl knew it was the defining moment in the young beaver's life up to that time.

No matter what else happened, he not only had defeated the young otter but made up a ten-yard deficit.

Victor Running Deer wasted no time in getting started. As he reached the edge of the dam, however, the Rogue Deer was running right beside him. "This will be a foot-race to the finish," mused Winston, as the two animals jostled and bumped their way along River Road. When they crossed the first bridge, Rodney forged a little ahead, but by the time the second bridge was under their hooves, Victor had pulled even again.

Wendell Red Breast looked terribly nervous when the two deer finally reached the Wooded Walk. It was the little robin's job to see that neither buck used his hands or tried to trip the other one. Being so small, Winston wondered if there was anything Wendell could do to stop them if they decided to break the rules. As the two animals matched each other stride for stride, the little robin flew directly behind them with his whistle in his beak.

Without warning a loose branch came swinging down from the foliage overhead, grazing Victor on the chest and just missing Rodney.

"Hey, watch out!" Victor screamed, as the branch managed to slow down both runners.

Wendell Red Breast was not so lucky and crashed right into the overhanging obstacle. The freak accident also caused the surprised holder of the branch to fall from the tree, leaving both the robin and the perpetrator in a tangled heap on the ground.

Sandy Antelope was fast approaching the fracas and

had to jump over the mound in order to stay on his feet. By the time Winston reached the scene, the bewildered bird was sitting in the middle of the path, and a shaken Rattlesnake Pete was slithering quickly away.

As Winston winged his way under the branches, he could just make out an excited Melinda Doe standing on top of a bench to the right of the finish line. On the other side of the line, he spotted Billy Bones and Georgie Beaver urging their teammate on.

The two deer, as before, were running neck and neck. They appeared to be completely spent, but neither would give an inch to the other. Just before the finish line, with an unknown stimulus Victor surged ahead and crossed the finish line first.

Victor was immediately inundated with cheers and congratulatory remarks. "For this moment in time," smiled Winston, as he tried to find a place to land, "he's everyone's best friend. Well, he deserves it. He's just defeated the fastest animal inside The Enchantment."

After the ribbons were awarded, the owl observed that the victorious deer kept his distance from Melinda Doe. Instead of seeking her out, he attended a lunch Gladys Beaver had prepared for all the participants and marshals.

Lenny Coyote accused Wiley Weasel of tripping Billy Bones after the contest was finished, but after some debate the owl and the other marshals decided not to investigate the matter further, since Georgie's team came out victorious. Sheriff Lone Wolf, however, did arrest Wiley Weasel and his friend Rattlesnake Pete for disturbing the peace, but he put off their incarceration because the jail cells were already full.

The marshals during the Great Medley never really found out who was responsible for dropping the net below the bridge. Winston Wise Owl was almost positive that Johnny Otter tripped the mechanism himself. Even Alvin Muskrat thought he saw an arm go up just as the otter went under the bridge but could not swear to it, so the matter was eventually dropped.

After the race Winston spied Rodney Wild Deer standing silent and aloof at the edge of the pond. As he approached him, the unhappy buck turned away and headed south toward the thicket. Winston saw the hatred in the disgruntled buck's eyes, and he feared that one day that pain and loathing would yield terrible consequences.

CHAPTER FORTY

THE FATEFUL ELECTION

A comfortable old armchair made especially for Winston Wise Owl's library was the owl's favorite place to read his books on a rainy Saturday morning. He was finding it hard that day to concentrate because of the elections at City Hall. He knew they could be turning points in the social structure of the Prairie. He felt guilty that he had not done more to ward off the influence of Brother Fabian Lynx in the little community.

When Brother Fabian came through the portal over a year ago, Winston had seen the hatred in the cat's eyes when he saw the owl's library. The lynx's experiences in the Wildlife Zoo must have been horrific. Apparently his keepers had kept him in a small cage and often taunted him and deprived him of food. The owl should have realized that anything written by humans would be abhorrent to Fabian. Even though he was immediately aware of the large cat's intelligence, he did not fully recognize the intensity of his loathing or the scope of his ambition.

As the old clock on the landing struck ten, the owl finally rose, took off his robe, and put on his long coat.

He had promised Hester Groundhog that he would escort her to City Hall and the voting booths. Later that evening they would retrace their steps to City Hall and attend the Summer Concert that traditionally ended the Grand Fair. The songbirds, including Councilor Wendell Red Breast, had worked for a number of months to make a fitting ending to the important week. After the concert the election results would be announced on the stage of the Great Hall and then posted on the door.

Winston retrieved his umbrella near the entrance and took one last look at his library. Earlier that morning he had reacquainted himself with many of the ancient books, running his fingers fondly over them as if they were old friends. He could not imagine life without them. He knew that if the election went the wrong way, there was a possibility that he could lose them.

When Winston Wise Owl and Hester Groundhog reached City Hall, they had to wait in line for some time to vote.

"Ah, I was hoping the rain would keep the turnout light!" sighed the owl, as he looked at the long line. "I'm afraid this can only favor Elmer Prairie Dog."

"Hush now, Winston. You don't want the others in line to know who you're voting for. After all you're the great gatekeeper, remember!" chuckled Hester, tapping her old friend on his wing.

"I'm sure they're all well aware of my feelings on the matter," continued the owl, looking around at all the prairie dogs. "My goodness, where do they all come from anyway?"

"Let's just say that the generations have been good to the little rascals!" giggled the groundhog again.

After Winston and Hester finished voting, they crossed the street to the old hotel and went into the dining room for lunch. A number of their friends also enjoyed this pleasant tradition. As they entered, Counselor Thaddeus P. Turtle and Wendell Red Breast beckoned them over to their table.

"I see that the weather hasn't kept our good citizens from voting," smiled the robin as Winston held a chair for Hester. "I just hope it stops raining before the concert tonight."

"Does everything seem to be ready?" inquired Hester Groundhog.

The robin laughed, "Yes, I believe so, but I'm concerned about the weather. I don't like the competition of raindrops on the roof."

As Wendell Red Breast and the other songbirds had hoped, the rain did abate in the late afternoon. By six o'clock the sun came out, and the ballots were taken over to the hotel to be counted behind closed doors.

Winston Wise Owl and Hester Groundhog arrived at the concert fifteen minutes early and found the Great Hall packed as usual. Thaddeus P. Turtle had saved seats for them on the second row behind the mayor and his wife.

The old owl allowed himself to get caught up in the beauty and excitement of the concert and for a time forgot about the election. During the second half, baritone Wendell Red Breast, mezzo-soprano Gloria Meadowlark, tenor Hosea Brown Thrasher, and soprano Melba Thrush were especially well received and got standing ovations.

Winston was quickly brought back to reality when Farmer Jason Crow and the rest of the voting committee entered the hall, walked in single file down the center aisle, and stepped onto the stage. The crow invited everyone to sit while he read the final tally for each race.

On the way home after the results of the election had been announced, Winston Wise Owl walked silently beside Hester Groundhog. He was still partly in a state of shock. As he had feared, Elmer Prairie Dog and three of the candidates for City Council from the strict constructionists—Phineas T. Fox, Charlie Pheasant, and Olen Buck—had won. Only two moderates, Wendell Red Breast and Cornelius Van Mink, had been able to hold their seats.

"Ah me, what's to become of us?" Winston finally whispered to Hester, as they crossed over to the beaver dam.

"Now Winston," soothed Hester, "maybe things won't be so bad. Wendell and Cornelius are still on the council, and Olen Buck is no fool. Maybe you can persuade him to be reasonable."

"Ah, but the look Brother Fabian Lynx gave me after the results were read – the sneer on his face. It was almost frightening," said the owl sadly. "Well, his lackeys won't take office until the new year. At least we'll have time to do some regrouping."

"And to think Elmer won by only four votes!" mused the groundhog with a sigh.

"I understand that Brother Fabian talked Sheriff Lone Wolf into allowing Rodney and the three coyotes to make the trip over to City Hall," recollected Winston.

"There are your four votes," concluded Hester. "Well, we have to be sure to go to the Old Meetinghouse tomorrow and show our support for Mayor Beaver. I have an idea that many of our citizens will decide to stay home.

"Yes, you are right of course. We must attend…."

During the rest of their familiar journey back to Land's End, neither creature spoke at all.

CHAPTER FORTY-ONE

THE NEXT DAY

Billy Bones awoke the next day to the clear opulent tones of Gloria Meadowlark's voice. She had gone out into the fields early and was singing one of the lovely folk songs passed down to her from her mother and her mother's mother before her. The melody came wafting through the top Dutch door, left open the night before.

Billy was immediately struck by the clarity of the morning and the beauty of the meadowlark's voice. It seemed ironic to him that such splendor could follow the foreboding he felt the night before when the results of the election were announced. Finally he rose, trotted down to the river and bathed, returned to the cottage, and put on his clean white shirt. Sandy Antelope, Arnold Big Horn, and Alvin Muskrat had promised to drop by on their way to the Old Meetinghouse.

Alvin arrived first. The muskrat always took time to come inside and stare at the old corner cupboard that had belonged to his grandmother.

"Granny loved that old cupboard!" he stated again, as he surveyed it carefully. "I can't imagine destroyin' it. I'm glad Percy gave it to you!"

Billy looked cautiously at the muskrat before he spoke. "Alvin, if I should ever have to move it to a safer place, would you be willing to help me?"

"Why, yes…yes, of course, but why? Do you think there's still a danger that someone from inside the new government might try to have it destroyed?"

"It's just that…" the shepherd dog began.

At that moment a knock on the door caused the two friends to look around abruptly, but they were relieved to see it was only Sandy Antelope and Arnold Big Horn. The antelope had a big basket covered with a checkered cloth.

"Hey, good mornin'!" called Alvin. "What's up with the basket?"

"It's for lunch after Thaddeus's talk. I brought corn-bread. There's enough here for everybody!" The antelope chuckled as he put the large basket on the table and pulled back the cloth.

Another knock drew everyone's attention back to the entrance as Victor Running Deer poked his head over the bottom door. "May I come in?"

"Why Victor, of course. Come on in!" greeted Billy, as he moved to the doorway.

"I just thought maybe I'd go to the Old Meetinghouse with you four this morning. Do you mind if I tag along?" inquired the deer.

"That would be great," said Billy, trying not to look surprised. Everyone in the room knew that the Rogue Deer was escorting Melinda to the New Meetinghouse this morning, but no one expected Victor to react in such a radical way.

"Victor, we're coming back here afterward for some cornbread. Are you interested?" asked Billy, smiling

"Yeah, count me in," answered the deer, smiling back. "I'd like that."

"Well, come on then. We don't want to be late," laughed Billy, as he started for the door.

By the time Billy and his companions arrived at the Old Meetinghouse, they were shocked to discover that only a few brave souls had bothered to attend. The dog surmised that most of the regular members must have felt embarrassed about Mayor Beaver's defeat and decided not to show up. As far as George P. Beaver was concerned, Billy could see no indication that he was demoralized, as he sat calmly with his wife in their usual spot in the second row. Hester Groundhog and Winston Wise Owl were seated close to them. Billy could see that the owl was trying to put on a brave front although he was devastated. In back of them Justin, Gladys, and Georgie Beaver were near the edge of the row. When Georgie spied his friends, he excused himself and took a seat next to Billy. Together the six animals filled an entire row behind Georgie's parents.

After the service Billy and his friends shook hands with the mayor and his wife, and then Billy approached the discouraged owl.

"I'm sorry, Mr. Wise Owl, about the election. I know you were counting on a win to safeguard your books," sympathized the dog.

"Ah yes, Billy, I am very disheartened. I know how much Fabian Lynx hates the human books in my library, and now he's got the upper hand. I'm afraid of what he'll try to do to them. But we can't give up hope, can we. We must find another way to protect them."

"I will do everything I can, sir. I promise," answered Billy.

Winston only shook his head and tried to smile.

"Come on, Winston. There's nothing we can do right now," joined Hester, as she smiled at the shepherd dog and led the old owl out of the meetinghouse.

After the owl and groundhog departed, Billy invited Georgie to join the group for lunch. When Gladys Beaver found out, she added two more baskets of fruit and vegetables.

Even though the companions were subdued, there was a cool breeze off the foothills, and the walk was pleasant. Soon Georgie and Alvin pushed on ahead with the baskets, as was their nature, and the usually serious-minded deer, the tough square-jawed ram, and the amiable antelope began jostling one another to break the somber mood. After a time they included Billy in their fun, and before long they were all laughing and enjoying one another's company. In fact, Billy could never remember a time when the comradeship of the six animals was any stronger, and it gave him a feeling of real contentment in spite of his earlier melancholy.

Back at the cottage Billy decided to eat outside at the makeshift table that Justin Beaver left after the construction was finished. Most of the cornbread that Sandy Antelope brought and all the food that Georgie's mother provided were completely devoured in less than half an hour.

After the meal Alvin and Georgie decided to nap under the large shade tree just to the west. Billy, Victor, Sandy, and Arnold sat around the table reminiscing about the different races during the week of the Grand Fair.

"Victor, how did you ever manage to come up with enough energy to get ahead of Rodney at the end of the Great Medley? You must have been completely exhausted!" exclaimed Sandy. "I know I was."

"Do you really want to know?" asked Victor, smiling at the antelope.

"Yeah," said Sandy.

"Yeah," said Arnold, sitting up and leaning toward the serious buck.

"Well…it was because of Georgie," responded Victor. "And Billy here…."

"Me?" barked Billy, sitting up himself.

"Yeah, you," grinned Victor. "When I remembered you getting up and runnin' through your pain, and Georgie's words, 'Let's do this in the name of friendship,' I couldn't do much less. I'd never hear the end of it!"

During the good-natured laughter that followed, Victor suddenly became serious and addressed the shepherd dog. "Billy, I couldn't help overhearing most of your conversation with Mr. Wise Owl at the Old Meetinghouse. Do you really think that Brother Fabian would try to convince the new City Council to destroy Mr. Wise Owl's books?"

"You heard what he said on our first day inside The Enchantment, Victor…that he wouldn't rest until Mr. Wise Owl's books were burned!"

"But that was in the heat of anger," countered the deer.

"But what if he tries to go through with it, Victor? Those books are our only link to human intelligence in the other world. If anything happened to that knowledge…it would be irreplaceable!"

"I still don't think Brother Fabian would go that far," insisted the buck, looking away.

"We can't take that chance, Victor. You heard what the creatures in the Hill Country believe—that our awareness may have come from those very human artifacts."

"But Brother Fabian says that's just superstition! And anyway, that happened a long time ago."

"But what if he's wrong?" countered Billy.

Before Victor could answer, Olen Buck suddenly appeared around the end of the cottage. He seemed agitated.

"Victor," said Olen, gritting his jaw, "I hate to interrupt you when you're with your friends, but I need to talk to you."

Victor Running Deer rose, walked a short distance from the table, and beckoned for Olen to follow him. The creatures that remained could not help but hear the concern in the old deer's voice.

"It's Melinda! Rodney took her to the New Meetinghouse this morning. Of course Sheriff Lone Wolf had to go along. After the service Melinda refused to let Rodney take her home. She said she only promised that she would go with him <u>to</u> the meetinghouse," explained the old stag. "As you can imagine, Rodney was furious. He grabbed her by the arm and started screaming in her face and threatening her. It took the sheriff and me and Brother Fabian to restrain him."

"And Melinda… is she all right?" asked Victor, feeling concern for the doe who had snubbed him after the Big Race.

"Yes, but she wants to see you… to tell you how sorry she is for hurting your feelings."

"Where is she now?" asked Victor, glancing down at his hooves.

"Right over there," said Olen, pointing to the path east of the cottage.

As Victor Running Deer turned to look at Melinda, she lowered her head slightly. The breeze billowed around her long blue skirt and scarf, accenting the exquisiteness of her face and body. He half stumbled over to her as she raised her eyes and looked straight into his.

The young buck and the doe stood talking to one another for some time. Billy Bones and the other animals could not hear what they were saying, but they could see that Victor was completely enveloped by her charm. Finally without looking back, Victor took Melinda's hand, and the two deer sauntered slowly southward along the East Wagon Trail.

After allowing a few moments to pass, Olen Buck crossed over to Billy Bones. "Mr. Bones, I know I have not always been kind to you. I mean, at the Old Meetinghouse when I doubted your experiences inside the mist. However, you have always been a loyal friend to Victor, and I appreciate that." Just as Olen excused himself and started down the path, Billy suddenly remembered his conversation with Victor and found himself chasing after the old stag.

"Mr. Buck, one quick question if I may," began the dog.

"Yes, what is it, Mr. Bones?" the stag asked, as he stopped on the path.

"I just want you to know that I'm worried now that the elections are over. I mean, about Mr. Wise Owl's books and the other human artifacts but…but especially about the books. They are the only record we have, you see, of what went on…before. And I feel there's a potential for much violence, sir, if the new City Council votes to remove them by force. So I'm compelled to ask you, sir…what is your feeling?"

"I cannot tell you at this moment, Mr. Bones, but you have a good point. I will give your concern considerable thought, and I will discuss them with Victor. Yes, that I will do." He started walking and then halted a second time. "And I will let you know what I decide. That I promise."

With those hopeful words, Olen continued his journey down the path toward the thicket, careful to follow discreetly behind the two young deer.

Soon after the three deer departed, Billy's other guests left for their own homes. Only Georgie stayed around for most of the afternoon. Toward evening when the young beaver felt it was time to leave, he invited the dog over for supper.

"Thank you, Georgie, but tonight's Sunday, and the little guys will be comin' around. We've got a deal. I should stay here," explained the shepherd.

CHAPTER FORTY-TWO

THE SHERIFF'S INVITATION

When Nosey Coon and Needles Porcupine came to spend the night, Billy Bones was especially glad to see them. He gave each a little cornbread and told them how he first met William Stuart III in the human's world. Afterward, Nosey climbed up to his bunk, and Needles curled up with his blanket in front of the cupboard.

When Billy blew out the candle and crawled into his bed built sturdily into the wall below the loft, Nosey peeked down over the rail beside his mattress. "I'm glad you're with us now, Billy," he whispered loudly, "and not with the human boy and his grandfather."

After a short time, the shepherd dog heard another even louder whisper from across the room by the old corner cupboard: "So am I!"

When the dog finally succumbed to sleep, he had another dream that concerned the human pioneers. This was as vivid as the first one, but this time he saw everything through Jimmy Stone's eyes rather than seeing it from above. As before, Jimmy was following the other wagons along the Old Wagon Trail and was discovering that the slope was much steeper than he had expected.

As Jimmy drove his covered wagon up the trail, he was becoming aware of the tragedy that was taking place all around him. Hundreds of household articles and pieces of furniture had been discarded on both sides of the trail. As he looked around at these precious belongings, the young man realized that most of them held the hopes and dreams for a better life in this new territory called Oregon. He could also tell by the weather-beaten condition of many items that they had been cast away by previous pioneers. In fact, the entire area on both sides of the trail resembled a graveyard of lost treasures.

Among the settlers struggling desperately to lighten their wagons, Billy Bones learned that Jimmy Stone had recognizable friends. The name "Mrs. McNeil" came to him, for instance, when he saw this lady weeping uncontrollably as she unloaded her antique Irish furniture and covered them with old rugs and pieces of canvas.

Another older man called Cortland Witherspoon was clumsily trying to wrap a grandfather clock with an old tapestry turned inside out. The man's hands were shaking, and his eyes had a fixed stare. As Jimmy gazed at these items, Billy realized in his dream that the clock was the one that Mr. Wise Owl had in his tree house, and the tapestry now hung in George P. Beaver's castle.

Billy watched as Jimmy Stone passed the Witherspoon wagon and suddenly heard the frenzied scream of a woman and the warning shouts of men on the trail just ahead of him. He looked up in time to see a team of horses lose its footing, and an overloaded wagon break free from its controlling harnesses. Amid a cloud of dust, the screeching wagon barreled down the steep slope, just missing Mr. Witherspoon and his clock. Finally it careened off the trail and crashed into the hillside.

When Billy woke, he realized that he had just lived through the scene that he had witnessed before coming out of the mist during his second day inside The Enchantment at the west end of the wagon trail. Now he knew where the human artifacts came from and why the name Cortland Witherspoon was on the Bible that sat in the place of honor in the Hill Country's Sacred Chamber.

For another hour the shepherd dog lay awake staring at the bunk above him. From time to time small bits of straw fell from the little mattress, seen between the rough boards that formed the floor of the loft where Nosey moved about with his own dreams.

"Why've these dreams been given to me?" Billy wondered. "What am I supposed to do with them? And what's my connection to this Jimmy Stone? Maybe Lucinda can help me. Well anyway, I'll see her at the Autumn Equinox, and I'll ask her then. Yes, that's what I'll do. Maybe she'll know…something…."

On the morning of September first, three days after the Grand Fair, Billy Bones was still tossing and turning on his little bunk built into the west wall of his one great room. Nosey Coon was again sleeping on the loft above the bed, and Needles Porcupine was curled up on a blanket in front of the old corner cupboard. Usually the raccoon and the porcupine were allowed to sleep over only on Sundays, but because Nosey had helped him in the Overland Race, Billy had decided that he owed them an extra night.

The shepherd dog was dreaming he was Jimmy Stone again. This time, however, he was riding through a mountain pass in the same wagon as his friend Ben and his wife. He was feeling a great sadness, as if he had just lost someone very close to him. Suddenly one of the front wheels gave way as it hit a rut in a ravine, and Jimmy went tumbling off the wagon.

At the same instant Jimmy fell, Billy was awakened by a voice from the loft above him crying, "Billy, Billy, wake up! You're havin' a bad dream!"

Billy struggled to sit up on the edge of his bed. "I'm sorry, Nosey. I didn't mean to wake you. Come on, we might as well get up. I'll find us some breakfast."

"Is everything all right?" said Needles, peeking out from under his blanket. "I thought I heard Billy yell."

"I think he was havin' one of those magic dreams again," explained Nosey, leaning over the loft.

Billy smiled up at the raccoon. "I don't know how magical it was, but it was certainly pretty intense. Come on. Let's have some breakfast, and I'll tell you about it.

As soon as the invitation to eat was extended, a scramble for the table ensued. Nosey crashed into a place on one side, and Needles plopped himself down on the other, both animals grabbing knives and holding them in an upright position.

While Billy Bones related his dream, a small loaf of wheat bread quickly disappeared, as did a dish of apple butter from Gladys Beaver's cupboard. After Billy finished his strange tale, Nosey peered quizzically over at him. "Do you think it means anything?"

"I don't know," admitted the dog. "It's almost like this Jimmy Stone is trying to tell me something."

At that moment the silhouette of a tall, well-built creature wearing a black felt hat partially blocked the sun-filled doorway. Since he stood with his back against the light, Billy could not immediately discern who it was. When he stepped inside the room and removed his hat, the dog realized it was Sheriff Walter Lone Wolf.

"Billy Bones, I'm sorry to interrupt while you're eatin', but the City Council is meeting tomorrow morning. They want to handle that matter of the three ambushes that took place before the Grand Fair. They'll need your testimony. I've already spoken to Victor Running Deer, Sandy Antelope, and Arnold Big Horn. Please be at City Hall by nine a.m."

As the wolf turned to leave, he caught sight of Nosey's ringed tail sticking out from under the right side of the table. "Oh, and tell your friend Nosey that I'll need his testimony too. Since he was with you on the wagon trail when the stoning incident occurred, he's an important witness." The sheriff strode back to the door. His badge glistened when the sunlight fell upon it. "Remember, nine o'clock sharp!"

"You can come out now, Nosey," laughed the shepherd dog. "He's gone away."

Nosey Coon slid out quietly from under the table and peeked out the open door after the departing sheriff. Needles, who still sat at his seat with his hand up to his cheek, spoke for his friend. "Nosey tries to stay clear o' the sheriff. He's always after us about somethin'."

Billy Bones had agreed to meet Nosey Coon outside his cottage on Wednesday morning at eight o'clock. After waiting patiently for over half an hour, the dog decided he better find the little creature. When the shepherd dog reached the raccoon's little hollow, he knocked several times on the door and then called, "Nosey, get yourself out of bed! We'll be late, and we don't want the council mad at us!"

Receiving no response, Billy carefully scraped the door open on its sagging hinges and looked inside. It took the dog time to rummage through the mess, but he was finally satisfied that the raccoon was not there. As he poked his head outside again, he glanced across the way at Needles' little stump and saw the tarp being quickly pulled down over the opening.

"All right, what kind of game is this?" shouted the dog, as he drew open the covering. The young porcupine stood in the doorway with a surprised look on his face. He had already pulled his ragged overalls up with its single strap. "OK, Needles, where is he? Don't you think this is a bit childish?" The porcupine gave the dog a sheepish look and then stood aside. Billy looked at the empty bed and then underneath it saw a bushy tail sticking out the back end. The dog gingerly reached down and pulled the raccoon out by the back of his patched britches. "All right fellow, get yourself out here! We've got a job to do this morning!"

"That's just it, Billy, as I told ya' yesterday, he don't wanna go before no council," explained Needles. "He's been in trouble before, and he likes to stay clear of authority."

"Well for heaven's sake, why didn't he say something earlier? He's got nothing to be afraid of this time," assured the dog. "They just have to hear everyone connected to the case. You don't want the sheriff comin' after you, do you, Nosey?"

"Would he do that?" inquired Nosey, suddenly changing his attitude.

"Of course he would if he thought it was necessary to win the case. Now come on. You're one of the prime witnesses!"

CHAPTER FORTY-THREE

PANDEMONIUM AT CITY HALL

When Billy Bones and Nosey Coon reached City Hall, the clock in its great white tower read nine twenty-four. Sheriff Lone Wolf was waiting just inside the entrance hall for them. "I thought I told you two to be here at nine! It's almost nine-thirty! I had to stall them by sending Victor, Sandy, and Arnold ahead of you. Now get inside! They're waiting!"

Billy considered offering an excuse but then thought better of it and followed the perturbed sheriff into the Great Hall. He had to grab Nosey by the strap of his pants to keep him from escaping.

Inside the hall the council members were seated in a row across the back of the raised platform. As usual, Cornelius Van Mink and Mayor George P. Beaver sat in the center with Wendell Red Breast and Sylvester Turtle on their left and Phineas T. Fox and Charlie Pheasant on their right.

The sheriff seated the raccoon part way up the center aisle and sent the dog up onto the platform. Victor Running Deer, Sandy Antelope, and Arnold Big Horn had already testified and were sitting in the front row facing the platform. As Billy passed them, he smiled and nodded, and they smiled and nodded in return. To his surprise he noticed that the council had asked for a closed session. Only those giving testimony and Olen Buck were present.

After Billy's testimony and while the nervous raccoon was recounting his version of the stoning incident, the dog noticed Lenny Coyote sitting alone in the back. The young coyote had reluctantly agreed to attest to the attempted assault on Sleepy Road. As Billy watched the wide-eyed Nosey Coon stutter before the council, he thought of the difficulties Lenny must be facing. He knew that the coyote's brothers might retaliate in some way for his cooperation in the matter. Fortunately the coyote was allowed to testify before his brothers arrived.

After lunch Sheriff Lone Wolf went back to his office, released Rodney Wild Deer and the three coyote brothers from their jail cell, and escorted them to City Hall. Calhoun Coyote came along with them and brought his spiritual adviser, Brother Fabian Lynx. When Rodney reached the front of the main hall, Victor suddenly stepped into the aisle and confronted him.

"I understand you were rude to Melinda," Victor snarled. "I hope they lock you up and throw away the key!"

"What happens between me and Melinda is none of your affair, you jackass!" yelled Rodney, as he pushed Victor so violently that he smashed up against the edge of the raised platform that ran across the front of the hall. He then threw himself on top of Victor and began pummeling him in the face and chest.

Seeing his friend being so brutally attacked, Billy raced up the aisle, grabbed Rodney by the shoulders, and flung him back down the center aisle. Witnessing this, the three coyotes jumped on top of Billy, and then Sandy Antelope and Arnold Big Horn rushed to the dog's defense. Unfortunately, by this time the two deer were swinging wildly at each other as they rolled back down the center aisle.

At this critical point Olen Buck jumped to his feet, let out a loud bellow, and helped Sheriff Lone Wolf pull the two young bucks apart.

The pandemonium finally subsided when Councilor Cornelius Van Mink stood on his chair, pounded the table, and screamed, "We'll have order in this place, or I'll have the whole lot of you put in jail for the rest of the year!"

After Sheriff Lone Wolf, Brother Fabian Lynx, and Calhoun Coyote were able to usher a struggling Rodney Wild Deer and the three coyotes over to the far west wall, Cornelius glared down at them. "Brother Fabian, I understand you represent these four animals. I suggest you explain to them that their actions this afternoon did not help their cause." He looked around at the other councilors just beginning to regain their dignity. "And after a short break, I will expect an apology from each one of them before this council reconvenes."

Cornelius then turned his attention to Victor, who was still standing with Olen in the center aisle. "And as for you, Victor Running Deer, we'll have no more emotional outbursts, or you and your friends will face charges as well!"

After a ten-minute break, Sheriff Lone Wolf returned with two of his deputies, Bison Bob and Milton Brown Bear, and together they lined up Lester, Leon, Leroy, and Rodney before the west side of the raised platform. At the same time, under the supervision of Olen Buck, Victor, Sandy, Arnold, and Billy were lined up on the east side. Billy noticed out of the corner of his eye that the sheriff and his deputies were having some trouble controlling Rodney. Unfortunately the Rogue Deer had ended up across the aisle from Victor.

Beginning with the coyotes, each animal in turn mumbled an apology to the City Council. When it came time for Rodney Wild Deer to offer his apology, he turned and glared over at Victor Running Deer. At that same moment, Victor glanced sardonically back at his archenemy. As their eyes met, Rodney started to sputter something that grew in intensity and finally evolved into a savage "Aaah!" as he threw himself toward Victor.

This time however, Sheriff Lone Wolf was vigilant. With utmost speed the wolf tackled the rogue before he could reach Victor, and with the help of his deputies managed to handcuff Rodney and drag him kicking and screaming out of the hall.

"No, no, let me at him! I'll kill him!" were the last cries Billy heard as the double doors slammed behind the law officers and the raging Rodney Wild Deer.

As before, Councilor Van Mink was standing on top of his chair and pounding on the table for order. After everyone was finally seated and harmony restored, Brother

Fabian calmly strolled up to the platform. The lynx's eyes flashed and his teeth sparkled as he began his defense. "Earlier this morning Lester, Leon, Leroy, and even Mr. Rodney Wild Deer all expressed a desire to me and to Mr. Calhoun Coyote to become better citizens. As for today's unfortunate upheavals, I believe the blame lies with unresolved issues that occurred during the time of the Grand Fair."

Although the shepherd dog was still smarting from his involvement in the earlier chaos, he could not help but be impressed by the skill and eloquence with which the attractive cat continued his summation. However, it was Brother Fabian's final statement that caught Billy Bones completely by surprise.

"Calhoun Coyote and I have convinced Lester, Leon, and Leroy to admit their guilt, and they have agreed to throw themselves on the mercy of the council," Brother Fabian concluded in an even tone. "They realize that they went too far in the three ambushes in question, especially in the unfortunate affair with Victor Running Deer when he was physically assaulted on the Timber Trail. Therefore they have already agreed to undergo counseling as well as community service and are truly sorry for their transgressions. As for Mr. Rodney Wild Deer, I believe he also desires to become a better citizen. In time, I believe Mr. Coyote and I can help him achieve that goal."

On the way back to his seat, Fabian walked over to Victor, put a hand on his shoulder, and whispered something in the deer's ear. Billy guessed that Fabian Lynx was not only concerned about getting the best result for Rodney and Calhoun's sons but with appeasing Victor Running Deer and Olen Buck, who were members of his gathering.

After another recess and considerable discussion by the retiring members of the City Council, all the concerned parties except for Rodney Wild Deer were called back into the hall. Cornelius Van Mink spoke for the council.

"Lester Coyote, Leon Coyote, and Leroy Coyote, we accept your plea of guilty, and despite today's transgressions, we have taken into account your desire to improve yourselves and your willingness to undergo counseling."

The mink stopped, glanced over at the charismatic lynx and then back to the perpetrators. "Therefore we have decided to put you all under probation, and you will be allowed to leave in the custody of Brother Fabian Lynx and Mr. Calhoun Coyote. However, besides living and working with Mr. Calhoun Coyote, you will be required to attend weekly counseling sessions with Brother Fabian, and you will be obligated to spend ten hours a week working for the community under his guidance. This will last for a period of no less than nine months. You will also report to Sheriff Walter Lone Wolf every Saturday morning at ten o'clock. If your probation is broken, Sheriff Lone Wolf is authorized to put you back in jail for the remainder of your time. As for Rodney Wild Deer, after hearing all the evidence in this case, we find he is guilty…and considering his two outbursts in this court, he will be required to spend the next three months in Sheriff Lone Wolf's jail. After that, with good behavior he will be permitted to fulfill the requirements of his probation."

Billy Bones was somewhat disappointed that Rodney would still have the opportunity to influence the three older coyote brothers, but he knew that the guilty verdict was a victory for Victor, Nosey, and himself, especially since Victor's remarks to Rodney had precipitated the first ruckus before the City Council.

"Can we go now, Billy?" asked Nosey, who had begun to fidget and was still wide-eyed from the violence he had witnessed. "I'd like to get out a' here!"

The dog nudged the raccoon playfully. "So would I. Let's go."

CHAPTER FORTY-FOUR

THE REVELATION

Billy tried to be jovial as he and Nosey walked out of the Great Hall but could not shake the apprehension he felt when he observed the three coyotes with the crafty lynx after Fabian's speech. Even though the coyotes pleaded guilty, the dog thought he detected an unholy camaraderie between them and the lynx, and he worried that one day that comradeship would come back to haunt him.

"You OK, Billy? You got one of them faraway looks in your eyes," observed Nosey, as he opened the hall's great double door that led out to Court Street. Clouds had covered the sun briefly, which seemed to add to the uneasiness of the moment. "I thought we won."

"Sorry Nosey, I'm just thinking ahead," replied Billy. "But yes, I'm very happy. It looks like we won't be bothered by Rodney and his friends for some time."

Before the two animals reached Court Street, Sandy Antelope's friendly voice made them stop and turn around. "Hey Billy, Nosey, wait up!" Sandy and Arnold Big Horn were just coming out of the big double door. Billy noticed that their white shirts were still rumpled and dotted with blood stains from the melee.

"Now that we've won and law and order has been restored, I'd like to invite you both over to my place on Sunday. We'll celebrate over a pot of soup and reminisce about the Grand Fair. I already talked to Victor."

Billy looked over at Nosey, who was wagging his ringed tail. The little raccoon had never been invited to join the likes of Sandy Antelope and Arnold Big Horn socially. "Well Nosey, how about it? Are you up for it?"

In his excitement Nosey jumped up into Sandy's arms, causing him to nearly fall over. "Yes, yes, you really mean it?"

"Yes, of course I do. But I think you better get down. I don't want to have to carry you around all day," smiled the good-natured antelope.

As Nosey climbed down and started scampering in the direction of the beaver dam, Billy noticed Victor Running Deer and Olen Buck coming out of City Hall. Both were smiling, even though Victor's left eye was starting to swell shut and his lip was bleeding.

"Nosey, wait for me at the start of South Court Street," Billy called to his friend. "I'll meet you there in a few minutes."

"I guess I owe you all an apology," began Victor, as he made his way over to the three animals still standing on the east lawn of the Court House. "Me and my big mouth.... It looks like I could have gotten us all thrown into jail."

"Yes, you might have," smiled Sandy. "But then of course, when Billy jumped in…."

"Yeah sure, blame it on me now," laughed Billy.

"Wait now. Let's give Mr. Bones his due. The way he sprang to Victor's defense…without hesitation…with no thought of his own safety…." interrupted Olen Buck, as he reached out and placed a big hand on the dog's shoulder. "It was an act of true friendship. I shall never forget it…." Olen paused for a moment and collected himself. "Well anyway, it's over, and it looks like Rodney and his crew will be occupied for some time to come."

At that moment a brilliant shaft of light broke through the clouds and illuminated the old stag as he continued to speak. "And Mr. Bones, I've just had a long talk with my friend Victor here, and we've decided that you were right. There is a great potential for conflict if the new City Council decides to take human artifacts out of anyone's home without their permission, and that includes Winston Wise Owl's books." Olen hesitated again. "Please tell Mr. Wise Owl that I will do everything in my power to see that no harm comes to them. In fact, I think the five of us should make a pact to do all we can to safeguard all our citizen's artifacts. That's how strongly Victor and I feel about stopping this invasion of privacy before it starts!"

Olen suddenly put out his hand with the palm down. He was joined quickly by Victor who put his hand over the old stag's. This was followed by Sandy, Arnold, and finally an elated Billy Bones.

"Thank you! Thank you very much," said Billy, feeling a lump start to well up in the back of his throat, as the group added their other hands and moved them up and down together.

Billy was especially appreciative of Victor's support. The dog knew that the deer still had a deep hatred toward the humans who killed his mother, and he feared that Brother Fabian had managed to drive a wedge between himself and the deer, especially since he had seen Brother Fabian and Victor whispering together after Fabian's talk.

"And I will inform Mr. Wise Owl in the morning," stated Billy, looking over at Olen Buck. His heart was fairly singing for joy, and he had a hard time containing himself.

"Good! But it's probably best not to tell him or anyone else about the pact we just made here this afternoon. I think we need to keep that between ourselves. I believe it will be safer for everyone."

"Yes, you're probably right about that," agreed the dog, still in high spirits. "But I'm sure he'll be greatly relieved by your decision. I know he was terribly concerned about his books and the irreplaceable knowledge they represent."

After another round of handshakes and several more pats on the back, the members of the extraordinary pact broke up and went their separate ways.

As Billy Bones rejoined Nosey Coon on South Court, they saw what looked like three huge crows circling above the beaver dam. When they got closer, they realized that the birds were not crows at all but something much larger.

"Nosey, it's Felix, Festus, and Floyd. What are they doing so far from the Hill Country?" queried Billy.

The dog's question was soon answered when the vultures stopped their circling and headed toward Billy and

Nosey. Festus was the first to swoop down directly over their heads. "Hey Billy Bones, we've been lookin' for ya'!"

"Momma's got a message for ya'!" shouted Floyd, diving in from the southeast, barely missing Nosey's head.

"See ya' at the dam!" yelled Felix, coming in from the northeast where the foliage was thickest.

"Are they tryin' to kill us?" cried Nosey, as he threw himself behind Billy and wrapped his arms around the dog's knees.

"No, I think they're just showing off," laughed Billy, as he peeled Nosey off his legs and lifted him back on his feet. "Now come on. Let's follow 'em down to the dam where there's plenty of room to land."

When the shepherd dog and wary raccoon reached the wide roadway that crossed the top of the dam, they saw that Felix and Festus had already landed. Floyd, on the other hand, was in the process of landing. Unfortunately he made some miscalculations on his descent and was headed straight toward Festus. The collision that followed caused the two brothers to tumble head over heels onto the very rim of the dam.

"Dang it, Floyd, ain't you never gonna learn to land smoothly?" shouted Festus, shoving Floyd off the edge of the dam and into the water.

"Help, help! I can't swim!" screeched Floyd, flailing about in the water.

As swiftly as he could, Billy threw himself on his chest, reached out as far as he could, and pulled the soaked bird back to the shore.

As Floyd shook the water out of his drenched feathers and Festus struggled to regain his feet, Felix tried to take charge. "Momma wanted us to remind you that the Tribal Council meets on the twenty-second," reported Felix.

"And Momma wants to know why you ain't told her about your dreams," continued Festus, remembering his instructions.

"Yeah, she said you're supposed to tell us so we can tell her," sputtered Floyd, still trying to catch his breath.

Billy smiled at the well-intentioned sons of Lucinda Vulture. "Explain to your mother that I plan to tell her about my dreams when I return to the Hill Country. Also explain to her that I had these dreams only a couple of nights ago and last night," confessed the shepherd dog. "But I'll tell you about them now if you like, so you can pass them on to her."

For the next few minutes Billy Bones related his dreams about the human pioneers along the trail, the discarded furniture, and the horses that lost control of one wagon.

"You say the horses stood on their feet and hands?" queried Floyd, who had a quizzical look on his wet face. "I ain't never heard o' nothin' like that!"

"No, Floyd, they have front legs instead of arms, and they have hooves on each leg," explained the dog.

"Yeah, you dummy," grumbled Felix, hitting his brother on the back of his head. "Don't you know nothin'?"

After Billy repeated the dream a second time, the three vultures flew off toward the Hill Country, still arguing and accusing one another of being ignorant.

As soon as the big birds departed, Billy started looking around for Nosey Coon, who had strangely disappeared. He finally found him hiding behind a gnarled old tree part way up the path toward City Hall. The dog could see that the hectic trial and the bizarre meeting with the vultures had somewhat unnerved Nosey. He felt he should do something to raise the raccoon's spirits.

"Say, how about you and Needles stayin' at my place during the Autumn Equinox while I'm serving on the Tribal Council? I'd feel better knowin' someone was in the cottage."

"Oh boy, you mean it? We'll be like kings!" whooped the little raccoon, jumping into the air and starting back down the path to the dam. "I can't wait to tell Needles!"

CHAPTER FORTY-FIVE

THE SPECTER

Sometime later when Billy and Nosey were within fifty feet of the dog's cottage, Nosey saw something eerie on the roof. He scurried back to the dog and pointed down the path. "Look, Billy! What's that?"

"Where?" questioned the dog, looking straight ahead of him.

"There, up on your roof! That thing all in black!"

Crouched on the edge of Billy's thatched roof was a specter-like creature, dressed in a black hooded robe that covered its entire head and body. Only the whites of its eyes showed through the opening where the face should have been.

"That's her, Nosey. That's Lucinda Vulture," explained Billy, whispering back over his shoulder.

Slowly the old vulture uncovered her head and flew down within a few feet of the dog. By that time the raccoon had already ducked behind the dog's legs.

"Nosey, why don't you run on home and tell Needles about staying at my cottage during the autumnal equinox," suggested Billy.

"I think…I think maybe that's a good idea," whispered Nosey.

As the raccoon made a wide circle around the dog and the vulture, Lucinda pointed a crooked finger at Billy. "Mr. Bones, I'm afraid that I was not aware of your dreams a couple nights ago and last night. For some reason I totally missed them."

"But Lucinda, you asked your sons to have me relate them for you," insisted Billy.

"No, no, they're not the ones. The dreams I refer to happened last Thursday. In fact, I felt them twice. They were so powerful that they shook my very being!" exclaimed Lucinda in an exasperated tone. "Surely you know what I'm talking about? That's why I flew down here. The dreams my sons told me about were not the ones I was expecting to hear. Think, Mr. Bones, think!"

Billy Bones finally realized that Lucinda Vulture was referring to the two visions he saw during the debates before the election.

"Oh," said Billy quietly, "those." It continued to amaze the shepherd dog that the old bird could sense most of his visions whenever they happened.

"Yes, those," continued the vulture, becoming less agitated. "Now suppose you tell me exactly what happened."

"Last Thursday during the debates on Main Street, I came across my friend Georgie and Patsy Prairie Dog," began the dog, concentrating hard on exactly what he had seen. "They were arguin' about who would be elected mayor. Suddenly I couldn't hear any sounds at all, and a yellow light began glowing around them. Almost immediately it seemed that Georgie and Patsy started shrinking. I must've screamed and covered my face, because Georgie came runnin' over to me. When I looked around again, everything had returned to normal. The same thing happened a little while later, only the light this time was around Gerard Crow, Jason Crow's son. I didn't scream this time but covered my eyes. When I looked back, Gerard was standing by his father again as if nothing had happened."

"These are indeed powerful visions, Mr. Bones, and I'm sure they are immensely significant," concluded Lucinda after a few moments. Her demeanor softened. "I'll take this information back to Omar Mountain Goat and the Tribal Council. When you meet with us during the Autumn Equinox, we can delve into them further. Now concerning your dreams about Jimmy Stone and the lost treasures, well, they certainly give us greater clarity as to what really happened to the human pioneers. As for their effects on you personally, that's another story. For some reason you have a very close connection with this ancient human. Perhaps there's some unfinished business there also?"

"Is there anything I should be doing? I…I mean about these strange visions?"

"It's only fair that you tell Mr. Wise Owl about them. And tell him about your latest dreams of the lost treasures along the trail. Perhaps he too has a connection with this Jimmy Stone."

"Lucinda, there is another bit of important information I have for you," said Billy. "It has to do with what happened at City Hall and with Olen Buck."

"Oh, what is that, Mr. Bones?"

"As you probably already heard, there was quite a ruckus at City Hall today. Because of this fighting and the ambushes before the Grand Fair, the City Council gave Rodney Wild Deer three months in jail and six months' probation, and the coyote brothers nine months' probation. After the meeting Olen Buck caught up with me and said he was tired of all this violence. Then he said he would do his best to keep the new City Council from taking human artifacts out of animal's homes without their permission. As you know, his vote would be enough to keep them out of the hands of Brother Fabian." Billy wanted desperately to tell Lucinda about his pact with Olen and Victor Running Deer and several of their friends but remembered the pledge of secrecy he had made with the old stag.

"Why Mr. Bones, this is indeed wonderful news. I'm especially happy about Mr. Wise Owl's books, for they are the most critical. But I'm still concerned about the artifacts that could be given up freely. If destroyed, it would be just as devastating," the vulture concluded.

"I hadn't thought of that," admitted the dog.

Lucinda paused for a moment and gazed in the direction of Land's End. "Well, maybe if Winston Wise Owl and Thaddeus P. Turtle do their part and safeguard all the artifacts here in the Prairie, we can still circumvent any kind of disaster."

The old vulture then turned her attention back to the shepherd dog. "But you are right, Mr. Bones. Mr. Buck's promise throws a completely different light on our future. Brother Fabian's desire to destroy the human artifacts has definitely been thwarted, at least for the time being. And the City Council's verdict has made the Prairie a much safer place with Rodney in jail and the coyotes serving probation."

Lucinda paused again and looked deep into Billy's eyes. "I know these past few weeks haven't been easy for you, Mr. Bones, and I admire your courage. Now go home and relax for a few days. I will need you when the Tribal Council meets during the autumnal equinox."

Before the old bird departed, she placed a hand extending from the tip of her wing on the dog's forehead. Billy was somewhat taken aback. He had never seen Lucinda touch another creature. More astounding than the contact, however, was the immediate connection the dog felt with the cool, deep waters of the vulture's mind. He was absolutely dazzled by its clarity. After she released her hand, she slowly turned westward, spread her great wings, and flew steadily away.

CHAPTER FORTY-SIX

BILLY STUART

Billy Stuart pulled up the extra blanket from the bottom of the old iron bed with its white paint and brass knobs. The September night air was chilly, and he had also been thinking of Bones again. He and his grandfather had spent Labor Day fishing down at the old beaver pond, and the subject of a new pup came up after a particularly good catch. The boy knew his grandfather meant well, but he stubbornly refused to admit that his shepherd dog was gone for good.

At that moment, a kind of barking caused the boy to bolt upright. He threw off the covers and rushed to the open window. "Bones, Bones, is that you?"

Suddenly a gunshot rang out near the chicken coop west of the farmhouse. Billy rushed downstairs and onto the back porch, nearly running into Will Stuart, who stood on the back step with his shotgun under his arm. "Those blasted coyotes! Got away with more of my chickens and the coop's a mess! It'll take me half a day to fix it!"

Back in the kitchen over a peanut butter sandwich and a glass of milk, Billy looked up at the older man. "You don't suppose the coyotes got him, do you, Grandpa?"

"You mean Bones?" Will glanced over at Billy. "I doubt it. He was pretty tough."

"Yeah, he was pretty tough," agreed the boy, with tears in his eyes in spite of himself.

Gently Will Stuart put an arm around his grandson and drew him closer. In the distance, the howl of a coyote rose from the vicinity of Sand Hill. Shortly afterwards, another howl answered from the hills beyond.

END OF BOOK ONE: *BEYOND THE TALL GRASS*

ABOUT THE BOOK

Beyond the Tall Grass is the first book with the general title *Billy Bones.* The next two books, *In the Shadow of the Lynx* and *Return to the Golden Mist,* continue the story. The books are outgrowths of bedtime stories that I told to my younger brother David and my daughter Laura when they were children. The hero of the stories is a shepherd dog, Bones, based on a dog that I played with on my grandfather's farm in Humbolt, South Dakota, when I was a boy.

Much of my inspiration for writing came from stories my older brother Irl told me when we were young. The most memorable times occurred when we lived in San Angelo, Texas. During the summer when we were ten and eight, we slept in an old open trailer in our back yard. I would coax him almost every night to begin a story, and then together we would make up an adventure. I would be remiss if I didn't also mention the stories my Great Aunt Ada Draper told my brother and me on the front porch of her old homestead near my grandfather's farm. She and her husband Charles were the second homesteaders in the Dakota Territory, and their many encounters in the late 1800's were mesmerizing.

Many ideas for the first book came from memories I had as a boy in various towns in eastern South Dakota. Especially relevant were the times my brother Irl and I raced down hills in old wagons with my cousins Bobby Joe Cleveland and Jimmy Cross on their fathers' farms near Montrose, South Dakota. Often we finished the run by crashing into the gullies below. Afterwards we would simply get up, brush ourselves off, and repeat the process. Later when we moved to Montrose, I recalled the summer festivals when many young people would enter the foot races up and down Main Street and around town.

The genesis for the three fantasies, however, really began when I stumbled across a number of abandoned trunks, plows, and other articles while hiking in Montana as a young man. I determined that these deteriorating antiques probably embodied the hopes and dreams of settlers migrating west to the Oregon Territory. This memory gave birth to the idea that the power of these cherished treasures caused a great rift, a bridge to another world, in which the creatures caught up in its magic were also profoundly changed.

ABOUT THE AUTHOR

Ron Oaks was born in Aberdeen, South Dakota. He earned a degree in speech and drama from Yankton College in Yankton, South Dakota; a degree in voice from the Peabody Conservatory in Baltimore, Maryland; and a master's degree in drama from Catholic University in Washington, D. C. Since then he has written a musical comedy, a religious opera, and a number of reviews, plays, and poems.

Ron has directed or performed professionally in over 100 operas, musicals, and plays from New York to Miami. He was the artistic director of the Garrison Playhouse in Baltimore County, Maryland, for 10 years and taught drama at Glenelg High School in Howard County, Maryland, for 16 years. More recently, Ron stage-directed seven operas for the Municipal Opera Company of Baltimore, Maryland, and a number of shows for the Woodbrook Players in Towson, Maryland. Ron was the bass-soloist with the Brown Memorial Presbyterian Church in Towson for many years and teaches voice in Washington, D.C., and at his home. Ron lives with his wife Janet in Howard County in Central Maryland.

ACKNOWLEDGMENTS

I began writing *Beyond the Tall Grass* on June 30, 2003. Since then my manuscript has gone through a number of revisions. Over those years I owe a special debt of gratitude to relatives, friends, and students who have patiently given advice and encouragement. We have discussed the lengths of the books, the divisions, the hidden meanings, the politics, the titles, the chapter lengths and placements, the history behind the fantasies, the art work, and many other aspects of the writing. These discussions were extremely valuable to me, and I will always be grateful to all of them for their time and consideration.

Initially, I want to thank Deborah Clayman, who taught classes on writing children's books at Howard Community College. Debra writes under the name Deborah da Costa and was very knowledgeable on the subject. Her two classes gave me the boost I needed to continue my writing projects. I also want to thank the writing groups I joined afterwards, especially Nancy Vaskuhl who read many early chapters and critiqued them. Also I want to thank Jean Israel, Ann Rudolph, Jane Wall, Pat Hooker, and my wife for allowing me to read and talk about various early chapters of the book when we were vacationing in Bar Harbor, Maine.

Next I want to thank Andrea Glaser and her book club in Olney, Maryland, including Alisa Austin, Mary McQueen, Patty Argyros, Patty Corridon, Alice Wertheimer, Linda

Krass, and Colleen Xydis. They not only read one of my earlier manuscripts in 2008 but took the time to meet me afterwards and offer recommendations and suggestions at Andrea's home. I also want to express my appreciation to Jan Chastant, Lynn Ellington, and Maysaa Alobaidi for reading later rewrites of my manuscript and discussing them with me at some length. Then I want to make special mention of Howard Garrett, Roger Thiel, and Jan Chastant who helped me with the front and back covers, and Sandy Rothberg who graciously agreed to take my photo.

I owe a special thankyou to two people who edited my book and encouraged me to continue writing. Anne Ostroff edited an early manuscript and did the final proof read, and her daughter Liora Ostroff read the book and gave a book report on it to her English Class. My good friend Louise Carlson graciously consented to edit my last two rewrites. I will be forever grateful for their expertise and professionalism.

Finally, I want to thank my wife and daughter. My wife Jan spent many hours reading chapters in my book after I initially wrote them and advised me on their content and flow. She also read an early rewrite during one of our summer vacations in Ocean City, Maryland. My daughter Laura not only reread the manuscripts as I made changes but offered a number of suggestions in the writing and is helping me publish the book.

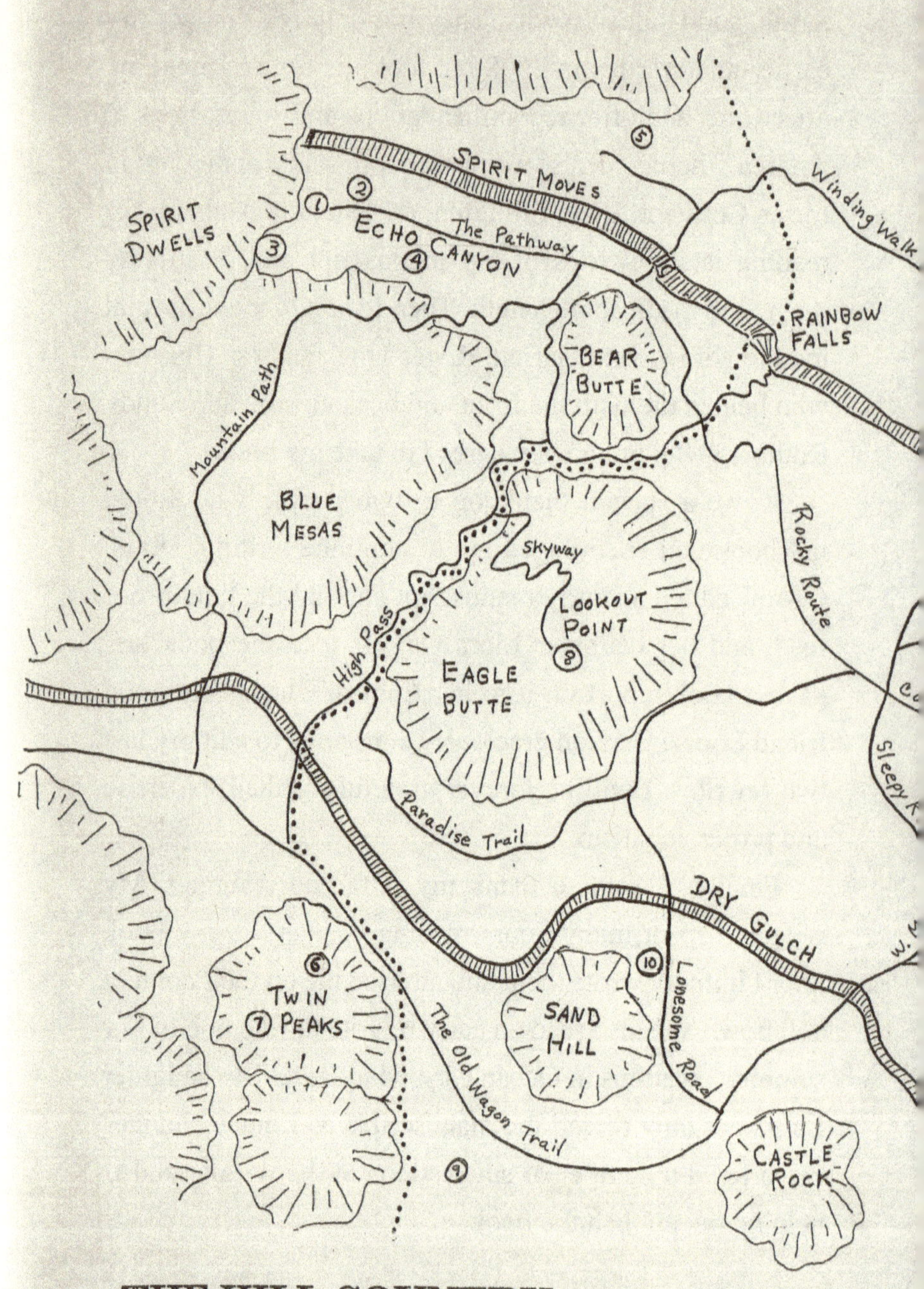

THE HILL COUNTRY

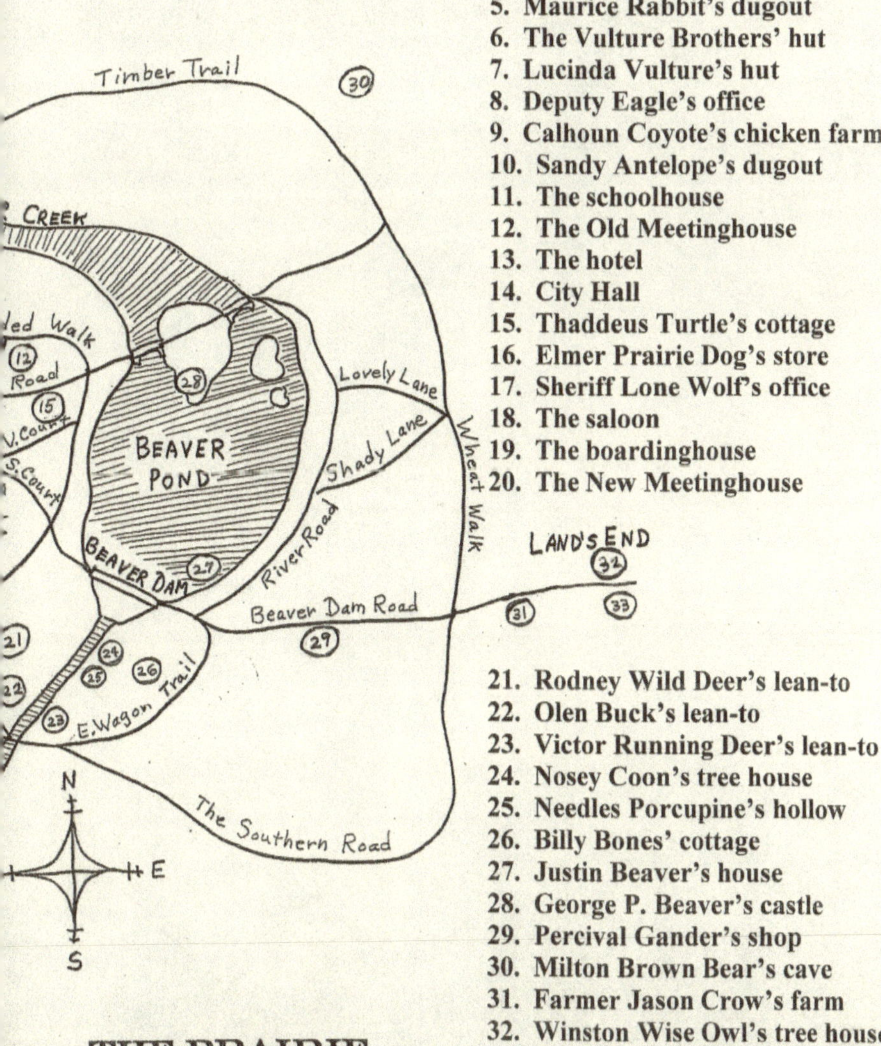

1. The lodge
2. Arthur Elk's hut
3. Omar Mountain Goat's cave
4. The store
5. Maurice Rabbit's dugout
6. The Vulture Brothers' hut
7. Lucinda Vulture's hut
8. Deputy Eagle's office
9. Calhoun Coyote's chicken farm
10. Sandy Antelope's dugout
11. The schoolhouse
12. The Old Meetinghouse
13. The hotel
14. City Hall
15. Thaddeus Turtle's cottage
16. Elmer Prairie Dog's store
17. Sheriff Lone Wolf's office
18. The saloon
19. The boardinghouse
20. The New Meetinghouse

21. Rodney Wild Deer's lean-to
22. Olen Buck's lean-to
23. Victor Running Deer's lean-to
24. Nosey Coon's tree house
25. Needles Porcupine's hollow
26. Billy Bones' cottage
27. Justin Beaver's house
28. George P. Beaver's castle
29. Percival Gander's shop
30. Milton Brown Bear's cave
31. Farmer Jason Crow's farm
32. Winston Wise Owl's tree house
33. Hester Ground hog's tree house